Double Image

Double Image

Don Searle

Bookcraft
Salt Lake City, Utah

All characters in this book are fictitious,
and any resemblance to actual persons,
living or dead, is purely coincidental.

Without Marie,
whose unreserved support made this possible,
as well as Sara and Laura,
who gave valuable help when it was needed,
this book would not have come to be.
To them, I express deep gratitude.

Chapter 1

The man in the booth on the far side of the restaurant looked up suddenly, gazing out toward the casino.

Paul Webber lifted his newspaper a bit higher so that most of his face was hidden. He shifted in his seat so he could still see the man without appearing to look at him directly.

The man stared past him in the general direction of the bar for a few moments, then went back to rearranging the packets of sugar in the small wire rack on his table. When that was done, he carefully repositioned the salt and pepper shakers so that they sat precisely in front of the condiment bottles.

Whatever was keeping James K. Delaroi here must be important, Paul thought. Delaroi was not known to his staff or to his colleagues at the bank in Los Angeles as a patient man.

Today, in tan cotton pants and a casual golf shirt, the banker was just another tourist in Las Vegas. But he sat well apart from the others scattered at tables in the hotel-casino restaurant.

Paul lounged on the padded bench just outside the entrance to the restaurant, watching to see what Delaroi was waiting for.

Watch and wait. It was part of the job, and Paul had plenty of experience at it.

Right now, experience told him to believe the woman who had called him at the wire service office in Los Angeles to talk about this banker.

She had seen Paul's byline on a newspaper article about the cost of corruption in business. Would he be interested in a case involving one of the largest banks in California, with branches in several other states?

1

Definitely interested.

Would he talk to her if she couldn't give her name?

Yes—for now. But if she was right about this story, the two of them would probably have to meet sometime.

A long pause. Maybe she shouldn't have called, she said.

Why not? If there really was something wrong, wouldn't it be best for the truth to come out?

Again, hesitation. And then—yes, that was what she had been thinking. She was afraid that her boss, the bank's director of administrative services, might have made some kind of secret deal with a Nevada company whose business practices were question-able—even illegal.

When a representative of the company called on him several months ago, her boss had dismissed the man angrily, fuming about greedy people who give business a bad name. So she had been sur-prised to learn two weeks ago that the bank was now doing busi-ness with the Nevada company, Business Line Office Machines.

Her boss said he had misunderstood their original offer, and that Business Line had turned in an unbeatable bid on new copy machines. But it was surprising that some larger, Los Angeles-based company hadn't been able to beat them. She wondered if her boss could have written up the specifications for the machines to favor the Nevada company.

Possible, Paul answered. Was there evidence of some kind of deal?

Maybe. As Delaroi's administrative assistant, she saw the tele-phone and travel bills for the department. The weekend before the Nevada company submitted its bid to the bank's purchasing department, her boss had told his staff that he was going up to his cabin at Big Bear Lake. But his company credit card showed that he had charged a room and meals in Las Vegas. And there had been three calls to Business Line's Las Vegas offices on his office phone in the two days before that company's bid came in.

Did she have any idea what had happened in Las Vegas that weekend when he said he was going to the lake?

No. But this week he had told her he was going to Big Bear again on Friday.

So Paul had done a little checking of his own with some sources in the business community. And then he had been waiting down the block from the Delaroi home in Altadena at five-thirty this morning when the banker backed his burgundy Lexus out of the driveway. Paul had not been surprised when Delaroi passed up the Big Bear turnoff, near San Bernardino, and continued on Interstate 15 toward Las Vegas.

Now that they were here, what was supposed to happen? So far, Delaroi had just sat at his table in there and—

"I have a *business* obligation to you, Wes. That's all. You should understand that by now."

A few of the players at nearby slot machines turned to look as the woman's angry words cut through the casino noise. Shocked, Paul turned too. He knew that voice! It belonged to someone he had talked to at church last Sunday—someone he wanted to know better.

The man and the woman stood in front of the elevators. They made an attractive couple. He was handsome, olive-skinned, dark-haired. His casual slacks and sport shirt looked expensive. The woman wore an eye-catching deep green dress—not tight, but, belted as it was, it showed that she had a figure. Her blonde hair was the wrong color for the woman Paul knew, yet the profile of her face seemed unmistakable.

"We'll talk about this later," the man said to her. "Wait here." He headed in the direction of the bar. The look that the woman gave him suggested she was in no hurry for him to come back.

Paul stood and stepped closer to her, next to the elevators where he could not be seen from Delaroi's table. "Kay? Kay Reston?"

The woman looked startled for an instant. Her eyes widened and her body tensed, but she seemed to will herself to take control even as she turned toward him. "Were you speaking to me?"

He had never heard another voice like hers. "Yes. Kay? . . . It is you, isn't it?"

"You must have me confused with someone else." The timbre of her voice was different this time.

Her eyes were brown—the wrong color. But the brown seemed too uniform and her irises seemed too large. As though to keep him from looking more closely, the woman turned away; she

3

opened a small clutch purse she carried, took out a pair of sunglasses, and put them on.

They didn't hide her facial profile. She had the same cheekbones and fine features as the woman he knew. "I'm sorry," he said, "but it's amazing how much you look like Kay—except, uh, that her hair is brown, and . . ."

The woman turned toward him once more. "You can see that mine is not." Now there was the hint of an accent in her voice. New York, maybe? Her tone was not unpleasant, but something about it said the conversation was over. She turned away again. Paul retreated to his bench.

She had almost made him forget why he was here. Glancing into the restaurant to assure himself that Delaroi was still at the table, Paul picked up the newspaper he had left on the floor.

He had just settled behind it again when the woman's companion came back from the bar. The man took her by the arm and guided her into the restaurant. The hostess led them toward a booth in the corner, three down from Delaroi.

A man in a suit had come from the direction of the bar and followed them into the restaurant. The blonde woman and her companion were just being seated when the man approached their corner, and the woman looked up as though she recognized him. Her companion said something angrily to her. She looked at him as though he had struck her, then retreated into the corner of the booth on her side of the table, put her back against the wall, and folded her arms across her chest.

The man in the suit ignored them and walked past the hostess to take the seat across the table from James Delaroi. The banker smiled slightly, and the two men were instantly involved in conversation.

Paul sat behind his newspaper wondering how close he would have to be to pick up what they were saying. Getting closer shouldn't be a problem. *Delaroi doesn't know me . . . and I look like any other tourist.*

Slowly, he folded the newspaper and put it down on the bench, then stood and walked into the restaurant.

"One?" the hostess asked.

He nodded, and she started toward the nearest small table.

"I don't think I want to be this close to the casino," Paul said. "What about over there?" Walking to a table just one removed from the banker and the man in the suit, he sat down facing them. The hostess followed, and handed him a menu. "Your server will be with you as soon as she helps those two gentlemen," she said.

Paul made a show of studying the menu. Over the top of it, he saw that the other two men glanced at him, then went back to their conversation. He caught only an occasional word or two as the man in the suit spoke: "every month . . . your share . . . account . . ."

Delaroi's reply was too soft for Paul to make out any of it.

The man in the suit took a keno ticket from the rack next to the table, pulled out his pen, and carefully circled several numbers. Planning to place a bet while they had lunch? No—he shoved the form across the table toward the banker.

Delaroi studied it, took his wallet out of his pocket, extracted a business card, and spoke to the man in the suit, who handed over his pen. Delaroi looked at the form once more, then began writing on the back of the card.

He had just finished when the server approached their table. She reached for the keno ticket, but the man in the suit quickly wadded it up. He smiled at the young woman, and Paul could hear the last few words he said: ". . . not feeling lucky today."

After the woman had taken their orders, she walked over to Paul's table. "Are you ready to order, sir?"

"Ah . . . sure. Patty melt sandwich, I guess."

The woman—Cindy, her badge said—looked at him strangely. "I'm sorry, sir, that isn't on the menu."

Paul glanced down at the menu he held open in his hands. Nothing jumped out at him instantly. "Burger and fries, then—whatever's quick."

"Yes, sir." Cindy walked away.

The restaurant was beginning to fill up for lunch. The hostess had just seated four older people at the next table, and at least two of them seemed to have difficulty hearing, so all four spoke loudly. Paul could no longer make out anything that Delaroi and his companion were saying.

He continued watching them unobtrusively, always keeping his eyes moving around the room, then coming back to them every few seconds. The two men were simply talking; there was no other exchange of any kind.

Paul reached into the pocket of his jeans and pulled out his palm-sized 35-millimeter camera. He had practiced taking photos in situations like this without getting caught at it. Sometimes the pictures had been used only to augment his own memory, but a few times they had been used with stories.

Fast film made a flash unnecessary, but the trick was to not call attention to yourself in any other way. While there was no reason a tourist might not have a camera in plain sight, he could not let Delaroi and the other man notice what he was doing with it. Casually he placed it on the table facing them, but directly behind the salt and pepper shakers. Then he moved the shakers apart about an inch and a half to make an opening for the lens.

The two men were paying no attention to him. Paul pushed the shutter release with his finger. The *click-whir* as the camera took a picture and advanced the film was almost inaudible over the noise in the restaurant. Delaroi and his companion went on with their conversation uninterrupted.

Paul continued to gaze around the restaurant, shooting another picture each time he glanced at the two men. He had almost finished his roll of film when Cindy arrived at the other table with a large tray of food. She served Delaroi and the other man, then turned toward Paul. He quickly palmed the camera and hid it under the table, resting his hand on his leg.

Cindy placed his food in front of him and walked away. Paul was about to put the camera into his pocket when he glanced to his left and noticed the blonde woman and her companion. The distance between them was obviously far greater than the width of their table. They sat staring in different directions, as though they were trying hard to ignore each other.

There were two frames left on the roll of film, and Paul needed to finish it so he could get the photos developed right away. Positioning the camera carefully so it pointed in the direction of the couple in the booth, he squeezed off the last two shots, then slid the camera back into his pocket.

He continued to watch the two men in front of him discreetly as he ate. The man in the suit seemed to do most of the talking.

Delaroi quickly finished the small salad he had ordered and leaned back with his arms folded, listening, nodding occasionally in response.

The man in the suit was still eating—and so was Paul—when Delaroi stood up and strolled toward the back of the restaurant. There had been nothing resembling a farewell between the two men, and the one in the suit paid no attention as the banker walked away. Where was Delaroi going—men's room? Phone, maybe?

Paul kept glancing toward the back of the restaurant, wondering when Delaroi would come back—or *if* he was coming back. Finally, after more than five minutes had passed, Paul stood up, dropped a five and a one on the table to cover his meal, and strolled in the same direction Delaroi had gone, trying to look unhurried.

At the back of the room, on the wall that he had been facing away from, there were two doors, one marked "Kitchen" and the other marked "Exit." Mentally berating himself for not paying closer attention when he had looked around the room earlier, Paul pushed through the exit door out into a hallway, and then through a glass door that opened into the parking lot in back of the building.

Stepping into the heat of midday Las Vegas, even in September, was like walking into a heavy curtain that seemed to wrap around him, smothering him. The heat was one thing Paul hadn't missed when he had moved out of this city. He forced himself into a jog, quickly moving around to the side of the building.

The space where the banker had parked his Lexus was empty. Delaroi was gone, and there was no way to know where he might be headed.

Paul jogged back around the hotel, entered the rear door, and walked into the restaurant again. The table where the two men had sat was now unoccupied; a busboy was clearing it off.

Paul made his way quickly toward the front of the restaurant. As he maneuvered past the tray of dishes behind the busboy, he spotted a flash of color on it—the wadded-up keno ticket that Delaroi's companion had left on the table. Paul picked it up smoothly with two fingers as he passed, palmed it, then slipped it into his shirt pocket as he walked out of the restaurant.

He scanned the casino. There was no sign of the man in the suit. He had lost them both.

Dumb! Beginner dumb! . . . Half a day sunk into this, and not much to show for it! Shaking his head, he turned to walk out to his car.

The woman who had Kay's voice was standing in front of the elevators with her companion, their backs to Paul. The bell *dinged*, one set of doors opened, and they stepped in. Paul watched them for a moment as they stood not looking at each other, and then, on an impulse, he walked toward the elevator and squeezed through the closing doors. Delaroi had left him with more questions than answers, but maybe he could still solve the mystery of this woman. It was hard to believe there was someone else who looked so much like Kay.

The button for the fourth floor was lighted. Paul pushed the button for the third floor.

The doors closed, and the three of them stood against the back wall of the elevator as they ascended, Paul in one corner, the other man in the middle, then the woman. She still wore her sunglasses, so Paul had not been able to see whether she had looked at him when he stepped into the elevator. She had shown no other reaction to his presence.

When the doors opened on the third floor, Paul stepped out nonchalantly into the small elevator lobby, then turned the corner into the main hallway that ran the length of the hotel. As soon as he was out of sight of the elevator, he broke into a jog toward the fire exit at the end of the corridor. He shoved open the fire door, and ran up two flights of stairs to the fourth-floor landing.

He eased the stairwell door open a crack so he could see the length of the corridor. The woman in the green dress and her companion were coming toward him; they stopped in front of a room three doors down. At least he hadn't lost *them*—one good break today.

He could easily hear the woman's angry words.

"No, Wes! It's never going to be that way between us again, and I know I don't have to tell you why. Did you think giving me this dress to wear and putting me up in a hotel room would make me forget about everything you did? Do you think I'm that cheap?"

The voice *could* be Kay's—it was hard to be sure because there was so much anger in it. Paul could not hear the man's reply, but the woman's laugh in response was short and bitter. "Why don't you go tell that to Barbie!"

Again, Paul could not make out what the man said. The woman seemed to make an effort at patience this time when she answered. "I'm sure that being dumped is a new experience for you, Wes, and I understand how hard it is to be alone. But that doesn't change a thing between *us*."

Now Wes raised his voice. "You *need* me, Kristina, and you know it."

Kristina took one step backward. She seemed shocked. "You really can't make yourself understand that I don't, can you?"

Wes reached for the room key she held in her hand. Kristina put it behind her back and put her back against the door. She put her other hand over the doorknob to keep Wes from taking hold of it. "If you try to come in, I'll scream. And if you don't go away right now, I'll call hotel security."

Wes drew back his arm as though he were going to hit her. Kristina tensed her body as though she expected it. Paul could see fury on the man's face.

But Wes relaxed suddenly and stepped back. "When are you going to face the truth? If you won't make a life with me, you won't have a life at all."

"Is that a threat?"

"Just think about it. I'm sure even *you* are smart enough to figure out what it means." The words were heavy with contempt. He turned to walk away.

"I played the partner for you just like you wanted, Wes," she called after him. "Now don't forget to phone Max and tell him where to meet me."

"*You* do it," Wes called over his shoulder. He reached the middle of the corridor and stepped into the elevator lobby, out of sight.

Kristina held her position, back rigid against the door, until Wes was gone. Then she seemed to sag as she turned slowly to put her key in the lock, steadying her trembling right hand with her left. She opened the door just enough to squeeze through, then quickly shut it behind her. Paul could hear the deadbolt click into place.

What would she do now—collapse in tears? Or was she strong enough not to let Wes beat her down?

And why, Paul asked himself, was this any of his business?

Because he was a news reporter? No. There was no story here—nothing anyone else *needed* to know. Wes and Kristina seemed like just one more sad pair with little left between them except hate.

When he had followed them into the elevator, he had still been angry with himself, wanting to prove that losing Delaroi had been only a fluke. But journalistic bravado had faded away as he listened to the conversation between these two people.

There was no reason for him to hang around . . . except that this woman looked and sounded so much like someone he couldn't get out of his mind . . . and she seemed to need somebody on her side right now.

A distant *ding* indicated that Wes's elevator had arrived. Paul waited for a few seconds, then opened the stairway door, stepped out into the corridor, and walked toward Kristina's room.

What are you doing, Webber? This is crazy! You're confusing this woman with Kay. There may be a close resemblance, but . . .

But one more close look at her would help him know whether he was wrong or not. He stopped in front of her door and raised his hand to knock. *So how are you going to tell her why you're here? "Excuse me, but I was eavesdropping on your conversation. Is there anything I can do to help?"*

He lowered his hand and stood looking at the little round peephole in the door.

There had been no trace of an accent in the woman's voice just now. Why had it suddenly disappeared?

He knocked lightly on the door and waited. The peephole in front of him turned dark, stayed that way for several seconds, turned light again, and then—nothing. She had looked out at him and walked away!

He raised his hand to knock once more, then hesitated. She had already told one man to leave her alone or she would call hotel security.

Paul turned and walked slowly down the corridor toward the elevator.

On his way out of the hotel, he stopped at the registration desk. "I'd like to leave a message for Kay Reston," he said when the clerk looked up from his computer terminal.

The clerk tapped a few keys on the computer, watched the

screen for a moment, then frowned. "We have no one by that name registered at the hotel."

"It may be listed as Kristina."

The clerk typed in that name, then looked up at Paul and shook his head. "No, sir. Sorry. Perhaps she hasn't checked in yet?"

"I thought she was already here. I must have been mistaken."

Chapter 2

He let his car idle along for a mile or so in the crawl of Saturday afternoon traffic on the Las Vegas Strip, then turned off on Tropicana Avenue, heading for a shopping center where he knew there was a one-hour photo shop. He dropped off the film he had shot in the restaurant, bought a news magazine in a convenience store, and found a bench in the shade where he could sit.

Pulling out the small cellular phone he usually kept in his car, he dialed a number and waited.

"News desk," a voice answered.

"Scott Pike, please."

"He's editing something for the six o'clock news. I'll see if he can take a call." A few seconds later another voice answered: "This is Scott Pike."

"I suppose you'll tell people tonight that you're giving them the latest, up-to-the-minute stories?"

Scott laughed. "And I suppose you want to sleep on my couch again?"

"I'll buy dinner. You like microwave, or microwave?"

"Yeah, with Canadian bacon. I'll be home between seven and seven-thirty."

Paul read for forty-five minutes, then picked up his pictures. They were adequate, given the circumstances. Delaroi and the other man showed up well.

What to do now? Scott wouldn't be home for five hours or more.

Paul got into his car and headed across town. There was one place where he knew he could do something worthwhile with an afternoon.

Less than half an hour later, he walked through the entrance to the Las Vegas temple.

Peace . . . like putting on a coat, or a wraparound robe.

What happened inside these walls always left him ready to believe again in the possibility of a world where everything that anyone did could benefit someone else—a world where no one would be motivated by pride or greed or the other sicknesses of society. He needed this spiritual refreshing to take the hard edges off of life. It was like washing off dirt from outside—from some of the things he had to see and hear and touch every day.

After the session was over, he sat for a long time simply absorbing the feeling of the place.

When he finally left the temple, he made a stop at a supermarket, then drove to Scott's apartment. Twenty minutes after his friend came home, they were sitting at the dinette table in the kitchen, feet up on the two vacant chairs, enjoying the pizza, salad, and soft drinks that Paul had bought.

"What brings you to Vegas this time?" Scott asked.

"An investigative piece—maybe."

Scott raised his eyebrows.

"So far, I don't have much more than two guys talking in a restaurant." Paul took the packet of photos from his shirt pocket and fanned them out on the table. "Does this man look familiar?" he asked, pointing to the one who wore the suit.

"No." Scott wiped his fingers on a napkin and spread the photos apart to examine them. "Who's the other guy?"

"Director of administrative services for CommerceBank of California."

"Hmm. With branches in Arizona and Nevada."

"Right. And his administrative assistant believes he made some kind of under-the-table agreement with a Las Vegas company that sells office machines and supplies. She thinks he gave them help on winning a contract with the bank."

"Or maybe it was all just good business. What makes her believe there was some kind of deal?"

"He was in contact with the company secretly before they got the bid—some calls, and maybe meetings here in Vegas. Today may be part of it."

13

Scott frowned. "In his position with the bank, he must be pretty secure. Why risk something like that?"

"He was passed over for promotion to vice president last year. And he's got a new wife—twenty years younger, expensive tastes."

Scott sighed and shook his head. "I know it comes with the territory, but I always hate finding out things like this about people." He leaned back in his chair and took another drink from the can he held. "Do you have anything else from today, besides the pictures?"

Paul took the crumpled keno ticket from his pocket and smoothed it out on the table.

Scott studied it. "Three pairs of numbers circled, and then—is this a dash?"

"And another pair of numbers. Not a legitimate keno bet."

"Looks like some kind of account code."

Paul nodded.

"And that would mean they were talking money."

Paul nodded again.

Scott slid the keno ticket back across the table. "This is your story, so I won't ask any more questions. But can I trust that if the suit from Las Vegas and the tourist with the Beverly Hills look turn out to be doing something illegal, I'll be the second to know?"

"Right after I file my story on the wire. I'll share everything I can."

Scott bent over the photos again. "Who's the blonde here? And the guy with her who looks like he thinks he's pretty important?"

Paul looked down at the picture for a moment. "I . . . don't know. I was just finishing off the roll of film."

Scott held up the soft drink can and spoke as though intoning his words into an imaginary tape recorder: "Subject hesitated before answering. Could there be more to this than he's admitting?"

Paul laughed. "She looked a lot like someone I know from Los Angeles."

Scott inspected the photograph more closely. "Salon hairdo, expensive dress—not usually your type, as I recall."

"Well, this woman doesn't look *exactly* like . . . I mean, her hair is the wrong color, and her eyes—I saw them before she put on the glasses. But her face looks the same, and when I heard her talk, at first I was almost sure . . ."

"Hmm. Could be wearing a wig," Scott said, looking at the picture once more. "And colored contacts?"

"Could be. But I asked to leave a message for her at the registration desk—for the woman I know. They didn't have anybody by that name."

"Maybe she's not using her real name, either."

"Maybe not." Paul frowned. "I don't think it could be the same woman, though. She was with a man—sounded like he was her ex—and from what I heard them saying . . ."

Scott raised his eyebrows. "Ugly?"

"Yeah."

"So—tell me about the woman in Los Angeles."

"I don't know much. She moved into the ward a few weeks ago. She's quiet, and she doesn't do anything to call attention to herself."

Scott smiled. "In a singles ward, she wouldn't have to."

"Yeah, but there's something . . ." Paul wasn't sure what it was that made Kay seem so attractive. She dressed conservatively, modestly, and, apparently, cheaply. She was average height for a woman; he was five foot ten, and he could almost look over the top of her head. Her hair was an average light brown. Yet there was something about her that made him look again when she came into a room.

It was more than that—there was something that made him want to be where she was.

"You've talked to her?" Scott asked.

"A couple of times. Last Sunday before church we talked for about fifteen minutes." But he had been intrigued by her the first time he had seen her, and that time they hadn't talked at all. During a Sunday School lesson on repentance, she had raised her hand several times to ask questions. Paul had been impressed by her earnestness—and fascinated by her voice. It was low and musical, and each time they had talked since then, he had enjoyed just listening to her.

"And?" Scott used a television director's gesture, the signal that told performers on camera to keep things moving along.

"She's an artist, and she lives in Westwood, not far from where I do."

Scott smiled slowly. "Could it be that veteran reporter Paul Webber has had his head turned by a woman? That's news!"

Paul smiled weakly. "*That's* not news, and you know it."

Scott studied his friend's face for a moment. "Sorry. I, uh . . . I thought what happened last year was nothing but history for you now."

"Yeah . . . except . . . well, after something like that, you have to wonder if it was the chemistry that just wasn't right—or if you're the problem."

"It wasn't you, my friend. You're a prince of a guy." Scott raised his soft drink in salute.

"Not the prince *she* was waiting for. Maybe there was more to it than what she told me, but she said when we broke up that she needed a stable home life and a reporter's hours are too crazy."

Scott traced a circle around the rim of his soft drink can with his forefinger. "That's funny, in a way. I saw her a couple of weeks ago working at Wal-Mart. Her husband the musician has a day job managing a sandwich shop while he tries to pick up singing gigs at night, waiting for his big break in show biz." He looked up at Paul. "She says she's happy. For her sake, I hope it's true."

"I do too. I wouldn't change things—now. I've had fourteen months to think about it. Marriage would have been wrong for the two of us."

Scott tipped his soft drink can up and drained it. He put it down and pushed the pictures across the table toward Paul. "Well, then, best of luck with your mystery woman here—or at least with the one who looks like her in Los Angeles."

"I wouldn't mind finding a way to know her better."

"Bake some cookies and take them over to tell her welcome to the ward."

Paul laughed. "If she tasted *my* cookies, that would end everything before it began."

Scott laughed too. "You need to sign up for a cooking class, Webber. If the timer on your microwave ever goes bad, you'll be in serious danger of starvation."

Three years ago, Scott Pike had come to a Las Vegas television station from a smaller one in Arizona. Paul had already been working at the *Review-Journal* for three years by then. He had been pleasantly surprised to see Scott at a stake conference a few months after they first met on the job.

They had seen each other frequently in the course of covering local news, but as competitors, they had avoided talking about stories they were working on. The discovery that they were both Church members had broadened the range of things they could discuss. First it had been growing up in the Church—Paul in California, Scott in New Mexico. Then their conversation had turned to other things—missionary experiences and people they knew from singles activities. Sometimes they had talked about trying to live the gospel in a world—and in a career—that put little emphasis on eternal values.

The two of them had become good friends. They had double-dated together several times. When Paul had started going steady with a woman five years younger, Scott had kidded him about being nearly twenty-eight and desperate. But when the breakup had come, Scott had deliberately kept close, trying to be sure his friend was all right.

A few months after the breakup, Paul had accepted a job in the wire service's Los Angeles bureau. Three times since then, he had come back to Las Vegas to follow a story, and each time, he had stayed with Scott instead of going to a hotel.

"Mind if I watch football?" Scott asked as he turned on the television.

"No, go ahead." Paul suppressed a smile. "I hope you can find a good game. Sometimes the cable channels fill air time with podunk teams."

"I know it doesn't rate much copy in the big city," Scott answered, "but New Mexico's playing UTEP tonight."

"See, what did I tell you? These cable channels—" Paul laughed and ducked away as Scott tossed a throw pillow at him.

"Wait till they play San Diego State. This year it'll be a wipeout!" Scott said, pointing a finger at Paul.

"You want to back that up with a steak dinner for me and my date?"

"Yeah—you and the mystery woman." The two men shook hands on it.

The game was already into the second quarter. They watched till the end—New Mexico won on a late touchdown—then Scott changed the channel to the local station where he worked. The news show was just beginning.

"All of today's news to your home at the speed of light," Scott said, and grinned at Paul.

"What you mean is, all of the headlines you could gather before five o'clock this afternoon and anything you may have gotten off the police scanner in the last few minutes."

"Ink-stained journalistic wretch!"

About halfway through the news portion of the broadcast, a story came on that Scott had done. "This is what I was working on this afternoon when you called," he said.

The story was good—well written and well handled on the air. When it was over, Paul asked, "How do you manage to do that so well?"

Scott smiled. "Talent, preparation, hard work. And did I mention talent?"

"Humility, too. But what I meant was, how can you be in two places at once—the handsome, glib TV newsman on the screen, and the guy who walks around in socks with his shirttail out at home?"

"Oh, that. Well, the truth is, I'm a twin. My brother and I have worked this out very cleverly so we can share the job and split the pay. No one knows, and neither one of us has to work so hard."

Scott settled back into his corner of the couch. "Maybe that's the way the blonde woman in your picture does it—she has a twin in Los Angeles. If you find out it's true, introduce me to the sister."

"This is real life, Scotty, not television. She'd probably turn you down."

Scott snatched up the other throw pillow from the couch and backhanded it at him.

Chapter 3

Paul watched her as she sat across the cultural hall talking to two other women. When the women drifted away, he walked over to sit down. These first-Friday-of-the-month socials were meant to help people in the ward get better acquainted, and that was what he intended to do.

"Hello, Kay."

"Hello, uh . . . Paul! It is Paul, isn't it?"

For a moment he thought her eyes had a hunted look—almost "Please, can I trust you?"—but then it was gone. "Yes—Paul," he answered. "We talked for a few minutes before church a couple of weeks ago."

"I remember. You're a reporter for the wire service."

"And you're an artist."

"Painter and illustrator—looking for places to sell my work in the big city."

"Where do you come from?"

She smiled. "You've probably never heard of it—a tiny little Mormon pioneer town east of Las Vegas."

"So that's why you sell your work in Vegas too?"

She frowned. "No, I don't. I'm concentrating on becoming known in this area."

"Oh." He tried something he would do in an interview when he thought someone was holding back on him. "I just wondered because I saw you in Las Vegas last Saturday."

Kay seemed surprised, and she answered without hesitation: "It must have been someone else."

"Could be. But she had your voice . . . and her face looked so much like yours that . . ." He pulled the packet of photos out of his sport coat. "I have a picture. I was shooting someone else for a story, but I had a few frames left, so . . ." He held out the photos, with a picture of the blonde woman and her escort on top.

Kay seemed hesitant to look—or maybe she just wasn't interested—but finally she reached out to take the photos from him. She glanced at the top photo, then laughed lightly. "Not even close, Paul." She pointed at the blonde, then patted her own brown hair. "And did you happen to get a peek at the eyes behind those sunglasses? Were they blue like mine?" She opened her eyes wide and batted her eyelashes at him.

Paul grimaced. "You've got me. The eyes were the wrong color too."

Kay moved the top photo aside. For a moment she seemed interested in the next picture—James Delaroi, the California banker, and the man in the suit who had joined him for lunch. But then she put the photo of the man and the woman back on top of the stack and handed the pictures to Paul.

"I guess it was her voice that fooled me," Paul said. "She sounded so much like you—at first. But . . . well, this wouldn't be the first time I've made a mistake."

Slowly, Kay smiled. "You mean journalists are human too?"

He put on a wounded expression and she laughed again.

"Some get pretty hardened," he said. "But they respond nicely to the gentle, artistic touch."

She looked at him strangely. The wariness in her eyes came back.

He searched for some glib, original way to approach what he wanted to say, but nothing came. Finally: "Kay, I'm trying to find a good way to ask you out."

She frowned as though he had just told her something disagreeable.

This wasn't going well; he could feel himself sweating. But maybe if he came up with an idea she liked . . . "Could I take you to dinner, or a movie?" Her expression didn't change. "Or I know a couple of art galleries . . ." If she said yes, he would find some quickly.

The look in her eyes was no longer wariness. It was more like panic. "Paul, I'm sorry, I, uh, haven't been out in a long time . . . and I'm sure it could be fun, but . . . but I just can't. I hope you'll understand."

He didn't. The color had drained out of her face, and she was nervously twisting the CTR ring she wore on her right hand. Apparently, something about the idea of going out with him made her very uncomfortable.

Try another approach? No. He didn't want to cajole her or make the situation more awkward. "It's OK. I thought we could find something we'd both enjoy. But maybe another time."

"Yes." Kay seemed relieved. "That would be . . . yes, thank you." She stood up. "Will you excuse me?"

Paul stood and watched as she walked across the room and out the door. He felt . . . what? Disappointed? No, it was more than that. Hurt, maybe? He had been turned down before, but never had a woman reacted quite like this. He looked down at his tie—old, like the other three in his closet—and his coat—a bit too baggy. He ran his tongue over his teeth. Nothing there. Was it something much worse—some flaw in his personality that was instantly apparent to a sensitive, intelligent woman? Was there some label on his forehead, visible to women only, that said "loser"?

He was still puzzling over what had happened when he felt a tap on his shoulder.

Phil Jarman, the elders quorum president, held a cup of punch out to him. Nick Karas, a Sunday School teacher in the ward, backed Phil up with a couple of cookies in a napkin.

"No luck?" Phil asked.

"What . . ."

"Kay Reston."

Paul took the cup from Phil's hand. "No."

Nick grinned and held out the cookies. "You're not the first. She turned white when I said 'date.' Maybe we just haven't got what it takes."

"Or maybe she's been burned in ways we don't know about," Phil said. "Nina Leman told me about some strange situations women in the ward have run into on dates."

Paul nodded. He had also heard the Relief Society president

talk about this. Considering what she had said, maybe Phil's charitable view was the best attitude to take.

Paul was still talking to the other two men a few minutes later when he noticed that both had shifted their gaze to something behind him. He turned to look and found Kay standing there.

She smiled tentatively. "Please don't let me interrupt, Paul—but may I talk to you when you're through?"

"Sure. This, ah . . . well, I wasn't saying anything important."

"I wouldn't want—"

"No, it's OK." He turned to Phil and Nick. "I'll see you guys later."

Kay walked across the cultural hall and out of the door again. He followed her. The music that was playing in the cultural hall, just in case anyone wanted to dance, faded into background noise. Kay stepped into the Relief Society room and sat down in a chair just inside the door without turning on the light. Paul sat down beside her.

"There wouldn't ever be another time, would there?" she asked.

"What?"

"You wouldn't ask me out again, would you? Please—I need to know the truth."

Paul thought about her request for several seconds. Did she *really* want honesty? Sometimes people who said things like this only wanted to hear what would make them feel good.

He didn't think Kay was one of those people. "No, probably not," he answered. "I could tell you didn't feel good about the idea, so . . ."

Tears started to slide down her cheeks.

Paul sat watching her, not sure what to do. *Blew it again, Webber. Looks like she didn't really want to hear the truth after all.* "Kay, I, ah . . . if it was something I said . . . or did, I—"

"No! It isn't you. I . . ." Her hands closed into fists. "I *won't* let this . . ." She bowed her head and wiped at her eyes with her fingers.

Paul reached into his hip pocket for the handkerchief he carried to polish his glasses and held it out to her.

She took it and wiped her eyes. "Thanks—and I'm sorry for being so emotional. I mean, if I embarrassed you . . ."

He smiled at her. "I'm not embarrassed. Are you OK?"

She stared at the empty blackboard on the wall for several seconds. Then she turned to look at him. "The truth is, I've met some fine men in this ward, but I was hoping that if any of them asked me out, maybe you . . . and then when you did . . . well, I panicked. I just . . ."

She stopped to take a breath and dab at her eyes with the handkerchief. Her voice was soft, almost a whisper, when she continued. "I was afraid. The last man I was close to hurt me badly, and it's been hard for me to deal with the idea of dating again." She wiped her eyes once more. "But if you still want to . . ."

He reached out to take her hand, wondering if she would let him. She tensed momentarily, then relaxed. "I wouldn't want to make it hard for you," he said. "We don't have to call it a date. You could tell me what movie you'd love to see on Friday night and we could just run into each other at the theater."

She smiled.

That's a start, he thought. "Or you could tell me where you'll be painting and I could drop by to give you my opinion on the form, the line, the texture. I'm fairly good at painting—those by-the-numbers things."

Kay laughed lightly. "I might take you up on the painting—but you'd be sorry."

"Why?"

"There's this place I've been wanting to go, in the desert out by Victorville, to do some sketches for a painting. I drove out there once. Some cowboys in a truck came by and wanted me to talk to them—and then they parked down the road, just watching me . . . so I didn't stay. But if somebody went with me . . ."

"I can handle desert. I was in the Scouts."

"We'd have to leave a little after four in the morning to get there for the sunrise."

Paul sucked in his breath and clutched his chest in mock pain.

She laughed again. "Don't tell me you've never gotten up at four in the morning for a good story."

"I'm off on Wednesday this week. If that's a good day for you, I'll psych myself up for it." He paused. "But this better be one really *great* sunrise."

She laughed once more. He liked making her laugh—liked the sound of her happiness.

They stayed in the Relief Society room for a few more minutes talking, until she handed back his handkerchief. "How about some punch?" he asked.

"I'd love it. But I need a couple of minutes to fix my makeup."

When they walked into the cultural hall together, he took her by the arm and she turned to smile at him.

Paul noticed Phil Jarman and Nick Karas watching from across the room. He smiled at them and shrugged his shoulders slightly.

There was still no sign of light in the sky when he passed the San Bernardino exit on the freeway.

Kay had said little since he picked her up at her apartment. She stretched and looked out into the darkness. "I'm glad it's *you* driving. I'm not awake yet." Then she turned to look at him. "Thanks for agreeing to bring me out here. I need a change like this from time to time."

"Yeah, it's nice to get a break from work."

"This *is* work for me. It just happens to be my favorite kind."

"But it must be a nice break from the commercial side."

He glanced her way and could not see her face very well in the darkened car, but he could tell that her brow was furrowed. Thinking about what he had just said?

"There's nothing wrong with being commercial," she responded finally. "Artists have to live by their work. I'm out there every week trying to turn up illustration jobs, and I've got a couple of portrait commissions. It's just that landscapes are my favorite thing to do."

West of Victorville, she directed him down a dirt road that ran into the high desert. The sky in the east was getting light when he pulled off the road and stopped at the spot she showed him.

They got out of his car and he spread the barbed wire of the fence apart for her while she climbed through with her sketchbook and 35-millimeter camera. Then he climbed through after her.

She started walking quickly up the small slope west of the fence, then turned to call back to him, "Come on. I can see color in the sky already."

"Yeah—gray on black. What's our hurry?"

She smiled at him. "We don't want to miss one glorious second of this, because the love of beauty in our souls is like water to someone dying of thirst in the desert. Come on! You're young and strong. I know you can make it." She turned and started uphill again.

He jogged past her, bounded over the two large rocks in their path, and waited for her at the crest of the rise. When she got there and stopped to catch her breath, he said, "You probably had no idea you could be so inspiring."

"Show-off!"

He grinned. "I run a little every other day or so and lift a few weights, just to keep in shape."

"Then you should be able to handle this," she said, handing him her camera. "Take pictures whenever I tell you. I want this view"—she framed a part of the panorama with her hands—"and this one."

Kay opened her sketchbook, pulled a pencil out of her pocket, and began sketching the distant scene. After a couple of minutes, she looked up, nodded toward the area where the sun was beginning to light the sky, and said, "Now." Paul snapped a picture. Several seconds later, she pointed toward the other vista she had indicated, and said, "Now that one." He took another photograph.

They went on this way for more than half an hour, with Kay sketching both scenes. Paul noticed that she made color notations on the drawings as the light changed. Occasionally she would point and say, "Now," and he would snap another picture. Once she said, "See that large cactus? Get it in the lower right corner." He noticed that it was in the same position in her sketch.

The sun was above the horizon when he said, "You're out of film. Want me to use my camera?"

Kay looked up and turned her head slowly to take in the panorama that lay in front of them. "No, I think you got the color I wanted."

"You've got goose pimples," he said, glancing at her arms, bare below the short sleeves of her blouse.

She looked down at her forearms. "I hadn't noticed."

"Do you want me to get your sweater from the car?"

25

"No, thanks, I'll be fine." She was quickly absorbed in sketching again.

Paul found a flat rock on the edge of the slope and sat down to watch as the shadows slowly grew shorter on the desert and on the mountains to the north. The only sounds were the whispering of the breeze and the occasional scratching of Kay's pencil on her pad. He didn't realize that the scratching had stopped until he heard her say, "Are you glad now that you had a chance to see this?"

"Yes. It's beautiful." He turned to look at her. "But I've enjoyed the company even more."

She laughed. "Flatterer! I haven't been much company. I'm afraid when I'm working I lose track of everything else that's going on around me."

"You make a nice picture yourself, just standing there sketching."

Kay blushed. "I'm, ah, ready to go—if you are." She took a racing stance. "Want to race *down* the hill this time? Maybe I'll have a better chance."

"Sure." Paul stood and stretched his legs. Then he began trotting down the slope. Toward the bottom, he went into a sprint and hurdled the barbed-wire fence.

"You've been holding out on me, Webber," she called as she strolled down the incline. "My brother was a hurdler when he was in high school, and I recognize the form. That's not something you picked up by doing a little running every day to stay in shape."

Paul laughed. "Want to know what I was thinking while I was in the air? 'Idiot! It's been years since you tried to clear anything this high.' I was lucky I had some elevation on the takeoff."

Kay stepped through the fence as he spread the wire for her again. "So, where and when were you on the track team?"

"Cross-country all through high school, and my first year at San Diego State." He opened the car door, closed it after her, and walked around.

Kay watched as he got in, buckled his seat belt, then started the car. "So—why didn't you go on with track?"

"I gave up the scholarship to go on a mission." He put the car into gear and pulled onto the road. "When I came back, I decided to put more of my effort into what I wanted to do for the rest of my life, so I switched to writing for the college newspaper and running just for fun."

"That was your start in journalism?"

"Not really." He chuckled. "When I was a junior in high school, I complained to the editor of the paper about the way they covered a track meet. She said, 'Why don't *you* do the story for us next time?' So I did, and then I found out I liked to write about a lot of things besides sports."

He paused. "What about you? When did you discover art?"

"In fourth grade. I started out drawing things around the farm." She laughed. "You should see the drawings my mother saved!"

"It's hard to imagine you as a farm girl."

"Are you kidding? I can ride a horse, milk a cow, drive a tractor—I was practically Miss Future Farmer. I'm not one of those city girls who goes to the market to buy a chicken and hasn't ever seen one on the hoof."

Paul laughed. "When did you realize you were hooked on being an artist?"

She leaned back and gazed out the windshield. "Mmm—by the sixth grade, I think. I found out that I really liked drawing scenes and still lifes. Sometimes, when Dad and Mom wanted to go for a ride out in the country together, I'd beg them to take me along so I could find something new to sketch. They'd end up taking all four of us kids, but while the others played, I'd draw."

"So where are you in the family?"

"My brother the track star is twenty-seven—two years older. I have a sister four years younger and a brother who's in high school. He's still living at home."

"Your big brother was lucky to have a sister who cared enough to watch him practice. My little sister always told me I was dumb to get up early and stay after school to run."

Kay smiled. "I wasn't as devoted as you make me sound. I was a cheerleader, and we practiced at the same time as the track team after school." She paused. "But I was always proud of him."

She turned to look at Paul. "Were you proud of your sister?"

It was an odd thing to ask. He wasn't sure how to answer. "Yeah—most of the time. For a while when we were younger we didn't get along too well."

Kay frowned. "I think it's sad when brothers and sisters don't get along."

"It's not like we fought *all* the time. It's just that . . . well, I think we were normal. She was four years younger—about the same age you are—and at fourteen, fifteen, sixteen I thought she was a tagalong. She felt like I just *had* to be the boss—telling her what to do all the time."

Paul smiled. "We're good friends now. She lives in Phoenix with her husband. She got married in spite of me."

Kay looked at him quizzically.

"I scared all her boyfriends off for a while after my mission. We didn't have a dad around, and there were a couple of those guys that seemed a little weird. I thought somebody needed to talk to them, so I—"

"You didn't!"

Paul nodded. He adopted a deep, authoritative voice. " 'You know, my sister is the kind of girl who has very high standards. A lot of young men would like to date her. Do you think your standards match hers?' "

Kay laughed. "Oh, Paul! Really?"

"Not in those words, exactly. But my sister finally told me she was going to inform her friends that I had serious mental problems—I wasn't always responsible for my actions. And my mother made it plain that I had to let Lisa learn to make her own choices, whether I liked them or not. I could be there if she ever asked for my help, but I had to let her deal with dating on her own."

Kay chuckled, then lapsed into silence.

They had traveled several miles, when she turned to look at him. "Thanks for asking me out." She paused. "Thanks for making it fun to be out with a man again."

Paul wondered if he should ask the question that came to mind. He chose his words carefully: "Sounds like you've had a rough time with men."

Kay said nothing for several seconds. Then: "Not men—*man*. Just one." She watched Paul's face as she spoke. "We were married. I was . . . too young, and he wasn't ready for marriage either. When it came apart, things turned ugly. He made the divorce as difficult as possible for me."

28

"You were . . . you, uh . . ." What was the right thing to say here? Paul didn't know. "I'm sorry."

"No need for *you* to be." She paused. "I'd like to put all of that out of my mind—but I can't. It doesn't just go away. And besides, it isn't something I can hide, because it might make a difference when I . . . to men I meet."

"Maybe—to some."

Paul wondered why she had responded as she did: "It isn't something I can hide, because it might make a difference" to men. It was almost as though she had been trying to test his feelings— and yet Kay didn't seem like the kind to play coy games.

And why had he answered the way *he* did? Just trying to help her feel good? No, not really; the words had simply come out without thought.

He had never dated a divorced woman. Should he feel any different about her? Probably not. Maybe he would if they . . . well, if two people were developing a close relationship, a divorce in the past might be something to know more about. But right now he and Kay were just two people enjoying the day together.

She was staring out the passenger window when he spoke. "So—we're not just going home, are we? There's a lot of day left."

She looked surprised when she turned to face him. "You, ah . . . you still want to . . . the two of us?"

Another strange response—as though she had thought he would shun her now. "Yes," he answered. "Unless you just have to rush home and get everything down on canvas before you forget it." He made rapid stroking motions in the air with his right hand.

Kay laughed. "That's why I had you taking pictures, silly—so I can remember later." She sounded relieved.

Paul glanced her way. "I've had fun with you this morning, Kay."

She smiled, almost shyly. "I was thinking just now when I was looking out the window that it would be nice if . . . well, I was hoping, really, that there'd be more to this day."

"What would you like to do?"

She hesitated. "You may not think it's fun. It's probably old stuff for you because you grew up here."

"Try me. Whatever it is, I'm sure I'll enjoy it with you."

"The beach!" Her smile was broad, expectant.

"Sure. I like the beach. I *love* the beach—never can get enough of it."

She laughed. "Me, too. The first time I saw it, I was eleven years old. My dad took four days away from the farm and brought us over here on a family vacation. I really liked Disneyland—but I cried when we had to leave the beach. I could have sat there forever watching the waves, and the birds, and . . ." She shrugged. "I've always loved the beautiful things the Lord made."

"Like sunrises on the desert?"

"Yes. A lot of people only see barrenness, but the desert has its own beauty."

She went on about some of the other things she found beautiful in the world. She seemed almost like a different person, Paul thought—less reserved, more relaxed, effervescent. It was as though he had broken through some kind of barrier by letting her know that he wanted to spend the rest of the day with her.

"We'll go by your place first," he said when he turned off the Santa Monica Freeway. "Then my place will be on our way to the beach."

"Give me a few minutes and I'll fix us a picnic lunch."

Her apartment was in the back half of a small bungalow, down a driveway off a narrow residential street.

She stepped inside and held the door open for him. "The nicest thing about this place," she said, "is the window light. It certainly isn't the space."

She was right. Large windows on two sides made the living room seem light and airy. But the worn old couch in the living room and the small refrigerator in the kitchen were both within his reach as he stood just inside her door, and it would be impossible to open the refrigerator all the way without hitting the two-person dinette table that was shoehorned into the kitchen space.

"I'll get ready for the beach and be right back," Kay said, walking across the living room. She opened a door facing him, and Paul could see the end of a neatly made bed. She shut the door behind her.

Between the kitchen and the wall of the bedroom there was a door leading into a cubicle that had to be the bathroom. Paul had seen larger walk-in closets.

He walked around the end of the couch to look at the half-finished painting on an easel in the middle of the living room. The painting showed a smiling, obviously vigorous older woman hugging a little girl.

There were two paintings side by side on the far wall of the living room—a finely detailed rendering of a desert cactus in bloom, and a scene that might be one of Kay's early efforts her mother had saved. Was it a desert landscape?

As he sat down on the couch, Paul noticed one more piece of art hanging in the corner where the outside walls met. The pencil drawing showed a smiling woman kneeling on one knee, her arms outstretched as a laughing little girl ran to her. Joy. It was as pure a joy as he had ever seen in one image. It etched itself in his mind.

Kay emerged from the bedroom a few minutes later wearing her jeans and a sweatshirt and carrying a towel. "Now for the picnic lunch."

Paul stood. "Can I help?"

She pulled a package of meat and a jar of salad dressing out of the refrigerator and reached for the loaf of bread. "Thanks, but I'm only making sandwiches. I hope that's OK."

"Sounds good. To a bachelor, a sandwich is a three-course meal—bread, meat, and lettuce for a green vegetable."

Kay laughed. She began spreading salad dressing on four slices of bread.

"What's that you're painting?" Paul asked.

She glanced over her shoulder toward the easel. "An illustration for a health magazine. You know—when a woman eats right and exercises, she can have a healthy old age."

"Right." He looked at the paintings on the wall again. "I like the cactus flower and the, uh . . . the desert scene."

She turned around to smile at him. "You don't have to spare my feelings. I didn't paint that last one. My younger sister did it for me three years ago when she was in high school. Art is hard for her, but she did it anyway, just to show me . . . to let me know she still loved me." Kay's eyes glistened.

Kay and her sister must be close, Paul thought. "And that drawing in the corner?"

She looked at the picture of the woman and the girl. "A figure study I did for a class a couple of years ago."

"It's very good—the kind of work I can't forget."

She turned back to making sandwiches. "My teacher tried to get me to sell it—that and four paintings of mine she liked. I sold the paintings and got my start as a professional, but I couldn't let go of the drawing."

"Is it something you saw somewhere—somebody you know?"

It was several seconds before Kay answered. "Sometimes artists just have to put things onto paper or canvas—things they see in their minds," she said over her shoulder. "Some of those things won't let you alone until you do it."

Paul sat down at the table. Kay worked in silence until she finished the sandwiches. Then she put down the knife she was using and stood for several seconds leaning on the counter, eyes closed. Finally, she stepped back and said, "There's a bag of chips up high in the cupboard. Could you get them down for me, please?"

He did it, and when he turned around, she was sitting on the couch, her back to him.

Paul walked around to sit beside her. He was startled by the pallor of her face. "Are you all right?"

"Yes." She put a hand up to shield her eyes from the window light. "No." When she squeezed her eyes shut, tears came out. "It's a migraine. I tried to ignore it, but I can't. When they come on this fast, they're the worst kind."

Slowly she leaned over until her head lay on the armrest of the couch. "I'm afraid I wouldn't be any good at the beach right now," she said softly. "Could you please close the blinds?"

He stood, took hold of her ankles, and gently put her legs up on the couch. "Stretch out and get comfortable," he said as he shut the blinds. "Anything else I can do?"

"Get me a glass of water? And there's a bottle of capsules in the medicine cabinet in the bathroom—a prescription for migraines."

She gulped down two of the capsules when he brought them. He put the sandwiches she had made into the refrigerator, then asked, "What else?"

"Nothing, really. I just have to sleep for a while. I'll go lie on the bed in a minute."

"Do you need help getting there? Do you need someone around?"

"No. I've learned how to handle this." She stretched her arm out toward him. "Thanks. Thanks for today. I'm sorry to drop out on you now."

He took hold of her hand, helped her up, and pointed her toward the bedroom door. "Go get the rest you need. There'll be another time."

"I hope so."

She disappeared into the bedroom.

Paul let himself out and made sure he heard the lock click into place when he pulled the door shut behind him.

Chapter 4

"I've got to get this on film," Kay said, rummaging in her bag for her camera.

She walked across the beach out into water above her knees and stood there shooting pictures of the breaking surf in the late after-noon sun. She bent low to shoot just above the waves, moving one way and then another as she tried to frame exactly the right view.

"Don't get the camera wet," Paul yelled.

"What?" she called back.

"Don't get the camera wet!" he yelled again, louder this time.

Kay cupped her hand around her ear.

Paul waved at her and smiled. She smiled too, then turned and went back to shooting photos.

He had never seen anyone enjoy the beach so much. Kay found beauty in everything she saw here—the texture of the sand, the occasional seashell worn smooth, the way gulls soared on the wind.

After the sun had sunk below the horizon, she came back to sit on her towel beside him. Rubbing her arms, she reached for the shirt she had worn to the beach. "It gets cool pretty fast out here after the sun goes down."

"Especially for someone who's used to the desert."

"I don't care. I want to drink in every last bit of this while I'm here."

He grinned at her. "Are you going to cry this time when you have to leave?"

She laughed.

"You can come back anytime you want. It's close."

"I know," she said. "But it won't be so much fun without . . . alone."

She leaned back on her elbows and looked out at the water. "I could watch the waves for hours. They fascinated me the first time I came here. They just keep coming and coming—forever. Did you ever wonder where they come from?"

"I used to. Then when I was about sixteen I found out."

Kay looked at him expectantly. He kept a straight face as he continued. "There's a big wave generator out there two miles offshore that makes extra-large waves for the tourists. It's operated by the state parks system."

Kay laughed, and pushed him down on his towel. "Too much sun today. You're delirious. Take another nap."

Paul laughed too, and raised up on his elbow again. "When I was a little boy, I used to think Heavenly Father made these waves just for me. I loved to let them chase me. Then when I was older, I played a different game. I built castles near the water, with moats, and I'd try to make the castles so strong and the moats so deep that the water couldn't break them down."

He paused, and Kay turned on her right side, leaning on her elbow too, so she could look him in the face.

"My mother lives down in Redondo Beach," he said. "The beach down there is perfect for sitting and watching the waves whenever I'm stressed or lonely. That helps me sort things out. It always reminds me that the Lord made this whole world work, so my problems aren't too big for him to help me with."

Kay looked into his eyes for several seconds, as though trying to read the thoughts behind them. Her own eyes shone with tears, but she didn't cry. Finally, she said, "I need to remember that too—the part about the Lord helping."

She reached out to touch his hand. "And please don't be lonely, Paul. I know about lonely—it's awful. You can always call me. I'm a good listener."

"That's an invitation I might not be able to resist."

"Don't try. I meant it."

She gazed out toward the waves again. They were nearly black now, with patches of white foam along the breakers. The sky had faded to a deep blue overhead, with a dark orange band just above the water where the sun had set. Kay sucked in a breath. "Beautiful!"

So is she, Paul thought. He lay studying her face.

He was close enough to kiss her right now. If he just leaned forward . . .

No. Not yet. If that ever happened, he'd have to feel sure it was something Kay wanted too. He had promised himself that the next time he began to get close to a woman, he would be sure of how she felt before he let his own feelings get away from him.

Kay sighed. "I suppose we really do have to go." She stood and pulled on her jeans over her swimming suit.

"Are you sure you're ready? We can stay and enjoy this as long as you want."

She held out her hand. He took hold of it and she pulled to help him up. "Come on, working man. You have regular office hours tomorrow, and I have work to do too."

They gathered their things and walked up the beach toward where his car was parked. Kay surprised him when she slipped her arm through his. "Thanks for giving us another chance at this."

He moved his hand down her arm and intertwined his fingers with hers. "Wouldn't have missed it."

"So—what *does* a wire service reporter do every day? What's the big item on your agenda tomorrow?"

"Well, I'll probably have some assignments from the bureau chief—breaking news. I also do political and business features. And there's the investigative story I was working on in Las Vegas a couple of weeks ago—but that one might be dead unless I can get more help from my source."

Kay's brow furrowed thoughtfully. "What makes something like that important, Paul? I mean writing about people when they're all tangled up in . . . when their lives . . ."

"I don't enjoy writing about people in those situations." He shrugged. "But it's part of the job."

"And you enjoy the other part enough to make up for it? I mean, what is it that makes you *have* to do what you do?"

"Just like something inside of you *has* to paint?"

"Yes."

Paul grinned at her. "It's the money—and the glory."

"Unh uh. You're not a money-and-glory kind of guy." She stood by his car looking at him expectantly.

"Serious, huh?"

"Serious. I really want to know."

He opened the car door for her. "When people ask that question, they're usually wondering if it's some kind of ego thing."

She shook her head. "Not you."

He shut her door after her, walked around to get into the driver's seat, and started the car before he said anything more.

"It's truth, I think—wanting the truth to come out. I used to believe the solution to every problem was truth, the way I saw it; if people had full access to the truth, they would see the way things ought to be, just like I did. But I've learned that truth can be subjective—very slippery sometimes. So now I'll settle for a free flow of information so people can make their own informed decisions about the things that affect their lives."

"Wow! That's . . . profound." She put her hands together and made a mock bow in his direction. "I feel unworthy of your wisdom, oh great one."

Paul laughed. He put the car into gear and pulled away from the curb.

Her smile faded. "I still feel sorry for the people who get caught on the other end."

"I do too. But sometimes writing about what they've done saves somebody else from getting hurt." He paused. "I hate seeing *anybody* suffer—even when they bring it on themselves. The part I hate most is when they get caught and start lying to cover up. It just hurts them more."

"Do you ever write about *good* things people do?"

The question took him off guard. "Um, yeah, sure. . . . Sure I do."

"What's the last story you did that made you feel really good about people?"

"A feature about businesses that put part of their profits into development of Third World countries. Before that, a story about a city councilman who kept his promise to listen to people and vote their way instead of his."

Paul was surprised at how easily she drew him out. He was used to being the one who probed for answers. Her questions made him think, and she had been right when she said she was a good listener. She made him feel like he could trust her with anything.

They were driving up her street when he asked: "Are you doing something Friday night? I'd really love to take you to dinner."

She hesitated before answering. "I'd love that too, Paul. But I have a big commissioned piece due next week and I have to spend the weekend working on it."

"That's a shame," he said as he pulled into her driveway. "I was planning a quiet little dinner for two on the beach—candlelight, silver, a dozen violins, *really* fresh seafood . . ."

Kay laughed. "I knew there was a romantic in you somewhere. Please ask me again sometime."

She sat looking at him, smiling. She was close. If he leaned toward her, would she . . .

"Thanks for making today so much fun," she said. "And thanks for being such a fine man." She put a finger to her lips and touched it to his cheek. Then she was out of his car and gone.

He wished he had taken a chance on kissing her.

"CommerceBank of California. This is the office of the administrative vice president."

"This is Paul Webber."

There was a small gasp on the other end of the line. "How did you . . ." She lowered her voice. "Why did you call me here?"

"I need more information. Can we meet for a few minutes on your lunch hour?"

Her reply was firm: "That won't be possible."

"I think you were right—Delaroi's into something that may be illegal. But the story isn't going to go anywhere unless you can help me."

She hesitated. "I have no further information."

"He met someone in Las Vegas. Are you interested in knowing who?"

There was a long pause. "Yes."

"I have pictures. I need you to tell me if you know the man."

Her voice dropped to just above a whisper. "I go to lunch at twelve-fifteen."

"All right, you pick the spot. When you come out of the bank building, look both ways up and down the street, then change your purse from one hand to the other. I'll follow you. I have light hair and glasses, and I'm wearing a light blue shirt and a patterned tie."

Paul was waiting in his car across the street when a woman in a conservative gray business suit stepped out of the bank building, glanced toward the south, then turned and started walking north. She shifted her bag from her left hand to her right. He got out of his car and started walking parallel to her.

There was gray in her dark hair, and she was beginning to look matronly. When they stopped for the traffic light on the corner, she glanced across the street in his direction, but he didn't know if she had picked him out of the crowd.

By the time he crossed to her side of the street, she was half a block ahead of him. She stepped into a small diner with a neon sign that said QuickiLunch over the door. Paul followed, and found her sitting in a booth at the back.

"Is this place taken?" he asked, gesturing toward the empty seat opposite her.

She looked him up and down carefully. "That depends on your name."

"Paul Webber." He slid into the seat opposite her. "Thank you for coming, Mrs. Leeds." He extended his hand across the table.

Her eyes narrowed, and she ignored his hand. "How did you know my name? How did you know I'm married?"

"I told the woman at the switchboard when I called that I didn't know your name. She volunteered it—trying to make the bank warm and friendly, I think." He glanced at her left hand. "And the rings say it's *Mrs.*"

Slowly, she relaxed. "I'm sorry, Mr. Webber. I'm a bit nervous about doing this." She extended her hand and he shook it.

"I'll do everything I can to protect you and your position at the bank—I promise. And please call me Paul."

She smiled. "Anna." Her expression was pleasant—she could have been the grandmother that somebody loved to hug—but she was wary. Her eyes kept looking around the room, checking out the scene behind him.

"Would you like to go someplace where there's no risk of being seen?" he asked.

"This will be all right. The food is awful, so no one from my office comes here. I ordered coffee and a bagel. If you want lunch, I'd advise you to put it off."

She looked at the small portfolio he carried. "You said you have some pictures?"

He pulled out the two best photos of Delaroi and the other man and slid them across the table to her.

She studied them for several seconds, then looked up at him and shook her head.

Paul frowned. "You don't know the man in the suit?"

"No. I've never seen him before. Who is he?"

"I don't know. I was hoping you would." Paul took the keno ticket out of his portfolio and put it in front of her. "But I heard him talking money, and he left this on the table. Does it mean anything to you?"

She puzzled over the paper, tracing her finger across the numbers, then looked up at him again. "Could be an account number—but not one of ours, unless there's more to it."

Slowly, Paul leaned back in the booth. "That's all I have."

Anna pushed the pictures and the keno ticket across the table to him. "Well, I have something new that might help us. This morning after you called, Mr. Delaroi told me that he's going up to the cabin at Big Bear for the weekend again. This time he said he's taking his wife."

Mr. and Mrs. Delaroi came out of the house early on Saturday morning carrying suitcases. A bad sign, Paul thought. Maybe this trip really would be just a visit to their cabin at the lake.

But when their Lexus passed up the Big Bear turnoff on I-15, he settled in, two cars back, for the drive across the desert.

In Las Vegas, the Delarois stopped at an automatic teller machine, where Mrs. Delaroi drew out some cash. Then they drove to one of the largest of the new hotel-casino complexes and made their way to its indoor mall.

Paul followed them to several exclusive shops where Mrs. Delaroi tried on what appeared to be expensive outfits. She had the build to make them look good; she might have been a model.

After lunch, they visited two western art galleries where James Delaroi took his time browsing. In the second one, it appeared that he was negotiating over a painting of a desert landscape, but he walked away without it.

Paul managed to stay out of their sight by wandering into businesses opposite the ones where the Delarois were shopping, then keeping an eye on them through the glass storefronts. Twice, with his camera at thigh level in the palm of his hand, he was able to snap pictures of them. Once they reversed course suddenly while he was following them down the mall, so he turned quickly to look into a shop window, his back to them as they passed. Mrs. Delaroi bumped into him and said, "Oh, excuse me." Paul heard her husband say as they walked on, "Anyway, the money is always here for us to use."

Late in the afternoon, they returned to one of the shops they had visited earlier, and Mrs. Delaroi purchased two dresses.

It was nearly eight o'clock when it became apparent that they were planning to stay the night. After a leisurely dinner in the hotel restaurant, they retrieved their suitcases from their car, then stopped at the registration desk. The clerk checked a reservation card and handed James Delaroi a room key. Standing at a pay phone nearby, Paul could hear the clerk say: "When you get out of the elevator on eleven, you'll find the room to your right."

He had been following the Delarois around for several hours. If they had noticed him, they had given no sign of it. Still, he didn't want to make himself too obvious. When they headed for an elevator, he took a different one to the tenth floor, then raced up the fire stairs to the eleventh. But that trick didn't work for him in this hotel. As he pushed the fire door open a crack, he found himself at the end of a short hallway branching off of a larger one; there was no straight corridor to afford him a view of everyone coming and going. After a couple of minutes, he stepped out into the hallway and went in search of the elevator. There were two dozen rooms to the right of it; the Delarois might be in any one of those.

He had lost them.

They had met no one today and done nothing that seemed significant. A whole day spent and he had nothing new—except the words Delaroi had said to his wife: "The money is always here for us to use."

Driving back to Los Angeles tonight was out of the question.

Scott laughed when he heard Paul's voice on the telephone. "Yes, the Hotel Pike has a vacancy, but I'm afraid the restaurant is already closed. I might have some leftovers in the fridge."

"That's OK, I'll grab something at a drive-through."

"Bring me a chocolate shake and I'll see that you enjoy all the perks of the executive suite."

"And what are those?"

"First dibs on the newspaper in the morning."

This sacrament meeting would be different from what Paul had grown used to—there were youth speakers on the program and children in the congregation.

The meetinghouse was on Tropicana, near Scott's apartment, and Paul had selected the ward on the 9:00 A.M. schedule so he could get an early start for Los Angeles after the meetings.

He sat next to the wall on a bench near the rear door of the chapel. A couple with two small children sat between him and the aisle. Their little girl, perhaps two years old, stood close to her mother on the bench and smiled shyly at him. Paul couldn't resist smiling back.

The little girl put her arm on the back of the bench and Paul patted her hand. She pulled her arm away, but then she put it back on the bench a few seconds later to see what he would do. He patted her hand again, and she giggled this time as she pulled it away. They played this game until the opening hymn began.

The hymn and opening prayer were over when Paul noticed two people making their way up the aisle on the other side of the chapel.

The blonde woman in the green dress! It was the same woman he had seen in the hotel the first time he followed James Delaroi to Las Vegas. She was leading a little girl by the hand, a beautiful child three or four years old with long, dark hair and dark eyes. The little girl looked around curiously at what seemed to be an out-of-the-ordinary setting for her. The woman led her to a vacant bench about halfway up the far side of the chapel.

Most of the rest of the meeting was lost on Paul. During the sacrament he tried to concentrate on why he had come to church today—tried to keep his thoughts focused on the Savior. But afterward he couldn't keep himself from watching the woman and child across the room.

The woman was tender with the little girl and seemed to be trying to orient her to what was going on. When the child's attention wandered, they played quiet finger games.

Adjusting his position from time to time so he could see past people in the center section of the chapel, Paul studied the woman's profile. He was sure—*almost* sure—it was the same face he had studied so closely at the beach just four days ago. The first time he had met the woman in the green dress, she had managed to convince him that she simply resembled someone he knew. But there was more than just a resemblance. With darker, shoulder-length hair and blue eyes, this woman would be Kay.

When the meeting ended, Paul stood immediately, but the family next to him was slow getting out of the pew. By the time he reached the other side of the chapel, the woman in the green dress and the little girl had stepped into the foyer and disappeared. As he made his way through the foyer, he could see them just going out the side exit door down the hall.

He walked to the door as quickly as he could and looked out into the parking lot. The woman and girl were getting into a dark blue Cadillac with a chauffeur. Paul noted the license number as the car turned out into the street, then hurried back to the foyer, dashed through the cultural hall and out to his car, hoping he would be able to catch the other vehicle.

Intent on weaving his way through the traffic on Tropicana, he almost did not see the Cadillac as it waited in the left turn lane at a traffic light. He braked hard and veered into the turn lane, two cars behind the big blue sedan. The left turn arrow went to yellow before Paul reached the intersection to turn, but he squeezed through the light anyway.

The Cadillac set a leisurely pace across town. When it turned the corner at a large park on Eastern Avenue, Paul sped up to keep from losing it. Rounding the corner, he could see the Cadillac pulling to the curb ahead. He took the first available parking space, several cars back.

The little girl was wearing jeans and a pullover shirt instead of her Sunday dress when she got out of the car. The chauffeur, a gray-haired man with a limp, retrieved a picnic basket from the trunk and followed the blonde woman and the child into the park.

The woman pushed the little girl in a swing on the playground for a time, then sat down in the swing beside her. The girl stopped swinging and made patterns in the dirt with her shoes as she and the woman talked and laughed together. Then they walked to the shady spot under a tree where the chauffeur waited with the picnic basket. The woman invited the chauffeur to join them, but he smiled, shook his head, and walked to the car.

The woman and girl bowed their heads and folded their arms, and Paul could see the woman's lips moving.

After they ate, the little girl went back to the playground and was soon involved in a game with three other children. The woman watched her for about half an hour, then beckoned her to the car.

The Cadillac headed into the eastern part of Las Vegas. Paul was following it up the long slope of Bonanza Road, one car back, when the car between them turned off into a subdivision. To avoid making it obvious that he was following, Paul turned off on the next street. He hoped that he had guessed right about where the Cadillac was headed; they were just two streets below the Las Vegas temple.

He quickly turned his car around and parked next to the low brick wall in front of the house on the street corner. The wall hid the lower two-thirds of his car, but he had a clear view up Bonanza Road.

The Cadillac had turned around and pulled to a stop in front of the temple. The woman and girl got out and gazed up at the temple's spires. Then, holding the little girl's hand, the woman led her around the corner in the direction of the temple gate. They were gone for about twenty minutes before they came back to the waiting car.

Paul slid low in his seat as the big sedan came back down the road past him. He waited several seconds, then pulled out to follow it.

Twice he almost lost the Cadillac in traffic but managed to catch up again. Finally it turned onto Alta Drive, off of Rancho. Half a mile farther on, it slowed to pull through a wrought-iron gate on the left.

Paul cruised past slowly and parked in front of a van across the street. Looking back through the gate, he could see most of the semicircular driveway and the front of the house—two-story white stone with a fountain in the middle of a front lawn that looked almost as smooth and soft as a billiard table. It would make a perfect picture for the cover of *Better Homes and Gardens.* There was a three-car garage on the far end of the house and a path down the near side that probably led to a pool in back, judging from the striped beach umbrella that could be seen through the wrought-iron fence.

This was "old money" Las Vegas. But, in a city scratched out of the desert largely over the past few decades, old money didn't have to go back very far; these homes probably dated from the 1960s. The name on the mailbox in front of the house was Riddley—familiar for some reason, but Paul couldn't remember why at the moment.

A large man with silver hair came out of the front door of the house. The woman and little girl stepped out of the car and the girl skipped happily up the sidewalk. The man gathered her up in his arms. She looked back at the woman still standing by the car, said something, and squirmed to get down again, but the man would not let her. The woman walked slowly up the sidewalk, seemingly wary of the man. She carried a small suitcase which she put down on the ground next to him. Then she stood on tiptoe to kiss the little girl. The girl hugged her around the neck. The man stood impassively.

The woman walked back down the sidewalk, opened the car door, and blew the little girl a kiss. The girl waved. The woman wiped at her eyes. The silver-haired man picked up the suitcase and stepped into the house with the girl.

Hugh Riddley. If you read the business news in Las Vegas,

sooner or later you'd run across the name. Riddley Construction, one of southern Nevada's largest privately-owned companies, was organized in the late 1920s when Boulder Dam was being built. Hugh was the son of its founder. Was this where he lived? Would that be him with the little girl?

The woman in the green dress got into the back seat of the Cadillac. It pulled slowly out of the gate and headed back down Alta Drive. Paul drove quickly to the next corner, turned around, and followed the other car at a discreet distance.

The chauffeur drove the woman to downtown Las Vegas, stopping in front of a small bus depot where a sign advertised twice-a-day runs to and from Los Angeles.

Twenty yards to the south, a double line of headlights flowed up I-15 toward Las Vegas. Ahead of him, red lines of taillights led the way toward Los Angeles in the dusk.

Ordinarily, Paul hated the monotony of this drive across the desert, but today the bleakness that stretched in every direction had hardly registered with him. His mind was focused on the vehicle ahead.

What did the people in this bus do with their hours on the way back from a weekend at the tables or slot machines? Try to figure out how to get along without the money they had lost? Work out a better system for next time?

What did the woman in the green dress do—think about the little girl in the big house on Alta Drive?

Nothing about this woman made sense. If it was Kay, why would she need a disguise? Why would she lie to him? And who was the little girl?

By the time he had crossed the state line into California, he had begun to wonder if he was a fool for following this bus. After all, he had never been closer than fifty feet to the woman in the green dress today. Maybe there really was someone who bore a very close resemblance to Kay. Maybe he should give this up before he made a complete idiot of himself. Maybe . . .

No! Her profile was the same, and this time, he was going to *know* whether he was right about her.

Paul glanced at his fuel gauge. Would the bus go straight into Los Angeles without stopping? He didn't have enough gasoline to make it that far. But he didn't want to risk getting to the terminal after the bus arrived, giving this woman a chance to slip away again.

He pulled alongside the bus hoping to find some clue to its destination. The art deco logo that ran the length of the vehicle proclaimed the name of the line: California Cruisers. Beneath it: "Weekend round-trips to Las Vegas. Call 213-GOVEGAS."

He pulled in front of the bus, then reached for his cell phone and dialed the number.

"California Cruisers," a monotone voice answered.

"I'm supposed to meet someone who's on your gambler's special from Vegas. Can you tell me what time it gets in and where your terminal is?" He made mental note of the answers, then asked: "Any stops before that one?"

"No."

He said thanks, hung up, and glanced at his watch. He could stop for gasoline and still be at the terminal well before the bus's 9:15 arrival time. He pushed his accelerator down and watched the bus grow smaller in his rearview mirror.

The passengers filed into the terminal slowly, as though no one were in any particular hurry to go anywhere. He watched from behind a video game machine—waiting for the woman in the green dress.

She was among the last to straggle through the door. Her sunglasses might have been simply a Hollywood touch, but when she paused just inside the terminal, Paul realized that the eyes behind the glasses were scanning it. He moved so that only a part of his face was visible from her vantage point.

She held her gray, hard-sided suitcase stiffly in front of her, as though ready to use it for a shield. What was she afraid of?

Her glance didn't linger on the video arcade area, and she seemed to relax a bit as she turned to walk toward the other side of the terminal.

Paul strode after her, ready to confront her before she could get out of his sight again.

He was not quick enough—not quite close enough to speak before she stepped through the door marked "Women." He had been close enough, though, to see the monogram on her suitcase: KR. *Kristina Riddley?*

He stood uncertainly in the middle of the terminal, then retreated to the game machine again, positioning himself so he had a clear view of the door she had entered.

After fifteen minutes, he began to wonder if she might have gotten out when he looked down momentarily at the game. But no—she couldn't have crossed the terminal that fast.

At twenty minutes, he began to wonder if there might be another exit from the restroom. He stared across the room, toying idly with the joystick on the game.

"It works better if you put a quarter in, man."

Paul glanced over his shoulder at the source of the voice. The boy was fifteen—maybe. Shaggy hair, wrinkled clothes, looked like he might have been sleeping in the terminal.

"I'm getting the feel of the machine," Paul answered. He pretended to study the movements of the electronic starship on the screen.

"Yeah, well, you been doin' that for at least five minutes. Why don't you let somebody play who knows how?"

"You can drop your quarter in as soon as I'm gone."

"I don't have a quarter, but I figure you could give me one."

Paul turned toward the boy again to speak, but the reply he had formed was instantly replaced in his mind by an image from the scene in the terminal—a woman carrying a gray suitcase. He swiveled to look again. The woman with the suitcase in her hand was just stepping out the door to the street. He had been watching for the green dress, but now she wore a plain brown skirt and beige top. Her shoulder-length brown hair was pulled back and fastened in a barrette, and she wore no makeup. It was Kay Reston.

"Enjoy," Paul muttered, walking away from the machine.

She was just closing the door of a taxi as he stepped outside. He sprinted toward the parking lot across the street, but by the time he got his car started, the taxi was out of sight.

No problem. He knew where it was going.

Chapter 5

He let the car roll slowly to a stop across the street from the house where Kay lived.

What was he going to say to her—"Who are you, really?" He wasn't sure he was ready for an answer to that question.

He took a deep breath and exhaled slowly.

The digital clock in the dashboard read 9:45. If he didn't do something quickly, she would be going to bed.

He walked across the street and down the driveway to her apartment, then stood on the porch looking at her door.

Cool off, Webber! Your journalistic ego's in overdrive. You want to pin her to the wall because she lied to you, but this isn't some politician, this is Kay, and her secret's not necessarily your business just because you're a reporter.

Slowly he raised his hand to the doorbell button.

Remember, she got away with feeding you a lie because you let it happen. You wanted things to work out so you could date her.

He rang the bell.

Think about her. *She probably needs a friend right now. She was hurting when she left that little girl this afternoon. What is it all about?*

The glass peephole in front of him darkened, then Kay opened the door. "Paul—it's good to see you! But it's so late. What are you doing here?"

"May I come in?"

"Sure. I was, ah . . . I was just getting ready to go to bed. But I'd love to visit with you for a few minutes."

Her yawn was too elaborate, he thought as he stepped inside.

49

"I won't stay long. I'll bet you're exhausted from the trip."

Kay's eyes registered surprise—but only for a moment. She put on a puzzled look. "Trip? What are you talking about?"

"The trip back from Las Vegas. You've had a long day."

She smiled at him, very deliberately it seemed. "You've been to Las Vegas again? I've been here all afternoon. I wasn't feeling well, so—"

"You weren't here. You were—"

"I *was* here." She looked at him indulgently, as she might look at a child who had said something odd. "There must be something about Las Vegas that makes you see strange things, because—"

"Stop it, Kay! Bluffing isn't going to work this time." The smoothness of her lying brought out the blunt, accusatory tone he would use in an ambush interview. "The first time I saw you in that blonde wig and those brown contact lenses, you managed to convince me that I was wrong, that I just *thought* you were somebody I knew. But not again."

She stood looking at him for several seconds, her face a blank. Then her expression changed slowly, as though she had decided what she had to do about this situation. Her brow furrowed and her lips became a thin line. She stepped around him and opened the door. "I think you'd better go." Her tone was angry. "This is sounding crazy!"

"Yeah—but it's true," Paul said evenly. "You went to church this morning in a ward on Tropicana Avenue in Las Vegas. You had a little girl with you, about four. After sacrament meeting, you ducked out and took her to Jaycee Park. There was an older man driving you, in a big, blue Cadillac."

Kay stood with her hand gripping the door handle. The look on her face was a mixture of fear and fascination.

"You took the little girl to a white, two-story mansion on Alta Drive," Paul continued. "Then the chauffeur drove you to the bus station. When you—"

"No! You're wrong! I—"

"When you got off the bus in Los Angeles, you went into the restroom in the terminal. When you came out, the wig and the sunglasses and the green dress were gone, and you—"

"Stop it! *Stop it! Please* . . . stop!" The muscles stood out in

Kay's slim forearms as her hands clenched into fists by her sides. "You have no right . . . you can't . . . I mean, you're wrong, about all of that! I want you to go now—or I'll call the police."

"Why won't you tell me the truth?" Paul demanded.

Her suitcase sat on the floor next to the couch. He snatched it up angrily and pushed at one catch, then the other with his thumbs. Kay almost leaped at him trying to grab the suitcase away, but as she pulled on the top, it sprang open suddenly and the blonde wig tumbled to the floor. The green dress was folded neatly on top of the clothing in the case.

Kay's look was anguish. She began to back away from him, past the couch, into her tiny living room.

"Want to tell me about it?" he said.

She sat down on the couch, put her face in her hands, and sobbed.

Mechanically, Paul shut the suitcase, put it down, and closed the front door. Then he stood looking at Kay.

Interviews didn't end like this. Politicians or business executives didn't break into tears after being caught in a lie.

He had watched people crumble in the face of tragedy; at times like that he had tried to do his job without adding to their suffering, but somehow he had always managed to insulate himself from their pain.

This was different. *He* had brought on the pain, for someone he cared about. *You went into automatic on being the reporter—forgot the part about being a friend.*

Slowly he sat down beside Kay. He reached out and gently stroked her hair. She surprised him by sitting up and leaning against his chest, leaving his arm draped around her shoulders. His shirt was quickly wet with her tears. He put his other arm around her and held her close.

When her sobbing finally subsided and she sat up straight, he hated letting go of her.

"I'm sorry for going to pieces like that," she said. She ran her fingers through her hair, brushing it back from her face. Even without makeup, her eyes red from crying, she was pretty, Paul thought.

Kay turned to face him. "And I'm sorry I didn't tell you the truth from the first, Paul. I've tried to keep *everyone* here from finding out about Las Vegas because . . . but the pressure has been . . . and now it feels good to know there's somebody I don't have to be on guard with all the time."

"I know how to keep secrets, Kay. I might even be able to help—if you'll trust me."

She frowned. "I don't think *anyone* can really help me. My ex-husband has too much on his side."

"That would be Wes? The man I saw you with the first time?"

She nodded.

"And the little girl you were with today?"

"Our daughter, Angela."

Paul looked up at Kay's drawing on the wall—the woman holding her arms open to the little girl. "That's her running to you?"

"She's the one good thing I've got in this world. I'm there to put my arms around her and protect her."

"From Wes?"

"Mmmm—that's part of it. But it's bigger than Wes. I need to protect her from the world—from the kind of life I got myself into." She paused. "Wes never cared enough about Angela one way or the other to hurt *her* deliberately."

"But . . . he hurt you?"

"He slapped me a few times. By then our marriage was already dead, and I didn't stay around long enough for him to get in the habit." She sighed. "Most of the pain in our relationship was emotional."

Paul put his arm around her again. "It makes me mad to think about him hurting you."

She looked up at the drawing. "The first version I made of that had me on my knees with Angela behind me clinging to my neck while Wes stood over us with his hands doubled up into fists. An artist I respect told me it was a very powerful piece; she thought I ought to enter it in a show. But I destroyed it. Every time I looked at it, I hated Wes all over again—especially because he took our daughter away from me—and I don't want to live with hate anymore."

Paul studied the drawing on the wall. "This one's powerful too. It says *joy* in ways I never felt before. Do you ever sit here and look at it on the bad days?"

"Sometimes. It helps. But there was so *much* . . . there's *still* so much that I can't seem to let go of."

Kay leaned against Paul's shoulder. She let herself enjoy for the moment the comfort of being close to him, of feeling that this man cared somehow what happened to her. "I got a migraine the first day you came here because you asked me about the drawing. I hit maximum stress almost instantly. That morning with you had been fun—but there's something inside of me that says I don't have any right to be happy as long as I let myself be separated from Angela."

"Ouch! Isn't it hard to live with that?"

"I'm working on it. But I keep that drawing up there to remind me of my goal—finding a way to live close to her again and be a real mother."

"Why did you let Wes . . . I mean, doesn't a court usually give the mother some preference . . ."

"You'd think so." Tears came to her eyes again. "Wes forced me to give her up. He's holding our daughter hostage."

"Hostage?"

Kay nodded. "Because I decided to hold onto my half of our business when we divorced."

"You liked being in business that much?"

She wrinkled her nose. "No. I was trying to be sure I'd have some income for my daughter and me. I didn't have any job prospects and I didn't think Wes would ever pay me alimony if he could duck it." She pushed her hair back from her face again. "Now I wish I'd listened to my lawyer. She told me to let the business go."

"But what kind of leverage does it give him to hold onto your daughter?"

"He can do whatever he wants with the company and I don't dare say anything about it. He blindsided me—let me think he wasn't going to fight me. Then the day before our divorce hearing, he told me if I was going to keep a hand in the business, he was going to keep Angela. I could either settle for weekend visiting rights, or he'd show the court I was an unfit mother and I might lose her completely."

"No judge would buy that. Without evidence—"

"Oh, there's evidence—thanks to Wes!"

"You mean . . . he set you up?"

"In a way. Angela fell and hit her head when she was learning to walk. Wes left the doctor thinking that I caused it. Then—"

"Wait a minute. He told the doctor you hurt your own daughter—and the doctor didn't ask *you* about it?"

"Wes got his chance to talk to the doctor first, while I was waiting with Angela in the examination room. He didn't bother to tell the doctor that *he* was the one who was with her when she got hurt. All I could ever get him to admit was that he said some things about how hard he thought it was for me to deal with a baby, how he wondered if I'd blow up sometimes when I was alone with her and yank her . . . or push her . . ." Slowly, she shook her head. "When the doctor came in and asked *me* how it happened, I said the same thing Wes had told me at first—that she fell against the coffee table. The doctor mentioned some classes for young parents. I didn't understand at the time why he brought that up."

The fingers of Paul's free hand curled into a fist. He willed them to relax. "Do you think Wes was covering for himself?"

"I don't know. He slips into lying so easily, but . . . well, at the time, I believed the coffee table story. It happens."

She looked up at her drawing on the wall. "Four months later, Angela broke her arm. She wiggled loose and fell on the steps while I was playing with her in Wes's father's swimming pool. I took her to the doctor again, and a couple of days later a state social worker showed up. She said she understood I might be having some trouble coping with parenthood. That's when I found out what Wes had told the doctor the first time." She bit her lip. "I might have been in serious trouble if Max hadn't been there to say he'd seen Angela fall and it was an accident."

"Max?"

"The chauffeur."

"What did your, uh . . ." Paul couldn't bring himself to say *husband;* Wes didn't deserve the title. "What did Wes say when you talked to him about it?"

"He denied everything, of course—said the doctor must have misunderstood. I talked to the doctor later and tried to convince him of what *really* happened. I don't know whether he believed me."

"So when you were going to divorce Wes, he brought this up again?"

"Yes. He said he could come up with other stories—that was the word he used—about how I'd abused Angela. He said his father would spend anything it cost to keep me from taking his only grandchild away."

"And whatever Hugh Riddley wants, Hugh Riddley gets."

Kay sat up straight and looked at him in surprise. "How did you know about him?"

"From working for the newspaper in Las Vegas. He has a reputation for getting things done his way."

"Yes—no matter what he has to do to anyone else."

"What do you mean by that?"

Kay didn't answer; she gazed at her drawing again. "Wes didn't really want Angela. She lives with Hugh. I think Hugh was behind the whole thing—or maybe Wes was just making points with him by playing the concerned father. Wes is a chameleon with people he needs to manipulate."

"Didn't your lawyer put up any resistance at all on the custody arrangements?"

"She wanted to, but I wouldn't let her. I wasn't strong enough to stand up to Wes and his father. I wouldn't risk losing Angela completely."

"Why don't you just give up the business now—tell Wes he can buy you out?"

"Believe me, I've tried! He won't hear of it. There's always some reason—it's too much money to raise all at once, or it's not a good time for the business, or . . ." There was bitterness in her tone. "He gets some perverse pleasure out of feeling like he still owns part of *me*—out of manipulating me."

"You stood up to him pretty well outside your hotel room the day I saw the two of you together."

Kay looked at him warily. "How much did you hear?"

"Enough to know what he wanted."

"It was so humiliating! He told me I needed to stay in the hotel because of a business meeting we were going to have. It never happened. He thought he could buy me a hotel room and then talk me into . . ." She looked away. "After you knocked on the door and

I saw you through the peephole, I went and laid on the bed and bawled. I needed desperately to talk to someone—but I couldn't face *you* that day."

"Kay, I—"

"You probably don't understand what it is to deal with somebody like Wes. When I met him in college, he was the most charming man I'd ever known. But it was all on the outside. He's a very little man on the inside. He *needs* to control people, and he'll do whatever it takes—flatter them, lie to them, threaten them. If he can't control them, then he has to get them out of his way somehow."

"But he wanted you back. And he hasn't tried to get you out of his way, so—"

"He wanted me back because he hasn't been able to control any other woman. Either they dumped him when he tried it, or he dumped them when he found out it wouldn't work. And after I started showing him it wouldn't work with me anymore, he *did* try to get me out of his way."

"What do you mean?"

Kay didn't answer; she put her fingers to her temples and began to massage.

"Another migraine?"

"It will be if I don't take something now to stop it."

Paul walked into the bathroom to look for her bottle of pain reliever. There was a new one, nearly full. He picked it up, walked into the kitchen to get a glass of water, and took the medicine and the water to her.

"Thanks." She shook three of the capsules from the bottle into her hand.

"Are you supposed to take that many at once? I thought two—"

"I've done it before. I'll be all right." She downed the capsules one at a time, with swallows of water.

Paul sat looking at her quizzically.

"What's wrong?" she asked.

"Just *thinking* about dealing with him brings on this much stress?"

"Sometimes—and he knows it. I think he puts me under pressure just to see what he can do to me."

"What did you mean when you said he's tried to get rid of you?"

"He tried to . . ." She looked away, frowning. "Well, he's done a lot of things—the divorce, Angela, the way he treats me . . ."

"Kay, it's me, Paul the reporter. You're dodging my question. Tell me what you were thinking."

She hesitated for a moment. "I can't."

"I heard him tell you that if you didn't have a life with him, you wouldn't have a life at all. Was that a real threat?"

"What do you think?"

"Stop it! I need to know what *you* think."

She didn't answer.

"Why are you so afraid of him?"

"You'd have to know Wes to understand."

"He's 250 miles away. You're out of his reach."

"Am I?"

"Why would he come after you?"

"He wouldn't. He'd send someone."

"Send . . . who? What are you talking about?"

She said nothing.

"You know I can find out more about him on my own."

"Leave him alone, Paul. Please. I'd be afraid for you."

"Why? I can take care of myself."

"That's what I thought too."

"What changed your mind?"

She was silent again.

"Come on, Kay! If he's threatened you, do something about it. You can't let him keep you living in fear."

"Don't you think I've tried to fight back? It's dangerous! If it weren't, I wouldn't be so far away from my baby."

"Then he *has* tried to get rid of you?"

"I can't prove he's behind it. It may be someone else."

"Tell me about it."

"Please don't make me! If you know too much, they might—"

" 'They' don't even know I'm alive."

"Let it stay that way."

"Listen to me, Kay! A friend of mine is afraid for her life. Most people don't have to live that way. I want to know why *you* do."

57

She sighed, and stared straight ahead for several seconds before she spoke. "One day about six months after the divorce, I came home to my apartment and found that someone had been in it while I was gone. Little things were out of place. There was a strange smell in my bedroom—like a man's cologne. I got scared and made the manager change the lock. Then the telephone calls started—no words, but I knew someone was there, listening to me."

"There are creeps who'll just keep calling when they get a woman who reacts. And the smell might have been some new cleaner you used, or something from outside. Are you sure—"

She moved away from him abruptly. "You sound just like the police! I was *not* imagining things. Someone *was* in my apartment. The calls kept on coming, but I didn't bother to tell the police because I didn't think they'd do anything."

Paul moved close to her again. "OK, you're right, I'm wrong—I'll shut up. Tell me."

"I finally moved and got an unlisted phone number. But it didn't take long for the calls to start again. Things got worse. . . ."

She knew there was something wrong when she opened the door. It wasn't the smell again—that didn't come until she went into the bedroom and saw the open drawers, things tossed on the floor. But there was something when she first stepped into the living room . . . some feeling.

Then she saw the picture on the kitchen counter—ragged edge, torn from a magazine . . . mother and little girl, smiling . . . mother's face crossed through with a large, red X.

After she found the mess in the bedroom, she was sitting in the middle of the floor, crying, when the phone rang. She picked it up and said hello. When he didn't answer, she said it again—and then screamed it in frustration. She thought she could faintly hear him breathing—or maybe she only imagined it.

"Listen, you creep, I know how to put an end to your fun—I'll move. You won't know where I am."

Hoarse whisper: "I'll find you again. You can't get away from me. We have to meet."

"Wes's voice?" Paul asked.

Kay shook her head. "Not a voice I knew. And it sounded like there was a slight accent—maybe New York."

"Who knew your phone number?"

"My parents. My lawyer, Cynthia. And Hugh Riddley, just in case there was some kind of emergency with Angela and they had to reach me."

"Did you call the police that time?"

"Yes. They asked a lot of questions and promised to send cars through the neighborhood more often. The phone company started tracing my calls. But then after the accident I knew I had to get out of Las Vegas."

The van in front of her skidded to a stop as a small boy on a bicycle wobbled into the roadway. She stomped on the brake pedal; it went clear to the floor—with no effect on her car! She whipped the steering wheel to the right just before her car reached the van.

Slam! car jumping the curb. . . . *Woman on the sidewalk, running—pushing a stroller out of the way. . . . Palm tree straight ahead. . . .*

Nothing. And then—arm shaking gently, woman's voice: "Are you all right?"

The police officer knelt, peered under the car, then dusted the knees of his pants with his hands as he stood. "When was the last time you had your brakes checked?"

"Last year. Why?"

"Your brake line's broken. It could have happened in the accident, or . . ."

"Or what?"

"Or before. The break's very clean. The line could have been cut—but there's no way to be sure." He looked at the bruise on her forehead. "I know you were only out for a few seconds, but I think we'd better send you to the hospital to have that checked."

Paul frowned. "You think Wes was behind it?"

"I'm sure he did it! Or he knows who did."

Wes opened the door when she knocked.

"What are you doing here on a Friday night?" she asked. "I thought you'd be out somewhere."

"Visiting my daughter," Wes answered.

"I want to see her."

He stared at the purple discoloration on her forehead. "What happened to you?"

"I want to see Angela, Wes."

"In a minute. Tell me what happened."

"I was in a car accident this afternoon. I was lucky it wasn't worse."

"Yes. You were," Wes said. There was no change in his expression, no visible response to her news, not even in his eyes. It was as though he had known about the accident already. But how could he possibly . . .

He smiled slightly. "Might be a good idea to have those brakes checked from time to time, hmm?"

She shivered, even though it was not cold.

"What do they gain by driving you out of Las Vegas?"

"What makes you think they just wanted me out? I'm afraid they want me dead! They just don't dare do it when I can be placed near them." She paused. "They probably know I'm in Los Angeles—they could learn that much by asking Max which bus I take. If they can find out where I live . . ."

"So the wig and the sunglasses, and changing clothes after you get off the bus—"

"Are a way to throw somebody off the track in case I'm followed. I don't always use the same bus line; sometimes I wait until Max drives away and go to another one. And I keep an eye on the people who get on the bus or hang around the terminal too. But I'm obviously not careful enough. *You* followed me."

"Luck. I already knew where to look after you lost me in the taxi."

Paul stared at the floor for a moment, thinking. "You're sure it wasn't Wes all those times on the phone, with a fake accent? When you put on that phony identity the first time I saw you in Las Vegas, you were very convincing."

"I was a drama minor in college, Paul. And I still feel bad about fooling you that way. Sorry." She smiled weakly, then it faded. "It wasn't Wes I heard on the phone. When the calls first started, I accused him of making them. He denied it. And then one came the next day while he was at my place dropping off Angela. *Very* convenient." She blushed. "Wes laughed because it upset me hearing the creep breathing on the phone. He said I needed to be more careful who I led on."

"You're sure it was a man that time, and not one of Wes' girlfriends?"

"I'm sure there's another man involved in this. My parents met him."

"When?"

"He went to their house after I moved here. He told them my lawyer had sent him to contact me, but when Mom went to call Cynthia, he got in his car and drove away. They said he was a couple of inches shorter than Dad—about five-eight, thin, and balding. And he had an accent—like he might be from New York, or somewhere back east."

"Did they manage to get his license number?"

Kay shook her head. "He drove some kind of gray sedan. They didn't pay much attention until it was too late."

"And he's never been back?"

"No. But I'm very careful because I know he's still out there. You're the only one here I've given my address to, except for the bishop and the Relief Society president. If Wes needs to contact me, he has to go through Cynthia."

Paul frowned. "Hugh Riddley's part in this doesn't compute for me. What does he gain by getting rid of you?"

"He keeps his granddaughter all to himself. I think there's no one in the world more important to him than her, and he's never trusted me to take care of her. He's always believed anything Wes told him about me. I think he hates me." Kay shrugged. "Maybe that's reason enough to get rid of me. It would be for some of his friends."

" 'Friends'?"

"Wes told me his father survived in the construction business when the mob was strong in Las Vegas by learning how to deal with them. Wes said a couple of them even have a stake in his father's company, and they like to keep a very low profile. He said

61

people like that would get nervous if I started talking about things that could draw the attention of the police."

"But what could *you* . . ." Paul thought for a moment, then slowly smiled at her. "You spotted something wrong in Hugh Riddley's business."

"No—in Wes's. But Hugh is tied to it."

Hugh leaned back in the big, black leather chair and looked at Wes across the desk. "Graduation in two months. Still no job offers?"

Wes settled back in his chair too. "One callback interview, tomorrow, with a company from Denver, and another interview next Tuesday."

Kay raised her eyebrows in surprise. Wes had said nothing to her about either of those.

Hugh glanced at her before going on. It wasn't a friendly glance—it never was. "You're a married man now—starting a family," Hugh said. "You need something solid right away. What are the chances one of those interviews is going to turn out?"

"I think I have a pretty good chance."

"To do what? Work for somebody else? That's no way to do well for yourself." Hugh waved his hand in an expansive arc that took in the den and, presumably, the whole mansion, pool, three-car garage out back, and even the construction yard across town with its array of huge machinery. "If you want to make it big, you have to have your own company."

"Yeah. That's something I've picked up in four years of business school."

Kay wondered if Hugh caught the sarcasm in his son's answer.

"But you have to have money to start a company," Wes continued.

"That's where I can help," Hugh said. He leaned forward, resting his arms on the desk. "Since your mother died, you're all the family I've got. If you take your wife and my grandchild"—he glanced at Kay's swelling stomach—"off to Denver or who-knows-where, I won't have anybody left here but Max. So I'm prepared to loan you the money to start a business of your own—if you'll do it here in Las Vegas."

"What terms and what conditions?" Wes asked coolly.

"Five percent interest for five years. You pay me off by that time and you're free and clear. If not, I own a third of the business."

"And the conditions?"

"Just one—it has to be a partnership between the two of you." Kay, shifting in her chair to make herself comfortable with the weight of the baby she carried, realized that Hugh was looking at her. "I think both of you need to work to earn whatever you get," he said.

"Why do you think he wanted to force you into a partnership?" Paul asked.

"I'm sure he believes I married Wes for money. Hugh wanted to be sure it didn't come easy."

"But I'll bet Wes wasn't exactly eager to have you involved in the business."

"No. He brought me the partnership papers to sign the day after Angela was born, while I was still in the hospital, and from then on he made all the decisions. I helped in the office sometimes, but Wes wouldn't even let me do that very much."

"Hmm. What could you know that worries them so much?"

"I'm not sure—maybe what I saw when I went down to the office one day and Wes wasn't there. I started looking through the books. There were some things that didn't seem right, so I told him later—"

"What do you mean—'didn't seem right'?"

"Charges on some contracts that didn't seem to belong there. Bills to the manufacturer for warranty repairs when it was only normal service. I told Wes it looked like the kind of business that could get somebody sent to jail. He scared me—he squeezed my arm until it hurt and told me we were in business *together* and I ought to think about what would happen to our daughter if we were *both* behind bars."

"I don't think it would ever happen, at least not to you, because—"

"It doesn't matter. I let it drop—but that's when I knew I couldn't stay with him. After the divorce, Wes's lawyer threatened me again—if I went around talking about dishonest business, they could sue me for slander, and if Wes somehow ended up in jail, then I would too."

"It's a bluff. They couldn't sue you if what you said is true, and anyway—"

"Paul! You're missing the point! I've left it alone because I can't risk being shut out of my daughter's life completely. I'm hardly ever there for her now."

"So you go up there every so often—"

"Every other weekend."

"And risk letting them do something to you while you're there, or follow you so later—"

"I can't stay away from Angela. I miss her too much. And I have to bring some things into her life that she'll never get from them. They're not going to teach her that God is her Heavenly Father, or how much Jesus loves her, or . . ." Kay spread her hands in a gesture of helplessness.

Paul thought for a moment. "Well, I admire you for what you're doing. And if it's any consolation, as long as they think they've got you running scared, you're probably safe. They don't have to worry about shutting you up; they have you right where they want you."

He looked at her drawing on the wall. "Have you thought about opening up the custody issue again? If Wes's attorney knew you'd be glad to give up the business, I'll bet he'd advise his client to work with you."

"You wouldn't say that if you knew Mitchell Harrison. He's an evil man. I think he enjoyed threatening me. He doesn't seem to worry about whether a job is honest or not so long as there's money in it. I wasn't surprised that you were taking pictures of him for the story you're working on."

Paul looked at her quizzically. "Taking pictures . . ."

"Of Wes's lawyer. When you showed me the photo you shot of me and Wes in Las Vegas, you had a picture of Mitch Harrison with some tourist."

"You mean . . . the man in the suit?"

"Yes, that's . . ." She looked at him curiously for a moment. "It wasn't him you were following, was it? It was the tourist. Who is *he?*"

"A banker. It looks like he's involved in a kickback scheme."

Paul was silent for several seconds, gazing at nothing in particular. Finally he realized Kay was watching him.

"I can almost hear the reporter's mind at work," she said. "What's going on up there?"

"Wes's business . . . it's copiers and office machines, isn't it?"

"How did you know? Is that part of your story?"

"Yes."

"I want to hear all about it sometime—as much as you can tell me." She yawned widely. "But suddenly I'm exhausted."

"And I've stayed too late." He stood. "I'll see you tomorrow."

"Paul, I . . . do you really mean that? You . . . well, I know how important the truth is to you, and I didn't tell it, so I thought maybe you'd, uh. . . . you'd decide . . ."

"I'll see you tomorrow," he repeated. "And anytime you need a friendly ear. Kay, I know how to keep my mouth shut when people share the truth with me."

She looked away. "Thanks. Sometimes I feel like I just have to talk to someone."

"But there's a problem."

Her brow furrowed. "What?"

Slowly, Paul smiled. "I need to know who I'm really talking to—Kay, or Kristina?"

She laughed. "Both. Kristina Kay Reston. When I was born, my brother couldn't pronounce Kristina, so I was always Kay to my family and friends. But when I started college, I was Kristina on the rolls, so that's how everyone knew me."

Her smile faded and she stared past him. "Kristina didn't do very well with her life—so when I came here I decided to be Kay again."

"Stop it! Don't beat yourself up over the past."

"I just hope that getting involved in my life doesn't put you in danger somehow."

Paul smiled at her again. "Try not to worry so much."

He stood and let go of her hand. "How about dinner at the beach tomorrow night? I know a great Chinese take-out place on the way."

"I'll be waiting with my chopsticks ready."

"About five-thirty." He opened her front door and stepped outside. "Now, get some sleep."

He shut the door behind him and walked down the driveway past her car. It was an old Chev sedan, too big for one person—a family car, really. It looked like something she might have picked up after the accident when she was desperate for transportation. Maybe something her family had owned?

He had nearly reached the street when Kay opened the door and called after him: "Paul?"

He walked back toward her. "Yes?"

"Thanks for caring enough to make me talk. I needed that." She smiled as she shut the door again. "Goodnight."

He scanned the photos of James Delaroi and Mitchell Harrison, spread out in front of him on the kitchen table so he could study them.

His mind had been racing when he left Kay. Now it was stalled. No amount of studying these pictures could tell him any more about what had passed between the banker and the lawyer.

His eyes kept going to the photos of Kay and Wes that he had laid to one side. She was a prisoner behind those glasses and beneath that wig—someone that young Kristina Kay Reston, just starting college, could never have imagined knowing.

How did a girl from a close-knit family in a small Mormon town ever find herself matched up with a man like Wes?

Studying the picture of her hiding her identity from the world, carrying so much pain, Paul hurt inside for her.

Looking at the picture of Wes made him angry. Here was a man who apparently offered nothing to anyone else, who only took from others, willing to suck them dry so long as he got what *he* wanted. Kay didn't have much of a life for herself as it was, and Wes would go on taking and taking and taking from her until she didn't have *anything* left . . . unless someone stopped him.

Paul scooped up the photos on the table and slipped them back into their envelope. Then he reached for the telephone and dialed Scott Pike's number.

It rang eight times before Scott answered with a mumbled, "Hello?"

"Sorry to call so late. Were you asleep?"

"You're kidding, right? It's, uh . . . a little past twelve. But that's OK—I still have four or five hours I can use to sleep."

"Remember the story I'm working on about the California banker?"

"I was just dreaming that I met this fantastic woman at a singles dance. You better be calling to give me the name of the good-looking blonde in your pictures."

"She's not really blonde. But—"

"You found out? How? Tell me about it."

"Next time I come up there. The story just developed a Las Vegas angle that's going to be a lot bigger than I thought. Are you interested?"

"The guy in the suit?"

"Mitchell Harrison. He's—"

"Wait a minute. Let me get something to write on." A drawer opened and closed, and then paper rattled close to the phone. "Go ahead," Scott said. "And we're working together on this story, right?"

Paul hesitated for a moment. He wasn't sure how he would explain this arrangement to his bureau chief. "Yeah—but I say when the story's ready to go. You know I have to give the wire-service the break on it."

"Understood. What's that name again?"

"Mitchell Harrison. Lawyer. Mean anything?"

"Not yet. But I'll get back to you."

"Scott? Check for any local investments—ties to businesses."

Chapter 6

"How can you eat that bagel without coffee?"

"Milk works for me," Paul answered. "And they always make it just the way I like it." He lifted the glass, took a sip, and made a face.

Anna Leeds laughed. "Sour?"

He nodded, and took another bite of the rubbery bagel to try to kill the ugly taste in his mouth.

"I told you this was no place to order real food." She glanced toward the counter of the diner as a man talking on his cellular phone sat down on one of the empty stools. "Fastest heartburn in downtown L.A." She pushed her coffee cup aside. "You have something new to show me?"

"No, I need you to take another look at the same pictures. There are a couple more questions I have to ask you." He pushed the photo of the banker and the lawyer across the table.

Anna studied it. "I still don't know the man in the suit. I've never seen him before."

"His name is Mitchell Harrison. He's a lawyer in Las Vegas. Does that mean anything?"

She thought for a moment. "No."

Paul laid one of the photos of Kay and Wes on the table. "Do you recognize the man in this picture?"

Anna glanced at the photo. "No, I . . ." She stopped to study it. "Well, maybe. I mean, he reminds me of the man that Mr. Delaroi threw out of his office, the man who came representing that company from Las Vegas. But I can't be sure."

"He looks like that man?"

"He has the same dark hair. The man was handsome like this one, but . . . I don't know. I only saw him for a few seconds, just one time."

"His name is Weston Riddley. Does that mean anything?"

"No." She examined the picture again. "Who's the woman?"

"Her name is Kay—*Kristina*—Riddley."

"I don't know that name either. But she's pretty."

"She's even better looking without the wig and sunglasses."

Anna looked at him quizzically.

"There are people who . . . well, she needs to keep them from getting a good idea what she really looks like," Paul explained.

Anna leaned back in her seat and studied his face as though she had missed something about him before. "You must do undercover work a lot more than I thought."

He shook his head. "Usually it's just a lot of digging in files and public records. This is more of a one-time thing."

"Who *are* these people that Mr. Delaroi's involved with?"

"I can't tell you much about them yet. But with these two guys, I think he's in deeper than he knows."

"What's the woman's part in it?"

"None, really. I'm sure she doesn't understand exactly what they're doing. She's being manipulated by the man you see in the picture."

Anna looked at him steadily for several seconds. "She's someone you care about, isn't she?"

Paul wondered how much to tell her. "You could say I have more than a professional interest."

Slowly she smiled. "Well, when you get all of this unraveled, I hope things work out for the two of you."

Kay pointed to a spot just short of Hugh Riddley's driveway. "You can let me out right there."

Paul pulled to a stop and looked at the Riddley mansion through the wrought-iron fence. "I can wait for you down the block. You and Angela can just walk out the gate and get into my car."

"No, I don't want them asking questions. Anyway, Hugh always insists that we have Max drive us."

"The chauffeur? So he can keep an eye on you?"

Kay wrinkled her nose. "Maybe—I guess that could be part of it. But Hugh knows that Max will watch out for Angela like she was *his* granddaughter. Max really cares about her."

"Well, you could tell them you left your taxi waiting this time."

"I don't think so. I don't even want them to suspect that I'm with someone and start asking questions. I don't want them to find out about you. I mean, because they might . . ."

"I'm not afraid of them—but I'll leave if that's what you want. I'm just trying to be helpful."

She reached over to touch his hand. "I know—and I appreciate it. It's more than enough that you volunteered to bring me up here."

"My pleasure. I loved the company."

"So did I. But I need to be on my own with my daughter this weekend, OK?"

Paul nodded. "I'll pick you up Sunday afternoon at your friend's place."

Kay adjusted her blonde wig, stepped out of the car and straightened the green dress, then walked up the driveway with her suitcase.

Scott took a bite of steak and savored it. "Mmm—sure beats store-bought pizza. You really know how to treat a friend, Webber."

"I owe you more than this for playing host so often."

Scott glanced around the restaurant. "Yeah, you're right. I think you should bring me here tomorrow night too."

Paul laughed. "Don't push it!"

Scott sliced off another strip of steak. "Your man Mitchell Harrison doesn't leave much of a trail."

"What does that mean—he's clean?"

"No, I didn't say that. I've talked to a couple of attorneys and a judge I know. None of them trusts him as far as they could throw him. He's got a reputation for doing anything, honest or not, to win a case. He's come close to being disciplined by the bar a couple of times over the way he handled clients' money. No ties to local businesses that I can find so far—but I've only been able to work on this between assignments."

"Yeah—me too."

"You have anything more to go on?"

Paul shook his head. "I thought I'd spend part of tomorrow digging into the background of the guy in the photo with the woman."

"Who is he?"

"Ex-husband. Abusive—likes to play ugly mind games with her. His name's Wes Riddley."

Scott raised his eyebrows. "Riddley Construction?"

"Son of the owner."

Scott frowned. "I've heard some things about Hugh Riddley . . ."

"Mob stories?"

"Yeah. Out of the sixties. I suppose no one could ever prove them now." He smiled. "So tell me about the woman."

Paul told him briefly about following Kay from Las Vegas to Los Angeles, and about her situation with Wes and Angela.

Scott shook his head. "She must be strong to handle all that."

"Stronger than she knows."

"You'd like to nail this guy and get her free from him, wouldn't you?"

"Yeah."

"Want me to do some checking on him too?"

"Stick with Mitchell Harrison for now. Wes Riddley is mine."

The woman at the desk looked up at him politely, then smiled broadly as she recognized him. "Paul Webber! I thought you were away in the big city making a name for yourself. Get tired of all the glamor?"

"I miss this place so much I couldn't stay away," he answered, smiling. "I came to look through some of the files just for old times' sake."

The woman glanced over her shoulder at the room where the newspaper's photo and clipping files were stored. "You mean you want to, uh . . ." She frowned. "I don't know, Paul. Margaret just came down hard on us about not letting anyone but employees into the library."

"Hey, it's *me*, Cassie. When I worked for the paper, I spent so much time in here that people thought you and I were going steady."

Cassie smiled. "Better not let my boyfriend hear that. He's big—and he's the jealous type."

Paul nodded toward the file room. "I'll hide out in back. He'll never know I was here."

Still she hesitated.

"Don't you think Margaret would let me in?"

Cassie grinned. "Probably, but not without hassling you first— so I guess I've done my job." She stood to step into the file room. "Tell me what files you want to see and let *me* pull them, OK?"

"Start with Hugh Riddley and Riddley Construction. Then we'll see if there's a file on Weston Riddley or his company—Business Line Office Products."

The file on Hugh Riddley was a thin one. There was a feature story on Riddley Construction and its long history in Las Vegas. There were newspaper photos showing Hugh smiling and shaking hands with people from a few of the organizations or projects he had donated money to—a hospital, the university, the Girl Scouts, even a shelter for homeless and battered women. Paul wondered if there was anyone else who would see irony in that last one.

There was no file on Wes Riddley or Business Line.

"That's all?" Scott asked.

"Yeah. I'm not sure where to look next. I was thinking of calling a few past clients of Riddley Construction and asking some questions—if I can come up with a reason that won't raise red flags for anybody."

Scott pushed his dinner plate away and leaned back in his chair. "From what you've told me about the Riddleys, Kay sounds like a complete mismatch. How do you suppose she ever got mixed up with a man like Wes?"

Paul shook his head. "I don't know. She's such a . . . she's a *sweet* person—quiet, almost shy. But she was a cheerleader in high school and a drama minor in college. It's hard to make those things fit together. It would have been interesting to know her when she was going to school."

Scott grinned. "Excuse me, did you say you're an *investigative* reporter?"

Paul looked at him questioningly.

"If I wanted to know what somebody was like when she was attending UNLV, I'd go out to the university library and see if I could find her in the yearbook. If she was in drama, she might have made the newspaper too." He glanced at his watch. "I'm sure the library is still open."

She was in the University of Nevada, Las Vegas yearbook three times her junior year—once in her individual photo and twice in photos of scenes from plays. Her role in the spring production of *You Can't Take It with You* was Alice, the beautiful, conventional daughter in a family of eccentrics. Angled across the cast picture in the yearbook was a closeup photo of the program, with a drawing that bore a small credit line: Kristina Reston.

Paul found her in the newspaper too, mentioned in a review of the play. The review read in part: "After Kristina Reston shone as Laura in last fall's production of *The Glass Menagerie,* it was expected that she might do well in another role. She exceeded expectations in this one. Her performance was smooth and engaging, and she obviously has a gift for comedy." Further on, the review said: "Kristina, who is well known on campus, shows a depth that promises outstanding future performances."

Paul wondered what "well known" meant.

In her senior year, she showed up in the yearbook only once, in her individual photo. She was listed as Kristina Riddley.

Paul looked for Wes Riddley. There was nothing—no photo with an organization or a fraternity, not even an individual photo. Obviously, Wes was not a joiner, and whatever he had done in college he had done without attracting much notice.

Sometime between the spring of their junior year and the spring of their senior year, Kristina Kay Reston and Wes Riddley had married.

How could a man like that have attracted someone like her? Unless Wes was very different then, it didn't make sense. Obviously, Paul thought, there was much that Kay had not told him about the relationship.

A reporter might be able to dig out more facts on his own. But a friend would let *her* share the information when she felt comfortable about it. Paul closed the yearbook and put it back on the shelf.

How soon after the wedding, he wondered, had she learned that their life wasn't going to be happily ever after?

Chapter 7

Angela seemed very small staring out the rear window of the big sedan as it drove away. Kay waved to her, fighting back tears. Angela smiled and waved in return.

The Cadillac rounded the corner and disappeared. Kay wiped at her eyes, then turned and walked back toward the building where Marcy lived. She glanced in Paul's direction—his car was parked at the curb in front of the building—but gave no other sign of recognition.

Marcy was waiting at the door of her apartment. "Do you have a few minutes to visit right now? Or is your ride already here?"

"He's waiting."

"Why don't you invite him in and introduce me?"

"I'd like you to meet him—but maybe next time. I'm late, and he has to be at work early in the morning."

"OK—next time. But I want to be sure this man is everything you deserve, just in case you're feeling the way I think you're feeling about him."

Kay smiled. "And how do you think I'm feeling?"

"Like you're ready to trust somebody with your heart again."

"Maybe—I don't know." Kay put her arms around Marcy in a quick hug. "Thanks for caring about me—but stop worrying. I learned my lesson with Wes. I don't know what will happen with Paul, but I *do* know this is a man that a woman could trust."

When Kay emerged from the apartment building ten minutes later, she was no longer wearing the green dress and blonde wig. She had on jeans, a pullover, athletic shoes, and a different pair of sunglasses. Her hair was pulled back tightly in a barrette. Hurrying to Paul's car, she opened the passenger door, pushed her suitcase over the seat into the back, sat down, and pulled the door shut behind her. "Let's go, before anyone has time to get a good look—just in case somebody's watching."

Paul smiled. "They'll never get onto you."

He drove out of the parking lot and through the residential area to Tropicana Avenue. They rode in silence until after they had crossed the Strip and turned onto I-15 headed out of Las Vegas.

"Do you keep Angela with you when you stay at your friend's?" Paul asked.

She smiled. "Sometimes. Marcy loves her. She spoils her."

Kay searched in her purse for her comb, then unfastened the barrette she wore and let her hair fall free. Paul glanced her way several times as she began to comb it. She looked at him questioningly.

"Your hair is beautiful," he said. "It almost looks gold when the sunlight hits it through the window."

"Thanks." She smiled at him and went on combing. "It was blonde when I was a little girl, but it darkened as I got older. It's always a mess after I pile it up under that wig."

"Doesn't Marcy worry about the Riddleys' knowing where *she* lives?"

Kay laughed and shook her head. "Marcy isn't afraid of Wes or his friends. She got one of those harassing calls after the first time she let me stay with her. She said, 'Listen, Wes, you're a jerk, you've always been a jerk, and you'd better leave me alone.' She threatened him with everything legal she could think of and told him if she could find him she'd make him eat the phone. I've never seen her so mad."

"Was it really Wes?"

"I don't know. But she didn't get any more calls."

"Maybe you could handle him the same way—you know, stand up to him, let him know you're not—"

"No." Kay shook her head. "Marcy doesn't have a daughter to lose. I do."

"Marcy's known Wes for a long time?"

"I just wish I'd listened to her when she was my roommate in college. She could see from the beginning that Wes was a phony. I don't know why I didn't."

Kay paused with the comb and thought for a moment. "But you have to understand that he was the smoothest, most ingratiating man I had ever met. He made it his business from the beginning to show me a good time, and he let me know that he thought I was *very* attractive."

"He was right about that. And he probably picked you out very carefully. He seems like the kind of guy that would deliberately go after a beautiful woman who was well known on campus."

Paul's last phrase sounded familiar—but Kay wasn't sure for the moment just why. "Where did you . . . what made you say that?"

"Well, you told me he likes women, and . . ."

"No, the part about my being well known."

Paul glanced her way. "I read it in a review of one of your plays."

"You read . . . you mean you looked me up in the UNLV paper? *You were checking up on me?*"

"No! It wasn't like that. I was checking . . . I did some research on Wes and his father, then . . . well, you hadn't told me much about college—"

"You just couldn't resist being the reporter, could you?" She wasn't able to keep the edge out of her voice.

It surprised him. Why was she irritated? "Kay, I was just interested in *you*. I didn't mean to do anything to upset you. Please—forgive me?"

She didn't answer. He finished passing a car and pulled back into the right lane, then glanced her way again.

She wiped away a tear that was sliding down her cheek. "How much did you learn about me, Paul? Tell me."

"Not much, really. The yearbook and the campus newspaper show that Kristina Reston did well in a couple of plays as a junior. As a senior, she was Kristina Riddley in the yearbook."

"And did you check the *Review-Journal* for my wedding announcement?"

"No, uh . . . why should I—"

"Or Angela's birth announcement?"

"No," he said slowly. "Would that tell me something I need to know?" He was afraid he already knew the answer to his question; he was afraid he knew where this was going.

Her hands trembled as she brushed away the tears that were

beginning to make dark water spots on her shirt. "You'll have to find out sometime. I hoped maybe later, not now . . . but I want you to hear it from me before you learn it some other way."

She turned to face him. "I was pregnant when Wes and I got married. Angela was born six months later."

Paul looked straight ahead and said nothing. Her confession brought back echoes of the past, but he wasn't sure how to explain what he was feeling just now.

Kay waited for him to respond—waited until she couldn't stand *not* knowing what he was thinking. "Does that make you sorry that you ever asked me out? Do you hate me?"

"*Hate* you? No! Why should I?" He paused. "You made a serious mistake. I wish you hadn't—for your sake. But 'hate'—"

"You're being awfully broad-minded. I couldn't blame you if you said you didn't want to see me anymore."

Later he would tell her why he needed to be "broad-minded." Right now, he wanted to help her get past the hurting. "This has been eating at you for a long time, hasn't it?"

"Years. And 'mistake' doesn't begin to cover what I did." Kay brushed at her cheeks with her fingers again. Paul handed her his handkerchief and she wiped away the tears.

"Whatever happened," he said, "it seems to me you must have punished yourself enough about it by now."

"Punished *myself*?"

"Who else is doing it?"

She thought about his question for several seconds. The answer seemed clear enough. Why hadn't she realized it before now? "Wes," she said.

"But you're divorced now. How could he—"

"He set me up for it. He was always very good at hurting me—more emotionally than physically. He made me believe that I wasn't good enough even for *him*. He said no other man would ever want anything to do with me if he knew all about me."

Paul glanced her way. "And you believed *Wes*?"

"It was easy at the time," Kay said softly. "I felt dirty. I felt worthless."

She was silent for several seconds. Then: "If you knew *everything* I've done . . ."

Paul hesitated before answering. "I don't really need to know—but I care about you. If it will help you to talk, I'll listen."

She leaned back against her seat and stared out at the sky ahead. "When you were younger—in high school, or starting college—did you ever do anything that went against your parents, just to show them you could make decisions on your own?"

"Well, yeah, little things—not very serious."

"I thought mine wasn't very serious either. My parents wanted me to go to a Church school—BYU, or Ricks—or maybe Dixie College, up in St. George. I wanted to go to UNLV because they offered me an art scholarship and I liked the galleries and theaters I saw in Las Vegas."

"Do you feel like it was wrong to make your own choice?"

"No. But I can understand now what my parents were worried about. I didn't have much of a testimony, even though I'd been through all the Young Women and seminary things. In Las Vegas, I quit going to church. My roommates did fun things all weekend—water skiing and partying—and I felt lucky that they let me go along, because they were popular. There was always a cooler full of beer, but I'd sip some kind of soft drink. I was sure I was in control because I stayed sober. It was all fun and exciting. I really got into it." She blinked away the tears that kept coming. "That's why the newspaper said I was well known on campus—Kristina the party girl!"

"Kay, if it's too hard to tell me—"

"I want you to understand."

She dabbed at her cheeks again. "I met Wes at one of those parties. We went out a lot, and the way he treated me in the beginning made me feel something I'd never felt with any other man. When I told my parents I thought I was in love with him, they were terribly upset because he wasn't a member of the Church. But I wasn't sure at the time how I felt about the Church, and I didn't want to give Wes up."

Kay stared out the windshield. She couldn't look at Paul and say this. "I let Wes talk me into sipping wine coolers with him, and it seemed like he was right about them—they didn't do much to me. Then one night he brought something stronger, and we . . ."

She balled the handkerchief up in her fist. "I'll pay for that one 'mistake' the rest of my life! But I found out later that Wes told his father it happened many times, that I did it so I could make him marry me when I got pregnant. That's why Hugh Riddley never trusted me."

"Why would Wes lie about *that*?"

"Because he asked me to get rid of the baby before it came— 'take care of the problem before it gets any bigger,' he said—and I wouldn't. So he lied, and hoped his father would tell him to dump me—maybe give me some money to go away. That's Wes's idea of handling problems. But Hugh surprised him. He insisted that Wes stand up to his responsibility—marry me and take care of our child."

"Why in the world did *you* go through with the marriage?"

"Remember, I only found out about all this later. At the time, I thought I was in love with him. I could tell *his* feelings had changed, but I thought the baby would make a difference, and I felt like I had an obligation to make things work between us." She paused. "Wes never felt anything like that, even though he put a good face on things when we were first married."

"What made you decide to come back to the Church?"

"Angela. I didn't want her to grow up to live the way I was— with nothing to hang on to. Really, I knew before she was born that I needed to come back. I knew the right way to live all along— I just conveniently ignored it. I was having too much fun being Kristina the campus queen!" She paused. "It wasn't until I felt like I'd lost everything important that I saw how precious the gospel could be."

"No doubt Wes didn't see it that way."

"No. He tried everything he could to keep me from going back to church. He wanted me to go on partying with him, he didn't feel any responsibility for the baby, he . . . well, when Angela was a little over a year old, I found out he was seeing another woman. I stuck it out another year, trying to make the marriage work, but he never had any commitment to it."

"And Hugh Riddley just looked the other way while all this was happening?"

"No. He came down hard on Wes when he found out about the other woman—told him if a man couldn't be true to his wife, he couldn't be trusted in anything. Wes dropped the woman and swore he'd change. But he found someone else a couple of months later. When I learned about it, I started sleeping in the baby's bedroom. That's when he turned vicious."

"Hitting you."

"That came later, after I started standing up for myself. What he did at first hurt more. He cut me into little pieces emotionally—told me I'd let myself go since the baby came so I wasn't attractive anymore . . . told me it was embarrassing to introduce me to his friends because I didn't fit in . . . told me I was stupid to believe in all that religion and God stuff. He said I'd already blown it in my church anyway. When I talked about leaving him, he told me to go ahead, but I'd live alone all my life, no man in my church would ever want me because I was, uh . . . well, I don't want to say what he said."

"Never mind. I get the picture."

She closed her eyes and tears spilled out from under her eyelids once more. "I'm so sorry for dumping all of this on you. My bishop in Las Vegas helped me work through it—starting on the repentance part, at least—and when I moved to Los Angeles, Bishop Taylor told me I could come talk to him anytime I needed. But he's so busy, and there hasn't been anyone else I could . . . a friend, I mean . . ."

"Kay, I hope you'll believe that I wasn't trying to pry out your secrets. I'd be honored to be the friend you can talk to any time, about anything." He looked her way and smiled. "How about if I drop by tomorrow afternoon to talk?"

"Paul, I . . ." Kay reached out to put her hand on his arm. "Please tell me you really mean it—that I'll still hear from you tomorrow."

"Sure. I'll—"

"Because I've had this nightmare that Wes was right—I'd meet new friends in the Church, and then, once they found out about my marriage . . . and my baby . . ."

He put his left hand on top of hers. "I'll be there. Count on me."

She smiled at him, and settled back in her seat.

He glanced in the rearview mirror and accelerated to pass a

semi so he could make way for a Porsche that was rapidly coming up from behind. Then he looked her way as she rubbed her forehead. "Headache again?"

"No. Just tired. These weekends are exhausting—trying to be everything to Angela in two days—and then . . . this."

"We'll have to stop for gas in a couple of hours." He reached into the back seat for his jacket. "Take a nap. You can roll this up for a pillow."

The car was slowing down. Kay opened her eyes and turned to look at Paul. It was almost dark outside.

"Still here," he said, smiling. "Did you have a good rest?"

"Ummm—yes!" She stretched. "Where are we?"

"Victorville. It's time to find a gas station."

"I hope they have a fountain. I'm thirsty."

"I forgot to tell you—I brought a couple of bottles of water and some oranges and cookies in case we got hungry. They're in a sack behind my seat."

When they were on the road again, west of Victorville, Kay reached for the sack and took out one of the oranges. "I'll share with you. Got a knife so I can peel it?"

He fished in the pocket of his jeans and brought out a Swiss Army knife, grinning as he handed it to her. "It's clean. I wiped the blade after I dressed the last deer I shot."

Kay laughed. "Somehow I don't see you handling guns or going hunting."

"I used to—when my dad was alive. He'd take me to Utah for the deer hunt every fall."

"What happened to your father, Paul?"

"Heart attack, when I was fifteen. He was young. He went out for a run on the beach. Someone found him lying on the sand."

"And your mother never remarried?"

Paul shook his head. "She lives by herself in a small condo."

"It must have been hard losing your dad that way."

"Yeah. I was lucky in one thing, though—I had him long enough to learn a lot from the way he lived. My dad was one of those completely honest men that anybody could trust. I admired that." He paused. "I missed him a lot. But it always seemed like Mom had more than enough love to give whenever I needed it."

Kay dumped the orange peelings into the sack and handed him a section of the orange.

"Umm—delicious. And the service is terrific," he said.

"It's the least I could do. There's no galley on this flight, or I'd cook you up something. I owe you for taking me to Las Vegas." She handed him another section of orange. "What about tomorrow night? When you come by, plan on staying for dinner."

"Kay, you don't have to—"

"I want to. Six-thirty." She held out one more piece of the orange.

"I thought you were going to eat some of this."

"There's another one, and I'm not very hungry yet."

He smiled as he took the section of fruit from her hand. "Thank you, friend."

Paul seemed not to feel any differently toward her because of what she had told him. Still, Kay wondered what was in his mind. *What does "friend" mean—friendship, and nothing more? . . . Is that what you can expect whenever a man finds out about Angela—just a friend? . . . Maybe it wouldn't matter so much with some other man— but with this one . . .*

When he had finished the first orange, she peeled the other one and nibbled at it in silence as they dropped down through Cajon Pass and headed into Los Angeles.

"Everything all right?" he asked finally.

"Yes. Why?"

"We were having a good time there—and then you got all quiet on me. Did I say something wrong?"

She smiled at him. "No." *Ask him. He said you could talk about anything.*

She could almost taste the fear. She tried to fight it back. "Paul, about what I told you . . . do you feel . . . is that something you would . . ." *Ask him what? "Does what I did make it impossible that a man like you could ever feel love for a woman like me?" . . . I can't.*

"Yes?" he said.

No. I can't. "About what I told you . . . it feels good not to have to hide it from somebody I . . . respect. But I'm not ready to share it with anyone else yet."

"Don't worry—journalists know how . . . *friends* know how to keep secrets."

She sighed. *"Friends."* . . . *Well, friends are good, Kay. You need all the friends you can get.*

They rode in silence again, until he passed up their exit in Santa Monica. She looked at him questioningly. "That was . . ."

"I know. But you've had a rough weekend, and I think you need something to take the edge off of it. Are you up for a little wave therapy before I take you home?"

"Sure. With the nap I had, I wouldn't be able to sleep now anyway."

At the beach, he parked the car and came around to open her door. "Bring my jacket. You'll need it."

Opening the trunk, he got his sport coat out of his garment bag and put it on. Then he led her to a spot halfway between the parking lot and the surf. They sat down on the sand to watch and listen to the waves.

Only the white, foamy tops of the breakers could be seen in the dark. The sound the waves made was not exactly a roar, she thought; it was more pleasant than that, more soothing. It seemed to envelop her, almost massaging her tension away with its power. Like the fresh breeze, it was comforting somehow in its constancy.

They had been sitting there for several minutes before Paul spoke.

"What you told me today . . . it's not the first time I've known someone who was pregnant and unmarried—not even the second.

"When I was a junior in high school, there was a girl in my seminary class—Cathy—who got pregnant. Suddenly the rest of us, all of her 'friends,' didn't seem to know how to talk to her anymore. I don't know why—but I know we added to all the hurt she was carrying around inside." He paused. "She finally dropped out and went away somewhere to have her baby. In my sixteen-year-old mind, I wondered if she'd be able to find a *good* man to care for her someday."

He stared out at the ocean. "Then while I was a missionary I was called to be branch president in a small town. It was a quick course in understanding how people can face their problems. There was this unmarried woman in the branch who had a baby, and I . . . well, I almost drove her away from the Church before I learned it wasn't a judge she needed—someone to tell her what she'd done wrong. She already knew that, and she was hurting. She needed *help*. And when she was willing to let the Lord touch her life, I saw how much a person could change. I heard later that she finally married a good man in the branch."

He tossed a small shell toward the surf. "Whenever I think of Cathy back in high school, I wonder why the rest of us lost sight of all the good things about her. For all I know, she could be married in the temple now and be Primary president in her ward. I hope so. She was really good with little kids."

Kay pulled the jacket tighter around her. *Where is this leading— "I know you'll find a nice life too—with someone, somewhere"?*

Paul went on. "I thought you were going to ask me earlier if I could forgive you somehow for your past. I can't do that." He turned to look at her. "I mean it's not up to me. That's between you and your Savior, and if you've taken care of it with him, no one else has anything more to offer." He smiled at her. "I'm trying to tell you that I think the Kay Reston I know right now is as good as any woman I've ever met."

She struggled to hold back tears, trying not to cry in front of him again. "Thank you. That means a lot to me."

"Have you ever thought about going to the temple?"

"I'd like that—if I could feel good about . . . if I could feel like I deserved to be there."

"Why can't you?"

She shrugged. "The bishop told me there's no reason I can't plan to do it soon."

"Then don't let anything stand in your way. After all you've been through, you need to go there and get a good look at who you *really* are. If there's anything I can do to help you get ready, I'd like to do it. Will you let me?"

"Of course. There's no one I'd like better."

Paul took hold of her hand and turned back to watch the breakers.

What he had told her the first time he brought her to the beach was true, she thought; there was healing in these waves. They just kept coming and coming, their power never seeming to diminish. They could wash anything away, eventually. Anything could be washed away by the right power.

Her hand felt warm nestled in Paul's. That was as comforting as the sound and strength of the waves.

He stood suddenly and began to go through the motions of selecting something from a spot in the air in front of him. Kay watched curiously as he pantomimed removing an item from a case and inspecting it. She smiled at him. "What are you doing?"

"I thought it would be nice to have some music suitable to the company I'm keeping. It's a CD from my collection." He went through the motions of inserting a compact disc into a player and punching the play button. "There—'Uptown Girl,' by Billy Joel."

She frowned. "Not that one! Wes used to sing that to me when we were first going together."

Paul ripped the imaginary disc out of the player, sailed it toward the surf, and watched it drop into the water. He made a sour face, held his nose with the fingers of one hand, and turned his thumb down with the other.

Kay laughed.

He went through the motions of selecting another CD and putting it into the imaginary player. "This one's better anyway— more like you," he said. "Nat and Natalie Cole—'Unforgettable.' "

"Now you're exaggerating."

"No. I'm not."

He pretended to adjust the volume. "Can you hear it all right?" She smiled again. "Yes."

He held out his hand to her. "Dance with me?"

She gave him her hand and stood. He began to dance with her, their feet moving slowly in the sand.

He sang softly in her ear, "Unforgettable, that's what you are, unforgettable, though near or far . . ." His baritone was smooth and mellow, and she enjoyed being in his arms.

He hummed to fill in words he couldn't remember, then continued, "Unforgettable, that's how you'll stay . . ."

Did he really mean what the words of the song said? One part of her was wary, after so much falseness from Wes, of believing words like these from any man.

But something stronger in her did not want to fight what was happening.

Paul started to repeat the words that he knew to the song, then quit. He stopped dancing and simply held her.

She looked up at him. "Paul, it's very flattering to have someone like you say those things to me, but—"

"It's not flattery."

He gently pulled her closer and kissed her. Then he let her go. "Kay, I've wanted to do that since the first time I brought you to the beach. But I didn't plan this tonight—I promise. It just happened. I—"

She put her fingers to his lips. "Don't tell me you're sorry—not when I enjoyed that."

Paul smiled. "I wasn't going to say I was sorry." He put his arms around her again and kissed her longer this time. She kissed him back.

When it was over, he brushed her cheek with his fingers, then stroked her hair lightly. "Nothing has made me feel this happy in a long time." He let go of her. "But it's late, and I'd better take you home."

He put his arm around her shoulders as they walked to the car.

She felt more than just the warmth of being close to him. Something inside of her was alive again—something she thought she had given up or lost forever because of her mistake with Wes.

It was a very loving Father, she thought, who would let her see that it was possible to find it again.

Chapter 8

"What are you doing for Thanksgiving?" Paul asked.

Kay sighed. "I'll have the privilege of dining with Hugh Riddley and family."

"Nice." Paul grimaced. "I'm sure *that* will be a festive occasion."

"It could hardly be worse than last year. Wes brought a girlfriend."

Paul groaned.

"They held hands and kissed a lot in front of the rest of us." Kay laughed lightly. "I think she and Wes were very, very close—for about three weeks."

She smiled. "The best part of next weekend is that I get Angela for an extra day. I'm taking her out to my parents' place. They're going to have Thanksgiving dinner on Friday so we can come."

"Does Angela know your family at all?"

"My parents—Grandma and Grandpa who have the horsey. She can remember one or two times that I've had her out there. And I think she remembers my younger sister and brother."

Kay paused. "When I married Wes, out of the Church, and my older brother found out that I was already pregnant, he . . . he was back from a mission, just married in the temple, and I think he was ashamed that his sister . . . well, anyway, he's never been there when I've gone home over the past three years because he and his wife live in Arizona, so I've never seen their little boy and they've never seen Angela."

Kay stopped at the door that led out to the meetinghouse parking lot and Paul held it open as she stepped outside. It made him angry to think that someone in her family had added to her pain rather than supporting her when she needed it—but he regretted the anger instantly. *Before you get too self-righteous, just remember how protective you were about your own sister back then.*

"I'm lucky again this year," he said. "I get the day off. I'll be at my mother's down in Redondo Beach. My sister and her husband are coming and bringing their two kids."

Kay stopped next to his car. "Ah. *Grand*children—your *younger* sister's children."

Paul smiled ruefully as he opened the passenger door for her. "Right. So my sister will ask me again if I have any prospects—just like last year. And my brother-in-law will offer to line me up with this great single woman in their ward—just like last year."

Kay raised her eyebrows. "And what will you tell them?"

"I'll say, 'I can handle it myself, thank you'—just like last year." Paul laughed, and Kay laughed too as she sat down in the car.

After he had walked around the car and taken his place in the driver's seat, he turned to face her. "If you *were* going to be here for Thanksgiving, I'd ask you to come to dinner at my mother's place."

She smiled. "You'd risk having your family meet me—and all those questions afterward?"

"I'd risk it." He paused. "There's a single adult Christmas dance and social the first Friday in December. Will you go with me?"

"Mmm. That could make the two of us an item for people in the ward, couldn't it? And a social . . ."

His brow furrowed. "It would bother you to have people in the ward see us together?"

"No! No, not that. It's just . . . I was thinking about being social with people I really don't know very well. That's a little scary. It's been a long time, and, uh . . ."

Kay smiled once more—a bit forced, he thought. "With you I'll risk it," she continued. "But that's more than two weeks away. I'm not going to have to wait that long before I see you again, am I?"

It was the kind of invitation to make him forget her reservations about the dance. "What are you doing Tuesday night?"

Paul groped for the phone in the dark, knocked it off the night-stand, and let his arm trail off the bed to feel for the receiver on the floor. He picked it up and rolled over onto his back. "Hello?"

"What are you doing in bed already?" Scott asked. "It's only eleven-forty-five."

Paul yawned. "Is this revenge for when I called you about Mitchell Harrison in the middle of the night?"

Scott laughed. "Not exactly. I need some information from you before tomorrow morning."

"What?"

"Do you still have that account number Harrison wrote on the keno card when he was talking to your California banker in the restaurant?"

"Yeah, in a file here at home. Why?"

"I'll be seeing a banker here tomorrow about another story. I could show him the number and see if he can match it up with a bank or financial institution."

Paul hesitated. "There's no chance he could mess things up somehow—tip off Delaroi or Harrison that we're onto them?"

"Paul, this is me, remember? I know what I'm doing. I wouldn't ask him for information about any specific account because he couldn't give it to me anyway. But maybe he can tell us where to start looking."

"OK, hang on."

Paul came back to the telephone in a couple of minutes and read off the numbers circled on the keno card.

"Thanks." Scott paused while he wrote. "Anything new with Kay?"

"No. She doesn't know anything more than what I've told you."

"Not that. You know what I mean—socially."

"We have a date Friday night for the single adult Christmas dance."

"Sounds promising. Think you can sweep her off her feet?"

Paul laughed. "The way I dance, I just hope not to *step* on her feet too often."

He caught his breath when Kay opened the door and then stepped back into the light. She was wearing a beige dress, in some kind of chiffon, that was not too tight, not too clingy, but the perfect compliment to her figure. Her soft, flowing hair just skimmed her shoulders. She had the appearance of not wearing very much makeup, but the lipstick and touch of eyeshadow she had chosen were exactly the right accents for her features. Paul let out a low whistle.

Kay blushed. "Would you like to come in?" she said.

"Just for a minute." Paul stepped in and shut the door behind him. "You're beautiful."

"Thank you. I treated myself to a new dress."

"It's nice. But you make the dress look good, not the other way around."

He reached into his pocket and drew out a flat box about six inches long. "I have something that I hope will go with it." He opened the box, took out a gold chain that carried a small gold disc, and let the engraved disc lay in the palm of his hand.

"Paul! You shouldn't have! It's very pretty. I . . ." She looked closely at the letters engraved on the disc—K.K.R., entwined—and a puzzled expression came to her face, then a small frown.

"Something wrong?" he said.

"No. No, I . . . nothing's wrong."

"Would you like to put it on?"

"Maybe later. Not now. I . . . I'm afraid I might mess up my hair."

It was Paul's turn to look puzzled, but he said nothing.

"Will you just hold onto it for now?" she asked. She was smiling, but he thought it seemed forced.

"Sure." He dropped the chain and medallion back in the box and put the box in his pocket.

She was silent as he drove toward the meetinghouse where the dance was being held. Finally he asked: "Did I do something wrong?"

"No. Nothing."

"You're holding out on me," he said after a pause. "What is it?"

"The letters you had engraved on that gold disc . . ."

"Yes? 'K.K.R.'—Kristina Kay Reston."

"I wish it had just been 'K.R.' You know I only go by 'Kay' here."

"You don't have to tell anyone what the other letter stands for. If they ask, just tell them you prefer 'Kay.' "

"*I'll* know what it stands for," she said firmly.

"Sorry. I didn't know you felt so strongly about getting rid of your first name. I'll take the disc back. I don't want you to wear it if—"

"You can't take it back—it's engraved." She paused, then spoke more softly. "I just wish you hadn't reminded me of . . ."

"Of what? Kristina?"

She nodded.

Why is she . . . does she really want to . . . "Kay, are you trying to *bury* that part of yourself—to bury Kristina?"

She said nothing.

"That's not healthy. That's . . ."

Kay folded her arms tightly across her chest and moved closer to the door.

He paused, then started again. "Let me see if I understand this. You feel like Kristina got in trouble, so for the rest of your life you plan to . . . tell me what . . ."

She spoke so softly this time it was almost a whisper. "I don't know, Paul. . . . I don't know if I can trust . . ."

"Kristina?"

Kay nodded. "I almost called you and backed out on this date. I worried myself into a monster headache over it before I decided . . . I mean, I didn't know if Kristina could . . ."

"You're talking like Kristina is someone else—like she's not part of *you*."

"Maybe I don't want her to be—ever again!"

Neither of them said anything more until he drove into the parking lot at the church building and pulled to a stop. He turned to look at her. "Do you really feel like Kristina the college girl was all bad?"

She looked down at the floor for several seconds before answering. "I don't know. . . . No, not really. But . . ."

"But you can't live with the mistakes she made?"

Kay nodded her head affirmatively.

Paul thought for a moment. "What was good about her?"

Kay considered her answer again before speaking. "She was friendly . . . more outgoing . . . good with people."

"What else? I'm sure there's more."

"She was, uh . . . happy. She loved life." Kay hesitated for a moment. "Maybe *too* much."

"Really? How much is too much?"

"Paul, will you stop trying to analyze me? Just stop it!" She turned away from him, staring out the window toward the couples and singles walking into the church.

Two or three minutes passed before he said anything else. "You told me once that you think the Lord has forgiven you. Is that right?"

She glanced toward him and nodded.

"Do you think he's forgiven Kristina too?"

She looked down at the floor. Again her answer was almost whispered. "I suppose so. But I can't forget what Kristina . . . what *I* did while I was so busy enjoying life that I forgot the way I was *supposed* to live it."

"OK, I suppose you won't ever forget those things that happened. But you learned from them, didn't you? I mean, you're not ever going to drink again, are you? Or do anything else that you learned you shouldn't do?"

Another whisper: "No."

"Then don't you think you ought to let Kristina out of the dungeon sometime soon?"

Kay didn't answer.

"Look, it's OK to enjoy life without holding part of you back. You already know the right way. All you have to do is let yourself—"

"Will you drop this? Please!"

Neither of them said anything for a long time. She looked away, out the window, and he stared out the windshield in front of him. Finally, he sighed. "Want me to take you home?"

There was another long pause before she answered: "No! I decided I'd have a good time tonight—and that's what I'm *going* to do." There was a firmness in her voice that he hadn't heard before.

She opened her door slightly so that the dome light in the car went on, then pulled down the sun visor in front of her and looked into the mirror on the back of it. Her eyes glistened, he noticed, but no tears had run down her face to spoil her makeup. She flipped the visor back into position, shoved the door open, stepped out of his car, and slammed the door behind her. She began walking toward the building.

Paul caught up just in time to open the door for her.

They walked into the cultural hall together and he led the way to two vacant chairs along the wall. They sat down and silently watched other people dance. Finally he said to her, "Would you like some punch?" She looked at him and nodded.

He came back from the refreshment table with two cups of punch, two cookies, and napkins. He gulped down his punch and ate his cookie in two bites. Kay sipped her punch and nibbled at her cookie.

He wished he knew what she was thinking as she watched others dance and studied the people along the far wall. But he didn't dare ask. After several more minutes of silence, he leaned forward, elbows on his knees, and looked down at the floor.

Kay's toe was tapping lightly in time to the music.

When her punch was gone, she stood and put her cup, napkin, and half-eaten cookie on her chair. "There are a couple of people here that I owe something to. Do you mind?" she asked.

Paul didn't understand what she meant, but he answered: "No."

She walked across the floor to where his friend Phil Jarman was standing, talking to two other men. She spoke to Phil. He looked at her in surprise, then smiled. They walked out onto the dance floor together and began to cha-cha to the number the band was playing. Phil was good at it—Paul envied him for having cultivated the skill—but Kay was better.

They danced two dances together, then Kay said something to him, smiled, and led the way as they walked off the floor.

Next she spoke to Nick Karas. It was his turn to look surprised. They walked out onto the floor together and began to dance.

She was a much better dancer than Nick. He said something to her and she laughed. She responded with something that made him laugh too. They carried on a lively conversation through two more numbers, with Kay laughing frequently. Nick was one of the most entertaining guys around, and Kay was obviously enjoying herself.

Paul tried to keep his anger down as he watched them. There was nothing wrong with her dancing with someone else, really . . . or enjoying herself . . . but . . . *Is this a game of some kind? Is she ignoring me just to show me she can do without my interference in her life?*

After the third number ended, she excused herself and walked back to her chair. She picked up her cup, napkin, and cookie, popped the cookie into her mouth, and devoured it. Then she sat down beside Paul and put her hand on his, which was resting on his knee.

He was surprised to feel her hand trembling.

"I hope you didn't mind," she said. "Phil and Nick tried to be friendly to me when I first came here, and I wasn't very nice to them. I felt like I needed to apologize."

"Yeah. Well, you looked friendly enough this time."

She squeezed his hand lightly. "I didn't forget who I came with, Paul. Dance with me?"

When he took her in the dance position, he held her almost at arm's length, but she moved closer. "This won't work very well unless we're *together*," she said, smiling.

He felt awkward at first. He had never done enough dancing to get good at it. On the beach with her alone was one thing, but here, with real music and other people . . .

She moved easily, lightly, in rhythm to the tune. Somehow she put him at ease without saying or doing anything special. He soon forgot about his awkwardness and enjoyed holding her.

When their third dance was over, she held onto his hand and led him toward the door. "Time for a break."

They walked down the hallway, past several classrooms and the Relief Society room, and turned a corner before they found a water fountain. She took a drink and then waited while he did too. When he started to walk back up the hallway, she took hold of his hand and stopped him.

"You made me do something hard tonight. I wasn't ready for it."

"I'm sorry," Paul said. "I didn't want—"

"But you were right. I *needed* to do it. I can't go on punishing part of me if I've really repented. It will take all of me to be able to move on."

"Kay, the truth is I had all three of your initials put on that disk for a reason. I wanted to tell you I think there's a lot of good in Kristina you need to let out, instead of keeping her bottled up inside. You'll never enjoy life that way. Maybe I pushed too hard tonight, but—"

She put her fingers on his lips. "I'm sorry I got mad. Thank you for helping me be somebody I didn't know I could be again— for helping me feel whole."

"That was something you had to do for yourself."

"Maybe. But in all the ugliness with Wes, before and after the divorce, I built a wall around myself, and you were the first person who made me want to break it down. It isn't easy—I'll still have to work at it. Help me?"

He smiled. "Sure—anything you want."

"Do you still have that gift in your pocket?"

"Yes."

"Put it on me?" She turned around and swept her hair away from her neck, gathering it up with her hand.

He pulled the box out of his pocket and took out the gold chain that held the engraved disc. She stood patiently as he fastened the chain around her neck.

Then she turned to face him. "If you had any idea how nervous I was about tonight . . ."

"Better now?"

"With you, yes."

"I have a feeling Kristina Kay is going to find a lot of good friends here who like her. I know *I* like her a lot."

"Good. You're the one I care about most." She put her arms around his neck and kissed him.

He held onto her when it was over, wondering what would happen if anyone walked around the corner and saw them just now. He didn't care.

Music floated down the hallway as the band started another number. Kay stepped away from him. "I love to dance. Do you?"

Paul realized the tune was another cha-cha. "I never learned this one," he said. "I don't know if I can—"

"Sure you can. It might not be easy at first, but it will come if you work at it. I'll help you."

Before the song ended, she had helped him settle into the rhythm of the dance. "You're better at it than you thought you were."

From down the hall they heard the bandleader's voice announcing an intermission. She took his arm. "Buy me another punch and cookie?"

"Sure." They walked around the corner toward the cultural hall. "Are you ready to mingle?"

She put her hand on her stomach as though trying to still butterflies inside. "I think I'm up to it."

Chapter 9

The couple strolling ahead of them turned in at the door of an exclusive dress shop. Kay stopped where she was and held Paul by the arm. "*Now* how do we keep an eye on Mr. and Mrs. Banker? We can't just stand and stare through the store window."

Paul nodded toward the shop on the other side of the passageway in the hotel-casino mall. "Let's go look at the Indian jewelry. You'll appreciate the artistry." He led her to the display window opposite the dress shop and stood there holding her hand.

She glanced over her shoulder. "What do we do—take turns looking back so they don't slip past us when they walk out?"

"No. Keep an eye on the reflections in this window in front of us. Watch for her yellow blouse."

Kay looked down at the jewelry. "This really is fine work. Have you ever given any thought to what it means to the people who make it?"

"No. It's pretty. I didn't know it had to mean something too."

"Some of those squash blossom necklaces are really intricate works of art. Women wear them because—"

"Hold that thought and fill me in later," Paul said. "Here they go."

"How did you know they were coming here today?" Kay asked as she and Paul strolled along about twenty-five feet behind the Delarois.

"I have a contact at the bank who put me onto this story. She calls me when he says he's going away for the weekend."

Kay raised her eyebrows. "Aha—another woman."

Paul grinned. "Nice lady—grandmotherly. I could introduce

you, but she likes to keep her distance from me and all of this, for the sake of her job."

They followed the Delarois for nearly an hour, until the banker and his wife walked into one of the hotel restaurants at lunchtime. Paul stopped Kay outside the door. "Wish I knew if they were going to have lunch alone."

"Who would they be meeting?" she asked.

"Do you think Mitchell Harrison would recognize you if he saw you?"

"In a second. He's seen me in my wig and sunglasses. But Paul, do you really think Mrs. Banker would know all about this deal her husband's involved in? I mean—would he tell her everything?"

"Hmm—good question." Kay was speaking from experience, he knew; men like Wes Riddley and James Delaroi didn't want their women too deeply involved in their business. "Even if he has told her all about it, I'll bet Mitch Harrison would be too careful to talk in front of a third party—a witness."

Would the banker find some way to make a one-on-one contact with the lawyer today? Not likely, Paul thought; so far the Delarois seemed to be following the same pattern as last time, withdrawing money from an automatic teller machine, then going shopping—nothing more. *No art galleries—but maybe she's not interested in art.*

"Come on," he said to Kay. "You didn't come here to play cloak-and-dagger with me. I'll take you to pick up your daughter."

"Anytime you're ready. I'm just grateful to you for bringing me along. I couldn't have afforded to drive up again this week."

"Did Hugh or Wes give you any trouble about seeing Angela on short notice?"

"No. They'd better not. I have the right to take her every weekend, if I can."

Paul smiled. "Way to go—stand up for yourself."

"Maybe I made a mistake letting them bully me into that custody agreement, but I'll never let them stop me from seeing my daughter—*never!*"

He hadn't heard that kind of determination in her voice before. "I like your attitude. That's progress."

Kay looked at him curiously. "Did you think I was a complete marshmallow, Paul?"

"No. I'm just glad to know you're not going to let them make you back down again."

As they neared the Riddley mansion, Paul slowed down and prepared to stop outside the gate.

"Pull into the driveway," Kay said.

He let the car roll to a stop at the edge of the driveway. "You're sure?"

She smiled at him. "Yes. If they don't like my being with someone, *they'll* have to deal with it."

He stopped in front of the door. "Wait here," Kay said. She stepped out of the car and walked into the house without knocking. She came out five minutes later holding Angela by the hand. They were followed by Max, the chauffeur, who stood by the front door looking Paul over carefully.

Kay walked to his car and opened the back door for Angela. The little girl stood looking uncertainly at him, making no attempt to get in. "Sweetheart," Kay said, "this is Paul. He's a friend of mine. He's a nice man. I think you're going to like him."

Paul smiled at her and Angela smiled back shyly, then climbed into the back seat. Kay buckled the seatbelt around her, shut the rear door, and got into the passenger seat in the front of the car. "Max is going to follow us," she said to Paul, making a face. "Hugh insisted. But it's OK—Max is not a problem."

Paul looked into his rearview mirror after he pulled out onto Alta Drive. The big, blue Cadillac eased through the gate and fell in behind them.

"Do you want me to take you to Marcy's?" Paul asked.

"You can if you want to. But we could go to a park—or something."

Paul understood. This would be a chance for him to get to know Angela—and for her to get to know him.

He drove to Jaycee Park—better stay with the familiar for now, he thought—and they went directly to the playground equipment.

Paul and Kay watched as Angela made a small circuit: climb up the steps of a wooden platform, cross the short, swinging bridge, slide down the slide, and go around to the steps again. But after a few minutes she came to an impasse; a boy of about two and his older sister were playing at the top of the steps, blocking her way.

Paul pointed to an opening between the chains supporting the suspended bridge. "Want me to boost you up there?" he said to Angela.

She looked at him, then at the bridge, and nodded. He held her up while she climbed through the chains. Then, on an impulse, he pulled himself up far enough to get part of his body through the opening and hung there, his legs dangling toward the ground. Angela giggled. "Big people can't come up here."

"Sure they can." Paul wriggled through the opening, climbed up onto the bridge, then followed Angela to the slide. She slid down and Kay caught her at the bottom. Paul followed behind. Kay made as if to catch him, then moved aside at the last second. She clapped her hands as he took a victory stance at the bottom. "Great form! Very athletic."

He grinned, and Angela clapped too.

"Swing me, Mommy," Angela said, and ran toward the swings. Paul and Kay followed. Angela sat down in a swing and Kay gave it a gentle push to get it started. Paul nodded toward the empty swing next to the little girl. "Sit down, Kay, I'll push both of you."

"Do it, Mommy!" Angela said. "Let's swing together."

He pushed Angela gently with one hand and Kay, in the small of her back, with the other. Angela's long, dark hair streamed out behind her. Kay seemed to enjoy the swinging, and smiled as she watched her daughter enjoying it.

When Angela tired of swinging, she took her mother by the hand and tugged her toward the merry-go-round. "Push us, Paul. Push us," she begged.

As Angela clambered onto the small merry-go-round, Paul looked up and noticed Max standing in the shade of a nearby tree, watching them. Max nodded, and smiled slightly.

How long would he stay with them, Paul wondered.

Max stayed until Paul delivered Kay and Angela to Marcy's. Angela had dozed off in the back seat, so Paul gently picked her up in his arms and maneuvered her out of the car. As he and Kay climbed the stairs to the outdoor walkway that ran along the second level of the apartment building, Paul saw the big Cadillac pull out of the parking lot.

When Marcy answered their knock, she looked at Kay, then at Paul with Angela in his arms and stood back to hold the door open wide. "Come in. You can put her on the couch."

As he laid Angela on the couch, she opened her eyes and looked uncomprehendingly at him for a moment, then at her mother and Marcy. "Hi, Marcy," she said. She smiled at Paul, then rolled on her side and closed her eyes again.

"I'd better go," Paul said to Kay. "I'll pick you up tomorrow afternoon."

He had shut Marcy's door behind him and was two apartments away when he heard Kay call out: "Paul?" He turned back toward her.

"Marcy wants me to ask if you'd like to stay for dinner."

"Well, that's, uh . . . but Scott's expecting me."

Kay leaned back in the door and spoke, but he couldn't hear her words. She leaned out again and said, "You can use Marcy's phone to call him if you want."

"Ah . . . OK, sure."

Marcy might be what some people meant by perpetual motion, Paul decided.

"I'll just add some more spaghetti to the pot and there'll be enough for all of us," she said, standing on tiptoe to search in her cupboard. She was short, blonde, and constantly busy. Not quite pretty but not plain, she had a warmth and personality that would draw anyone out. Was there a man in her life, Paul wondered—and if not, why not? *None of your business, Webber. Stow the professional prying for tonight.*

Marcy seemed to have no trouble juggling several tasks at once. Somehow she made spaghetti sauce and a tossed green salad at the same time and everything came out together.

They woke Angela for dinner. The meal began with Marcy telling Kay, "I know you'll want to say grace," then bowing her head for the prayer.

The little girl finished eating quickly and went immediately to the videotape rack beneath Marcy's TV. "Can I watch *Snow White?*" she asked.

Marcy nodded. "Of course. It's yours—I gave it to you."

When the three adults had finished eating, Marcy began gathering up the dishes—and began her examination of Paul.

"Kristina says you're a reporter. That must be interesting," Marcy started. "What do investigative reporters do?" she asked. The inquiries continued: How long had he been with the wire service? Did he plan to spend his career there? Did he plan to have a family someday?

To the last, surprise question, Paul stammered something to the effect that yes, it was in his plans. He said nothing more, even though Marcy waited expectantly. Kay turned red. When Marcy looked away to run the dishwater in the sink, Kay smiled apologetically at Paul and shrugged her shoulders.

He smiled back, and winked. "What about you, Marcy?" he asked. "What kind of work do *you* do?" He stepped up to the sink, took the dish Marcy had just rinsed out of her hands, and fit it into a slot in the dishwasher rack.

"Thank you," Marcy said, raising her eyebrows. "I didn't realize there were guys who knew how to do that." She scraped another dish and rinsed it as she spoke. "I work for the chamber of commerce—liaison with local companies and organizations that want to bring investors or convention business to Las Vegas."

"Do you plan to make that *your* career?" Paul asked as he took the next dish from her.

Maybe—she wasn't sure, but it was satisfying for now.

And where was she from?

Caliente—a small town northeast of Las Vegas.

From a small family, or large?

Five younger brothers and sisters.

Was that why she enjoyed children so much? Did she plan to have a family of her own someday?

Yes, and yes, she hoped to.

Watching, Kay marveled at how quickly Paul took over the interrogation, how easily he slipped into Marcy's rhythm, passing the plates and silverware from her hands to the dishwasher, grabbing the rag to wipe the table, then handing it back just as Marcy needed it. Kay recalled that in college it had taken her a couple of months to learn how to adapt to her roommate Marcy's accelerated pace in everything.

The three of them talked for almost two hours without getting back to Paul's work or his future plans. Did he deliberately steer the conversation to other things? Kay couldn't be sure. He seemed to enjoy listening to her and her friend. He drew Marcy out about herself and her hopes, and then somehow Marcy and Kay found themselves reminiscing about their past experiences together, encouraged by well-timed questions from Paul.

It was a quarter to nine when he thanked Marcy for dinner and excused himself. "See you tomorrow, three o'clock," he said to Kay as he stepped out of the door.

Scott leaned back in his stuffed chair and put his bare feet up on the arm of the living room couch. "Fine loyalty to a friend, Webber, letting a little bit of home cooking turn your head while I'm sitting here eating a TV dinner by myself, lonely . . ."

Paul put on a somber expression. "Sad. Terribly sad. What you need is someone to come home to. I think I just met her. Sharp, great personality, great cook."

"Ready to be baptized next week?"

"That's where you take over. I've done the scouting."

Scott laughed. "OK, chief scout, how are you doing with Kay?"

"Today was good—really good. I met her little girl and her—"

"Whoa! This sounds significant, meeting the family."

"It was her best friend, the one I just told you about, who was the real test. I got along fine with her little girl. Angela's a sweetheart—she takes after her mother." He paused. "Overall, I think I did OK."

Scott pretended to take notes. "As usual, subject is holding back. There must be more to this."

Paul laughed. "I certainly hope so."

"Anything more on the banker from L.A.?" Scott asked.

"Yeah. We followed him and his wife up here this morning. They went to an ATM and drew out some money, then went shopping—same as last time."

"And?"

"Nothing. That was all. Was your banker friend able to tell you anything about that account number?"

"It's from Cattlemen's Bank of Nevada, and I tried to test it out; I went into one of their branches and told them I needed to deposit some money I owed into the account of my good friend James K. Delaroi. They would have let me do it—but they don't have an account for anyone by that name."

Paul frowned in the direction of the far wall. "I wonder what name he's using? I'm not surprised he wouldn't have the account in his own name. But I wonder if there's any way we could tie him to . . . if he's used his home address, or . . ." The frown disappeared suddenly and Paul looked at Scott. "*Mrs.* Delaroi! *She* was the one who withdrew the money today—and it was at a Cattlemen's Bank of Nevada branch. Her husband handed her the card and talked her through it while she punched in the numbers."

"I wonder if she has any idea where the money's coming from? Do you know her name?"

"Margaret. Margaret Lynne—Lynne with an *e* on the end."

Scott made a note on the pad by his telephone. "I hope you're not in any rush on the story right now, because it will be a while before I can get back to this—but I *will* get back to it."

It was a quarter to four when Paul pulled into the driveway in front of Hugh Riddley's mansion.

"He's probably in there watching the clock," Kay said.

"We're late?"

"No, there's no set time when I have to be back with Angela, but whenever I have her out without Max along, Hugh lets me know that he's been waiting for me to show up."

Kay stepped inside the house with her daughter, carrying Angela's small bag. They were gone for about ten minutes. When they came back, Hugh Riddley followed them out the door and stood on the front steps scrutinizing Paul and his car. Riddley was a barrel-chested man of average height—maybe five-eight—with big biceps and forearms. He looked like he would have been at home behind a jackhammer or a shovel. He had sandy hair streaked with white, and a ruddy complexion. Wes, slim and dark-haired, must have taken after his mother, Paul thought.

Kay kissed Angela good-bye, got in the car, and said nothing as they drove away. In his rearview mirror, Paul could see Hugh Riddley watching them until they were out of sight.

Just before he turned off of Alta Drive onto Rancho, Paul glanced at Kay. Her face was flushed, her jaw was firmly set, and she was staring at something far away. "Anything wrong?" he asked.

"Yes," she answered curtly.

"Want to talk about it?"

"No." It was equally curt.

Half a minute later, she turned toward him. Her smile was obviously an effort. "Yes, I want to talk about it. You can help me. But—give me a few minutes?"

They were on the freeway headed toward Los Angeles when she sighed and said, "Just when I think I've got my anger under control, he hits me with some mean and low thing that's completely new."

"Wes was there today?"

"No. Oh, no, I don't think he sees Angela more than once or twice a week." She paused for a moment. "He stole something—something I gave to her."

"*Stole* it?"

"Yes. A painting—one of my best. It's a place on my dad's ranch where Angela likes to go. You can look out over the desert, mountains in the background. I wish you could see it when the sun's going down. It's . . ." Her voice rose. "Wes *took* it . . . he just . . . *took it, and gave it away!*" She paused. "I asked Angela, I said, 'Baby, where's your painting?' and she said, 'Daddy took it.' "

"What did he do with it?"

"He didn't tell Angela. But I asked Hugh where it went, and he said Wes told him it was part of a deal he made with a client." She held her arms tightly across her body as though she were cold. "And Hugh told me . . . he said, 'But you can just paint her another one'!"

Paul jumped as her fist suddenly smashed down on the padded dashboard. She drew her legs up tight against her chest, clasped her arms around them, put her head on her knees, and sat that way with her eyes tightly shut

Paul let the car roll slowly to a stop beside the highway. He reached out to put his hands on her shoulders and gently massaged her tense muscles. After a minute or so, she relaxed and leaned forward so he could massage her neck too. "Mmm, thank you. That helps."

She sat up and began to rub her temples. "Hugh has no concept of what that painting means to me—and I'm sure Wes knows *exactly* what it means." Slowly she shook her head. "A man who'd steal from his own daughter just to make a few extra dollars . . ." She massaged her temples more vigorously.

"Getting another headache?"

"Yes. Do you mind if I try to sleep for a while?"

Paul shook his head.

She took her bottle of prescription migraine medicine out of her purse, opened it, shook out two capsules, and held them up so he could count them. He reached behind the seat for his bottle of water and handed it to her. She swallowed the capsules with some water, then leaned her head back against the seat and closed her eyes.

He put the car in gear again and eased out into the traffic.

His palms were clammy and there was a knot in his stomach. He realized that he'd like to have Wes within reach just for a moment. He shook his head to try to clear the thought. What good would it do to take his anger out on the man? Then how would he be any different from Wes?

But how could anyone be so casually and deliberately cruel?

They were across the state line into California when Kay opened her eyes and looked around. "You didn't sleep very long," he said.

She sat upright, leaning her head back against the headrest. "I haven't slept at all. But the medicine is helping."

"I wish I could tell you something that would help with Wes. I'd like to do something . . . but everything I can think of right now involves getting him alone, and . . ."

"I know." She sighed. "He's done it to me again—slapped me around emotionally. I can just imagine what he was thinking when he took that painting knowing I'd find out about it!"

Kay closed her eyes once more. Paul didn't disturb her even though he didn't think she was sleeping.

She opened her eyes to look around when he stopped at the

California agricultural inspection station. After he spoke with the inspector and pulled back onto the freeway, he said, "Kay, I think it would help you to go through the temple."

She looked at him in surprise. "Help me with a problem like Wes?"

"Yes. There's a peace you can get that doesn't come any other way. What you learn and what happens there helps you face times in life when . . . well, especially times like this. It helps when you understand just how much Heavenly Father and Jesus love us."

"I've been thinking about it," she said slowly. "I have an appointment with the bishop Tuesday night. He said he wants to see me about the temple, and there's a class he wants me to take. It lasts six weeks." She paused. "But if it could be done faster than that—he told me he thought something could be worked out— then I could go after the Christmas holidays."

She turned to look at him. "Could you go to the Las Vegas temple with me the first weekend in January?"

"Me? I . . . sure. But isn't there somebody else you'd want to be with you?"

She bit her lip. "I don't know if they . . . but the bishop said I'd need to have a woman there, so I thought maybe Nina Leman . . ."

"Kay, your mother and your father . . ."

She was looking down at the floor. "I don't know whether they'd believe I could . . . or that I should . . ."

"You know they would. They'd probably give anything to be with you for that."

She squinted away tears and nodded her head.

Chapter 10

Kay was not waiting in the foyer of the temple when he arrived. Paul glanced at his watch. Probably she had already been ushered in to prepare herself for the endowment session. He showed his recommend at the desk and hurried to the dressing room.

After changing, he walked to the room where people in this temple session were to wait. There were several middle-aged men seated with younger men. Most of the younger ones looked like missionaries heading for the field; the others were probably bridegrooms.

One man who looked to be in his fifties sat alone. His hands and his cheeks were a dark brown, but his forehead was white—the telltale farmer tan. His cheeks had the wind-burned look of someone who spent a lot of time outdoors. This man would be a rancher, and he had blue eyes like Kay's.

Paul took a seat on the bench behind him. While he was wondering whether to introduce himself to the rancher, a younger man stepped into the room. He had sandy hair and blue eyes too, and he looked enough like Kay to be a brother. He sat down in front of Paul next to the older man, who put an arm around his shoulders.

Paul leaned forward and spoke softly in the older man's ear: "Would you be Brother Reston?"

The man turned to look at him, then slowly smiled. "Paul Webber?"

Paul nodded.

The older man reached over his shoulder to extend a hand. "Bill Reston. Kay was afraid you might not make it."

Paul shook the man's hand. "I had to work late last night. I didn't leave Los Angeles until a quarter to three this morning."

Bill glanced at his watch and raised his eyebrows. "You made good time."

The younger man next to him half turned in his seat and extended his hand for Paul to shake. "Doug Reston," he whispered. "I've heard a lot about you. If there's a chance later, I'd like to talk."

When the time came for the endowment session to begin, all three men filed into the room together. Kay saw Paul first and smiled at him with relief. She looked at her father, and then at the tall young man with him and began to cry. Her mother cried too. She put an arm around Kay and handed her the handkerchief she carried.

Kay hugged her brother around the chest. He had to reach down to put his arms around her. Standing five feet away, Paul couldn't hear what Kay said against Doug's chest, but her brother's whispered response was plain: "I should have talked to you long before now. I promise it won't be so long until the next time."

Her parents moved in to complete the circle; Bill Reston put one arm around his son and the other around his wife, and his wife put an arm around their daughter. The four of them stood like that for several seconds, drawn tightly together. Then Kay turned to look at Paul. She held out her hand toward him. He took it, and she drew him into the circle next to her brother. "You did this—or at least you helped a lot. Thank you for being here. I was afraid you weren't going to make it."

"You know I wouldn't have missed it. But I can't stay long; I have to be back tonight."

"Tonight?" Kay's smile faded. "I hoped this afternoon we could . . ." She squeezed his hand. "Well, I'm just glad you're here."

In the dressing room, Paul hurried to change so he could be waiting when Kay came out. He was aware that someone followed him out of the dressing room, but he paid no attention to the other person until Doug Reston sat down beside him on the couch in the waiting area.

"I need to thank you for what you've done for my sister," Doug said.

"I've just tried to help her find her way. Maybe you could have done the same thing if you'd, ah . . . if you'd had the chance."

Doug looked away. "No. I *had* the chance—and I didn't do it." He looked Paul in the eyes again. "When I found out that she was pregnant and not married, I was rotten to her—and I've been ashamed of that ever since." He hesitated. "I know I live pretty far away now, but I've been wondering if there are ways I could help her out."

Paul knew it was a question, not a statement. "There might be, from time to time."

"Money—or something else?"

"Maybe a little money, but a lot of that 'something else'— someone to listen, tell her she's the best mother she can be under the circumstances. Things like that."

"Well, I'll be calling her—often." Doug took out a business card and wrote a number on it. "There's my home telephone and my office. Call me, anytime, if you see something I can do."

Bill Reston sat down on the other side of his son and leaned forward so he could talk to Paul. "I can't thank you enough for what you've done for Kay." He glanced at his son. "She's a good girl. She always has been. But she's needed a little shoring up from time to time when things have been tough."

Doug put an arm around his father. "We've already been over that, Dad. I've told Paul I'm going to be part of it from now on. He says all he did was what we would have done if we were there."

"Maybe," Bill answered, looking at Paul. "But that's the trick—being there. Her mother and I prayed for a long time that there would be somebody close by who could help her. Looks like you were a big part of the answer."

The two women came out of the dressing room and the men stood. Kay took Paul by the arm as the five of them walked outside. "Dad's treating us to dinner—including you, if you have time."

"You don't have to—"

Kay's mother put her hand on his other arm. "Please? It's so little that we can do, and you've been such a good friend to our daughter. We'd like to get to know you better."

"Pick any place you want," Bill added. "Don't worry about the cost."

"Make it one of those places you like where a cattle rancher could get a good steak," Kay said. She reached out to loosen the knot in her father's tie. "A place for people who hate to dress up." Then she kissed him on the cheek. "Thanks, Daddy."

Paul grinned. "Good food, good prices, no tie—that's my territory."

As Paul drove away from the temple, Kay watched out of the back window until only the spire could be seen above the houses along the street. Then she turned to Paul. "I can still feel it."

"What?"

"What I felt in there—the peace. I've never . . . there's never been anything like . . ." She looked straight ahead for a moment, then took a tissue out of her purse and dabbed at her eyes. "You were right. He really loves me—no matter what."

"He always has."

"I want to hold onto that—what I'm feeling right now. And they told us before the session that we need to keep coming back to keep on learning."

"How about next Friday night, then—the Los Angeles Temple?"

"Yes. I'd love that." She reached her arm out to rest her hand on his shoulder. "I'm sorry you have to go back today. I was hoping maybe you could come out to see my parents' place."

"I wish I could. Are you taking Angela with you?"

"Just overnight. I promised to take her horseback riding before the holidays are over, and tomorrow was the only day Hugh didn't want to argue about."

"How was Christmas?"

"Wonderful! Max picked me up early in the morning and I was there when Angela opened all her presents." She paused. "And Wes didn't show up till just before dinner, at noon. He left a couple of hours later. I know he had a date—or something. Anyway, I got to keep Angela for two whole days."

"Tell her hi for me, and that I wish I could go riding with her."

"A city kid like you actually rides?" Kay smiled.

"Sure. Give me a chance sometime and I'll show you. I've done it at least two or three times before."

Kay laughed.

Paul's brow furrowed. "It's ugly that you have to fight them for every little bit of time with your daughter."

She put a finger over his lips. "I don't want to think about fighting right now—or about the Riddleys."

"Aren't you on television?" the teller asked, smiling.

Scott Pike made the effort to smile back. "Yes. Action News." He had hoped he wouldn't be recognized, but it had been a long time since he could count on being an anonymous face—someone she'd forget as soon as he walked out of the bank. Still, he had to do this himself; he couldn't bring anyone else in on the story.

"It's New Year's resolution time and I owe something to a friend," he said, shoving a twenty-dollar bill and a deposit slip toward the woman. It wasn't a lie; he hadn't specified which friend.

She read the account number off the slip, typed it on her computer keyboard, then frowned slightly as she read what was on the screen. "We don't have an account for a Margaret Lynne . . ."—she peered at the deposit slip—"Dee-la-roi." She looked up at him. "Did you mean Crowley?" It was pleasant, helpful. She waited for him to answer.

Crowley? Who is . . . never mind, she's waiting. Say something!
"She, ah . . . so she's still using her maiden name." It was a guess. He tried to sound casual. "I wonder why. She's been married for a while."

"Some of us don't feel like our identity changes just because we get married." Scott could see without breaking eye contact that there were rings on the third finger of the teller's left hand. "Or some women have already established a career in their maiden names," she continued. "That happens in your line of work, doesn't it?" She was still smiling—comfortable talking with him. That was good.

"Sure," he answered. "The name's her business. Either way, the money is hers."

The teller punched in more numbers on her keyboard, waited for the receipt to come out of her printer, and handed it to him. "I'm sure she'll appreciate it."

Scott laughed lightly. "I'm sure she'll be surprised to get it."

He was relieved to look back when he walked out of the bank and see the teller busy with another customer. Maybe she would forget, at least for the time being, that she had talked to him—and whose account had been of interest to him.

If Paul can verify that name, then we know how the money is funneled to Delaroi. Wonder if there'd ever be a way to tie it directly to Mitch Harrison? Or Wes Riddley?

Anna Leeds looked at the paper Paul put in front of her, thought for a moment, then leaned back against the cushion of the booth in the diner. "No, I thought maybe I recognized that name, but no, I can't say . . ."

"It sounded familiar? Think in terms of your boss."

Her brow furrowed for a moment. Then: "Of course! *Mrs.* Delaroi—Meg! Margaret *L.* Delaroi."

"And Crowley—is that her maiden name?"

"I think maybe . . . yes."

"Is there any way you can be sure—check somewhere?"

"Well, there are the personnel records. But it would be illegal for me to, uh . . ."

"I understand. What about something public? An article in the company newsletter? Maybe the bank's PR people have bio sheets on the top officers?"

"Hmm. Maybe that."

Back in his office a short time later, Paul immersed himself in a story he had to finish before the day was over. He had been busy for perhaps twenty minutes when his telephone rang. Anna's words when he answered were businesslike, but it was obvious she was trying to keep excitement out of her voice. "I have checked the bank's biographical file to update it. I can verify that the information you have is correct."

"Crowley is Mrs. Delaroi's maiden name?"

"Yes, sir. That information is in the biographical material sent out to people who inquire about possible speakers or seminar presenters from the bank. And our public relations department's records show that they sent the same information out to a lawyer in Las Vegas who made an inquiry about six months ago. I believe you already have his name."

"Mitchell Harrison!"

"Yes."

"Nice work, Anna! That's one of the links we need to—"

She cut him off. "Yes, sir. I'll put that information in the mail this afternoon." She paused briefly. "You're welcome." Then she hung up.

Obviously there was someone nearby who couldn't be allowed to hear the conversation. Delaroi?

What she had told him satisfied his curiosity on another point: the groundwork for involving the banker in this scheme had been carefully laid. Obviously, Mitch Harrison had studied the man, learning about the new young wife with expensive tastes before he sucked Delaroi in.

Anna had handled the situation coolly, intelligently, and he hadn't been able to thank her properly. He called a florist and ordered a small bouquet of flowers sent to her. When the woman at the floral shop asked if there was a message, he dictated a note: "I'm in your debt. This is on account." No signature, he said; she would know who they came from.

Kay stopped just inside the bus terminal and quickly scanned it. When she saw Paul, she smiled and walked toward him.

"How was the trip?" he asked.

"Long. Bo-o-oring." She put her hand in his. "I missed having someone I could talk to. So how about a little conversation at my place over sandwiches? I'm starved."

He took her bag as they stepped outside. "I couldn't turn down an offer like that—even without the sandwich."

As he stowed her bag in the trunk of his car in the parking lot, Paul glanced toward the terminal. A man at the curb was talking to a taxi driver and gesturing their way. He wore light-colored slacks, a red golf shirt, and what was either a cheap hairpiece or the worst haircut Paul had ever seen. When he noticed that Paul was looking in his direction, he quickly turned away and got into the rear seat of the taxi.

Paul watched his rearview mirror as he drove out of the parking lot. The taxi was not far behind. It stayed with them for more than a mile, always a car or two back.

Maybe it was only coincidence.

Or maybe not.

At a stoplight, Paul swerved into the right lane without warning and stopped behind a line of cars. The taxi was unable to change lanes. As it passed on the left, Paul tried to get a quick look at the passenger, but he couldn't.

After they drove away from the stoplight, the taxi fell back again into its position again one car behind them.

The next intersection was a T; a street coming from the residential area on their right dead-ended at the stoplight on the main road they were traveling. On the corner just before the stoplight there was a small convenience store, and just past the light a shopping mall. Paul cruised slowly through the light, then made a quick right turn into the mall parking lot without signaling. The driver behind him honked angrily as he passed. The cab, next in line, kept going. Paul had counted on that; if they were being followed, the passenger would have told the taxi driver not to make any panic moves. It was no surprise, though, when the taxi slowed to turn into the parking lot at the next entrance.

Kay was looking at him strangely. "What's wrong?"

"Nothing. I, uh, . . . I just remembered I need to make a phone call—back at that drive-in across the street."

"But you have a phone, don't you?"

"I—the battery's dead, I think. This will just take a minute."

"OK."

With other vehicles in the parking lot screening his car from the cab, Paul doubled back across an empty area, quickly crossed the street that ran between the mall and the convenience store, then drove behind the store and circled around to the far side of it. He parked there where his car could not be seen from the direction of the mall.

He got out of the car and walked to the phone shelter at the front corner of the building where he could look back at the mall. The taxi was cruising slowly away from him down one of the lanes in the mall parking lot . . . searching.

Lifting the handset of the phone, Paul fished a quarter out of his pocket, dropped it into the slot, and dialed his own number. He listened to his recording while he kept an eye on the taxi, and when the recording ended, he searched for words, then softly and slowly began reciting "Itsy Bitsy Spider" into the mouthpiece so that Kay would see him talking. The taxi came back toward him, to the street that ran between the convenience store and the mall. The driver stopped, waited, then turned left and drove slowly into the residential area behind the mall.

Paul watched the taxi until it was out of sight, then hung up.

Kay looked at him quizzically as he got back into the car. "Not at home," he said. "I left a message."

He kept an eye on the rearview mirror again as they pulled away from the convenience store and finished the drive to Kay's apartment. No taxi.

Paul walked her to her door, then hesitated as she stepped inside and held it open for him to enter. "I, uh . . . I have to be in the office very early in the morning—some business with the news desk in New York." He made a show of glancing at his watch. "Could we save the conversation until tomorrow night over dinner—your favorite fast-food Chinese-Italian-or whatever place?"

Kay laughed. "Of course." She stepped outside, wrapped her arms around him, and kissed him.

He held her close, wanting to cushion her head on his shoulder and stroke her hair—but she was still wearing the wig, along with the green dress.

At least the man in the taxi hadn't seen Kay without her disguise, Paul thought as he drove away.

Or did he already know what she looked like? The notes her tormentor had left in Las Vegas promised he would find her wherever she went.

Paul hadn't said anything to Kay about the man in the taxi because he didn't want to alarm her if there was no reason. But—how could he be sure there was no reason?

He made a series of left turns until he came back to her street, then parked fifty yards away from her house, on the other side, and turned out his headlights.

It was nearly ten, and there was little traffic. No taxi of any kind came down the street for the next forty-five minutes, and no one else parked on the street within a block of Kay's apartment.

Maybe his imagination was working overtime after all.

Chapter 11

Paul pulled into Hugh Riddley's driveway and parked just beyond the steps that led to the front door. "I'll wait for you here," he said.

Kay sat for a moment with her hand on the door handle. Then she wiped her palms on her jeans and took a deep breath. "No. I want you to come in this time." She turned to smile at him.

He reached out to take hold of her hand. "Are you sure? I wouldn't want—"

"Yes. If Hugh doesn't like seeing me with a man of my choice, that's too bad. He'd better get used to it." She adjusted her wig, then stepped out of the car. When Paul came around to her side, she took hold of his arm, walked up to the front door, and pushed it open.

Paul stopped just inside, but Kay kept on walking toward the middle of the large foyer. "Angela?" she called.

The floor of the foyer was of inlaid wood and the walls were paneled with oak. To Paul's right, next to a set of polished hardwood doors, was a faux Greek statue—a young girl holding a water urn that doubled as a planter. "I feel like I'm in some English country manor," he said.

Kay smiled. "Outside, it's a mixture of Greek and modern. And in the living room"—she gestured toward the open doors on Paul's left—"it's Park Avenue and Istanbul." From where he stood, he could see a modern sofa, in a muted floral print, situated on an oriental rug.

He turned in a circle to get the full effect of the place. "The choices of a man who knew exactly what he wanted."

119

She kept her voice low. "I think so. No decorator would have done this, and I never knew Hugh's wife, but I doubt that he let her—"

"Mommy! Mommy!" Angela called as she came running down the staircase at the end of the foyer. She leaped into her mother's arms, and Kay closed her eyes and smiled as she whirled Angela around. "How are you today, Sweetheart?"

"Fine." Angela looked at Paul and smiled shyly. "Hi, Paul. Are you going too?"

He nodded.

Angela grinned. "You can push us on the merry-go-round again!"

The double doors on Paul's right opened and Hugh Riddley stepped out of his office. The front half of a large wooden desk could be seen through the open door, and behind it, shelves of leather-bound books that looked expensive—and seldom used.

The older man studied Paul carefully, then turned to Kay. "Where are you going today?"

Kay glanced at Paul. "We'll be taking her to the park and then out to dinner. Angela and I will stay at Marcy's tonight."

Hugh gazed at Paul again, then spoke to Kay. "I'll call Max to go with you."

"There's no need," she answered.

"I'll take good care of them," Paul added.

Hugh Riddley's look made it plain that he wasn't interested in anything Paul had to say. Kay saw Paul's smile take on the hard set at the corners of the mouth that she had seen the night he confronted her about her dual life. Paul spoke softly but distinctly, the same way he had that night: "I'll bring them back safely—tomorrow afternoon."

Hugh turned to Kay. "I'll call Max."

"There's no need," Paul repeated.

Hugh didn't answer. He turned his back and walked into the study, picked up the phone on his desk, and pushed one of its buttons. "Max, Kristina is here with her, uh . . . *friend* to pick up Angela. I want you to go with them."

Kay looked at Paul. He was staring down at the floor shaking his head.

Hugh stepped out of the study, brushed past Paul, and knelt down by Angela. She put her arms around his neck and gave him a hug. "Bye, Grandpa," she said in his ear.

Hugh smiled at her. "Good-bye, Princess. Have fun at the park." He glanced up at Paul. "And remember what I told you—be careful."

When Paul opened the front door for Kay and Angela, Max was just pulling the Cadillac into position in the driveway. Paul helped Angela into his car while Kay brought her daughter's suitcase from the limousine.

As they drove slowly out of the gate, Max was close behind.

Paul said nothing for half a mile. He didn't even glance her way. Finally, as they were turning off of Alta Drive, Kay asked softly: "Are you OK?"

He glanced at Angela in the rearview mirror; she was looking out her window at the houses they passed. "What do you think he was trying to tell her—'Be careful'?"

Kay shrugged. "Don't let Hugh get to you. He's unfriendly with almost everybody. And you said it yourself—he's used to seeing things his own way."

Paul frowned. "I wonder if anyone's ever tried to teach him that he's seeing things wrong."

After stopping at a drive-through hamburger place to buy lunch, Paul drove to Jaycee Park. Max stayed with them, sitting in the Cadillac at the curb just outside the park while they ate lunch at a picnic table. Paul looked up occasionally to find the man watching them. He didn't like the feeling. *Hugh Riddley's watchdog. . . . Wonder if Wes has told Hugh stories about other men in Kay's life? . . . What do they think I am, some kind of . . .*

Angela finished eating quickly and ran to play on the slide.

Paul glanced toward the Cadillac. "Don't you ever feel like a prisoner with a guard?" he asked Kay.

"Sometimes." She gazed at the chauffeur for a moment. "I don't mind Max so much. He's good with Angela. The part that bothers me is wondering what Hugh asks him when he goes home."

Paul chewed a bite of his hamburger before he spoke again. "It doesn't say in the custody agreement that you have to be supervised, does it?"

"No. Hugh just sends Max along because . . ." She frowned. "I guess because he wants to keep an eye on me and what I do."

"How does that make you feel?"

"Not trusted." Kay shrugged it off again. "That's nothing new. That's Hugh." She gazed at Paul for a moment. "I suppose he doesn't trust anybody who associates with me, either. I'm sorry."

Paul finished his hamburger and milk shake before he said anything else. "Didn't you ever wish you could get away—take Angela anywhere you wanted without somebody tagging along?"

"Yes." Kay looked at Max, sitting very still in the car now with his chin resting on his chest. "But would that be . . ."

"Right?" Paul grinned. "What's wrong with it?"

She frowned. "Nothing, I guess, except . . . well, I wouldn't want to get him in trouble."

"Why should he get in trouble?"

"I don't know. Hugh . . ."

"Do you want Hugh looking over your shoulder wherever you go with your daughter for the rest of your life?"

Kay smiled. "No. But I thought before I ever took her away by myself, I'd tell him what I—"

"He'd just send Max to follow you anyway—wouldn't he?"

Slowly, Kay nodded.

"Well, then, why ask his permission?"

Kay turned to look at Angela, and so did Paul. Angela saw them and waved, then came running toward them. "Paul, push us now." She pointed toward the merry-go-round.

"How would you like to go horsey riding instead?" he asked.

"All right." She moved behind him and started to climb onto his back.

"No, I mean on a *real* horse, at your grandma and grandpa's place."

Angela lit up. "Yes! Yes! Yes!" She danced around them, clapping her hands. "Can we, Mommy? Can we? Can we?"

Kay didn't see that delight in her daughter's face very often—not since they had visited her parents at Christmas, two months ago. Still, that had been a holiday, and a special arrangement with Hugh and Wes. "Paul, we can't. It will take too long. It's—"

"An hour out and an hour back. That leaves three hours

there. We can still be at Marcy's by six."

Angela tugged on her arm. "I want to ride Grandma and Grandpa's black horsey! Can Paul take us?"

"Wouldn't your parents like to see her more often?" Paul asked.

Kay frowned. "Paul, I don't think I'm ready to—"

"Please, Mommy," Angela begged. "Please, please, please!"

Kay looked at her daughter for several seconds. She smiled weakly. "All right, Sweetheart, if you want to."

Paul stood quickly and lifted Angela up to ride on his back, her arms around his neck. She clung to him as he walked toward his car, parked two vehicles ahead of the Cadillac at the curb. Kay followed. Max's head was still bent forward on his chest when they drove away.

They had almost reached Tropicana Avenue when Paul looked into the rearview mirror and winced. Kay looked over her shoulder. The Cadillac was following them, about a block behind.

Paul turned right on Tropicana and wove through the traffic. He sped through a light just as it turned red. Kay looked back; if Max was still behind them, he was halted with the other cars at that light.

When Paul came to the ward chapel on Tropicana, he made a quick left turn into the parking lot, pulled around behind the building, and parked where he could just see past it. About a minute and a half later, they saw the blue Cadillac pass by on the street. Paul smiled.

"Why are we sitting here?" Angela asked. "Let's go."

"We'll go in just a minute," Paul answered.

When he pulled out onto Tropicana, he headed south—the direction from which they had come—then turned off on a side street and found another route to I-15 eastbound.

Kay felt a tightness in her throat as they drove out of Las Vegas. She stared straight ahead in silence, thinking—playing over in her mind some of the things Max might say to Hugh Riddley when he got home.

Once they had left the valley behind, she glanced back at her daughter. Angela had fallen asleep. Kay turned to look at Paul. "Don't *ever* do that to me again—please!"

Paul looked startled. "What?"

"Dangle something in front of my daughter like that and make me the meanie if I say no. I'd appreciate it if you'd ask me before you plan something involving her."

"I was just—"

"Doing something for her to make her happy?"

"Yes."

"Was that the only reason? Or were you trying to show Hugh Riddley that he couldn't tell *you* what to do?" She paused. "Think about it. Was this so different from what Hugh does to me when he decides what I can do with Angela?"

Paul said nothing.

Kay didn't press for an answer, but she wondered what he was thinking. *Wes would be looking for a way to get back at me. But Paul . . . well, I don't think he . . . he's mad, though, or he'd say something.*

It was nearly half an hour before he spoke. "OK, I'm sorry. It won't happen again."

"Do you see the problem it creates for me?"

"Yes. I've never had to think like a parent —but, yeah, I put you in a bad position. I'll be more careful."

She sat looking at him as he drove. "And . . . you're not mad?"

"I *was*. I really do like Angela, and I really was trying to do something nice for her. But what you said is true—I let Hugh get to me, and I had no right to drag you into a battle of wills with him."

She continued to watch him. "So it's over now? You're not holding back on me?"

"Why should I stay mad at *you*? I was the one who did something dumb."

"Yes, but . . . well . . ."

Paul grinned. "Wes wouldn't see it that way?"

"No—he wouldn't."

"I try to learn from my mistakes. You make it easier than some people do." He reached for his telephone, under the seat. "Want to call your parents and tell them we're on our way?"

She smiled as she took the phone from him. "The more I know you, the more I like you, Paul Webber."

There was much more to it than *like,* she thought as she dialed her parents' number.

She admired Paul for being able to admit his mistakes. With Wes, there had always been a price to pay if she crossed him, even when he knew she was right; he could not bear to be wrong. And somehow he *needed* to control every detail in her life. He would do it even now if she were in Las Vegas, and not constantly on guard.

With Paul, she felt free to be herself. He seemed to *want* it that way. It was just one reason she loved him.

When they turned off of the freeway a few minutes later, Angela woke. "Are we there?" she asked, rubbing her eyes.

Paul laughed, and Kay smiled. "Almost," Kay answered.

When Paul parked in the driveway between the small ranch house and the corral, Kay's father was already saddling the two horses. Her mother came out of the side door of the house. "Angela!" she called. "How's my favorite granddaughter?"

Angela jumped out of the car and ran to Kay's mother, who wrapped her arms around the little girl. "Mmm. It's wonderful to see you, Sweetheart. Shall we go inside and see if we can find a cookie or two somewhere?" She led Angela into the kitchen.

Kay squeezed Paul's hand. He looked at her questioningly.

"You don't know how much Mom enjoys having Angela here—or how much I like watching her enjoy it," Kay said. She kissed him on the cheek. "Thanks for thinking of this."

"Do you want to ride with Paul for a while?" she asked her daughter.

"Yes! Yes, I want to ride on the brown horsey too."

Kay maneuvered her horse close to his. Paul shook his head slightly. "I don't know. I'm a city kid—I'm still trying to figure out if I'm doing the right thing with this animal."

"Her name is Ginger. And she's very gentle, so don't worry." Kay helped Angela climb over to sit in front of Paul in the saddle. "You're doing fine."

Ginger followed Kay's horse up a draw and along a small ridge, then stopped as Kay reined in ahead. Kay sat gazing at the view in front of them—mountains receding into lighter shades of blue in the distance, with a foreground painted in warm shades of brown and yellow by the afternoon sun.

"It's pretty, Mommy," Angela said quietly.

"Paul, do you have your camera with you?" Kay asked.

He slipped it out of his pocket and handed it to her. She snapped three or four pictures showing slightly different views. "I'll pay you for these," she said as she handed the camera back to him. *And when I paint this one, I'll hold onto it until my daughter's old enough to keep it out of her father's hands.*

"Looks like it's about time to start back," Paul said, glancing at his watch. "It's four o'clock."

Kay sighed. "I'm in no hurry for this day to end." She turned her horse and let him start walking slowly down the slope. "And I don't care if we're late getting back."

It was just after six-thirty when they pulled into the parking lot at Marcy's apartment building.

Hugh Riddley's Cadillac sedan was parked in front of the building; Max stood leaning against it. Kay frowned. *Why is he here? And is that Wes's BMW next to the Cadillac?*

"Trouble?" Paul asked, glancing her way.

"I hope not." There shouldn't be. After all, as Paul had said, she didn't need Wes's permission for a visit to her parents' house with her daughter.

But Wes wouldn't be here unless he had something to say to her.

Paul parked three cars away from the Cadillac. When they got out of his car, Wes stepped out of the BMW and walked toward them. He glanced darkly at Paul, who was getting Angela's suitcase out of the trunk, then stopped in the middle of the sidewalk blocking Kay and Angela's path. "My father tells me you ditched Max and ran off with your friend," Wes challenged.

"We took Angela out to see my parents. We didn't think Max needed to drive out there."

"*I* needed to know where she was."

"You knew she was with me. And you know I take good care of her." Kay resisted the temptation to add that that was all he needed to know.

"When you take my daughter out of the area, I want to know about it."

"I don't think my parents' place is out of the area, Wes. And no one asks *my* permission when *you* take her somewhere."

She was still wondering whether to add that his sudden concern for his daughter was touching when Paul spoke. "I told your father I'd bring them home safely tomorrow afternoon. You don't need to worry about them in the meantime."

Wes sneered at him: "I should take *your* word for that?" He turned to Kay again. "I came to take her home."

Paul stepped up beside Kay so he could look into Wes's eyes. "You're not going to take her. Kay has her until tomorrow."

Kay gave him a warning look.

"Sorry," Paul muttered in her direction.

"She's going with me," Wes said, and held out his hand toward Angela.

Angela wrapped her arms around her mother's leg. Kay patted her arm reassuringly. "No, she's not. You don't have any right to take her away from me. She's my daughter too."

"I have every right to do what I think is best for her."

"Wes, I promise you, if you try to take her, I'll fight you for her, right here in the parking lot. Do you plan to drag her away from me screaming?"

The fact that Kay wasn't giving in to him seemed to take Wes aback for the moment.

Angela tightened her grip and hid her face against her mother's leg. Kay turned to Paul. "Would you please take her to Marcy's apartment so she can watch her movie? You can wait for me there."

Paul hesitated, looking at Wes.

Kay wanted to get Angela out of her ex-husband's reach before he tried to press his point again. She put Angela's hand in Paul's. "Please?"

Paul picked her up in his arms. She clung to his neck, looking at her parents over his shoulder, as he strode up the sidewalk carrying her and her suitcase.

Kay watched them go, then turned to face Wes. "Why can't you leave us alone?"

He laughed harshly. "You and your new *boyfriend?*"

"Me and my daughter!"

"She's my daughter too."

"Since when do you care—"

"And how do I know she's safe with some guy you've dredged up some—"

"She's safer than she ever was with *you!* At least Paul knows how to keep an eye on her when she's playing so she doesn't get hurt."

Wes's eyes narrowed. "Maybe it's time to review our custody agreement, Kristina. Maybe there should be some new limits—"

"Don't push me, Wes! If I have to take my chances in court to keep you from ruining Angela's life, I will."

"If I got married again so I had a wife at home to take care of her, and if I told them all about you and Angela's broken arm . . ."

"There's nothing to tell! You'd have to make it up."

He gave her one of his chilling smiles.

"You'd marry some other woman and ruin her life too—just so you could spite me?"

Wes reached out suddenly, cupped her chin in his hand, and held onto her tightly. She expected him to hurt her; she could see in his eyes that he wanted to. Maybe the fact that they were being watched by Max, and possibly others, stopped him. But he held her so she was forced to look into his eyes.

"I have a feeling it won't be convenient for you to see Angela when you come back in a couple of weeks. Maybe not the next time either—if you come with *him.* Angela and I might be so busy there just won't be time, or maybe we'll be gone somewhere, or—"

"You can't do that!"

"Watch me!" He lifted Kay's chin, forcing her to stand on her tiptoes. "Drop him—or forget about seeing her." He let go of her suddenly, leaving her trying to recover her balance as he turned and walked toward his car.

"Wes!"

He ignored her. Getting into the car, he slammed the door and put his key into the ignition. Then he glanced in the direction of Marcy's apartment and sat watching as Paul came down the sidewalk toward Kay.

"Angela's watching a video," Paul said, and looked at Wes, who was staring at them. "Why is he still here?"

Kay didn't answer. She looked at Wes too. *He meant it. He's waiting to see what I do.* Finally, she said: "I think you'd better go now."

Paul looked shocked. "Why?" He glanced in Wes's direction. "What did he say to you?"

"He said he'd keep me from seeing Angela."

"He can't do that. Don't let him tell you—"

"Paul!" She was still watching Wes. "Don't make me choose between you and my daughter."

"Kay, whatever he told you, he can't—"

"I don't want to talk about it right now. I have to think." *Think about what? He's always going to be there, watching . . . waiting. . . . He'll always find some way to . . . and there's nothing you'll ever be able to . . . nothing . . .*

Kay turned and started walking toward Marcy's apartment.

Paul stood watching her go. "I'll pick you up here tomorrow afternoon then," he called to her back.

"No!" Kay stopped and faced him. "No. I'll . . ." She glanced at Wes once more, and then at Max, still standing by the Cadillac. Always there was one of them around whenever she was with her daughter. It was impossible to make any plans that Hugh and Wes Riddley didn't know about. "Don't come by. I'll catch the bus," she said to Paul, then turned again and walked quickly to Marcy's door.

He could see her wiping at her eyes as she stepped inside.

He turned to look at Wes, who was still staring at him. Today Kay had stepped beyond the bounds Wes and his father had set for her and they had promptly slapped her down to regain control.

Paul started toward Wes's car. Wes smirked as he turned the key. He accelerated backwards out of the space, then made the tires squeal as he drove out of the lot into the street.

Paul watched, wondering what he would have said—or done— if Wes hadn't gotten away so quickly.

"Watch out for him. If he can find a way to hurt you, he will."

Startled, Paul turned to look at Max. "What?"

"I think he likes to hurt people."

The chauffeur was still leaning against the Cadillac, smiling slightly. Paul realized that Max was a big man—broad in the chest, muscular—but he had never seemed particularly threatening. Maybe it was because of his gentleness with Angela.

"I, uh—I'm sorry if we caused you trouble today." Paul hesitated. "Why are you telling me about Wes? I mean, you work for . . ."

Max frowned. "Not him." He opened the door of the Cadillac. "I coulda been mad when you lost me today, but I know how it is for Kristina, always havin' me around when she's with her little girl, 'cause Hugh . . ." Max shrugged. "Anyway, I'm tellin' you 'cause Kristina's good for Angela, and you're good for Kristina."

He got into the car and drove away, leaving Paul alone in the parking lot.

Chapter 12

The telephone was on its third ring and Kay hadn't answered. Paul glanced at his clock: 10:15. She should be home by now.

There was a click and the recording on her answering machine started. It was brief: "Hi. If you're calling about illustration work, please leave a message and I'll call back as soon as I can." Then the machine beeped in his ear.

"Kay, this is Paul, I'm just calling to see if you're OK, and, uh . . . because I wanted to talk. Please call me when you get in."

When fifteen minutes passed and she hadn't called, he dialed her number again. After the recording, he said, "It's me again. I was hoping—"

Her voice cut him off. "You'll keep calling until I talk to you, won't you?" She sounded tired.

"Well, ah, yeah, I probably . . . I'm worried about you. You—"

"I don't think I'm up to talking tonight." There was a pause. "And I don't know if I'm going to be up to talking tomorrow. I just don't know what to do . . . about us."

"What do you mean, 'about *us*'?"

There was silence for several seconds before she spoke. "If I go on seeing you, he's going to keep me from seeing Angela—and I can't give up my daughter."

"He can't do it, Kay. No court would let—"

"It doesn't matter what the court says, Paul. He *will* do it. I know he will."

"You can't let Wes tell you how you have to live your life. We can fight this thing. We can—"

"*We?* It's not *we* he's taking this out on. It's me—and Angela."

"Do you think that doesn't affect me too? I'm in love with you, and I care about Angela. No child ought to be caught in this kind of tug-of-war."

"You're right." Her voice was weak, almost a whisper. "But there's nothing I can do about it—and nothing you can do about it either without him punishing me and his daughter."

Paul wasn't sure whether this was the right time to say what came to mind. It could make her mad. He kept his voice even. "Wes got to you again, didn't he? You've got another migraine, you're feeling the pressure, and he's made you believe there's no way but his way. As long as you believe that, he's got you under his control."

There was no answer at first. He wondered if she might simply hang up on him. But finally: "He has no respect for law or decency. And no love for any living being, not even himself. I don't know how to fight that."

She was crying—he could tell without seeing her. "You can fight it with love, Kay. Fighting it with hate, his way, will never work. But you can go on loving your daughter and letting her feel it. You can let me love you. We'll do this together. Lean on me if you have to—for as long as it takes."

There was another long silence before she answered. "I want that. I want it so much!" She stifled a sob. "But I don't have the strength—I can't . . ."

"Yes, you can. But if you think you can't, *we* can. I'll be there with you, whether you decide to face up to him or not. But I still think you should—"

"Don't start telling me what to do! Not tonight. Please don't. I can't take somebody else telling me what to do." She paused. "I can't even *think!* I can't . . . I . . . please don't call me again tonight. Just let me rest. And don't call me tomorrow. I'll call you—maybe the next day."

There was a click as she hung up.

He held the phone in his hand for a long time, until he heard the operator's recorded voice saying, "If you'd like to make a call—" He cut her off and started to punch in Kay's number. But he stopped in the middle and slowly hung up the receiver.

She won't listen to me! She's going to let him keep us apart.

He picked up the handset again and touched the first three digits of her number. Then he stopped once more and slowly put the phone down.

No good. She won't talk tonight. And it probably wouldn't help anyway. There's no point until her mind's clear.

And yours too. You've got to think this out.

Kay pointed her toes toward the foot of the bed, put her arms above her head, and stretched. *Mmm—delicious.* She rolled over to look at the clock on the night table beside her bed: 10:22. *Twelve hours, almost. I must have been exhausted.*

Experiences like the ones with Wes over the weekend seemed to drain her emotionally and spiritually—even physically. It never got easier.

"Good-bye, Sweetheart." She gave Angela a last, tight hug, then turned quickly and stepped outside, where Max waited with the Cadillac to drive her to the bus station.

Wes followed her out the door and shut it behind him.

"I assume you won't be seeing your friend anymore—at least not with my daughter around," he said.

"Why shouldn't I? You take your girlfriends along whenever you go anywhere with Angela. Our daughter has never known what it is to have a father all to herself." She reached for the handle of the car door.

Wes put his hand on the door so she couldn't open it. "The women I date aren't any of your business, Kristina. I know that none of them is a threat to my daughter. I don't know that much about this man you're dating."

Kay felt her face getting warm. "All you need to know about him is that I trust him." She paused slightly, and then: "Trust is something I never could feel when we—"

Wes reached out suddenly and took hold of her arm, squeezing the muscle until she winced with pain. "Don't see him anymore with Angela—or I'll make sure you don't see her at all." He smiled malevolently. "It's a shame I still have to keep an eye on you to make sure you don't do things that are bad for her. And I am keeping an eye on you." He let go of her and walked back into the house.

Max, who could not have avoided overhearing the conversation, stood stoically beside the car, expressionless. But after Kay got into the back, Max slid into the driver's seat and slammed the door behind him. When he glanced into the rearview mirror before pulling out of Hugh Riddley's driveway, Kay saw that he was frowning angrily. Was he mad at her too?

Max was a puzzle—usually a silent presence who spoke to her only when spoken to. Kay had never been sure where she stood with him personally, but his tenderness toward Angela was a blessing. She had always felt she would rather have her daughter in his care than Wes's. But now, if she had alienated him too . . .

He surprised her when they arrived at the bus terminal by insisting on carrying her bag inside. As he handed it to her at the ticket counter, he smiled and asked, "Are you all right, Kristina?" Unsure what to make of the change in his mood, she simply nodded.

Had she misunderstood his anger?

But the puzzle of Max was gone from her thoughts almost as soon as he walked away. She couldn't keep her mind off of Wes's threat.

On the long ride back to Los Angeles, she had become more and more depressed as she replayed their conversation. There was no reason for Wes's dictatorial attitude about Paul—except deliberate cruelty. Somehow Wes would not be satisfied unless he could manipulate her life.

Would he really keep her from seeing Angela? She knew the answer. There was no legal justification for it, but that wouldn't stop him. If he learned that she was not doing exactly as he told her, he would find a way to make her pay.

Yesterday she had begun to believe that Wes would *always* be there, looking over her shoulder, wherever she went or whatever she did. The more she had gone over his words in her mind, the more she had despaired.

And then last night when she was emotionally wrung out, she had let depression do her talking to Paul. It was exactly what Wes would have wanted her to do.

Sometimes she felt like a rabbit being pursued by a coyote while her young in the den nearby were oblivious to danger. Fight back to protect her baby? No, that wasn't in the rabbit's nature.

She kept running, always running to lead the predator away.

But what if you decided not to be the rabbit anymore?

Startled, she spoke out loud: "What?"

The thought came again: *But what if you decided not to be the rabbit anymore?*

It was almost stunning, instantly clear and compelling, like an image that suddenly pops into sharp focus on a screen. Yet the truth of it seemed like something that had been there all along. Maybe she had simply not been ready to receive it until now. The meaning was plain in her mind: Wes would never *give* her peace— the coyote showed no mercy—but she could claim it for herself. The first step would be refusing to play the role of rabbit.

She had prayed often for strength to endure Wes's attempts to control and manipulate her—to ignore them as much as possible. Now the thought came that she wasn't required to endure any longer, and that she had never asked if there might be another way.

She slipped out of the bed and knelt beside it.

Prayer time was something she had come to love. When she was younger, her prayers had usually been the same words repeated day after day, though more fervently at some times than others. She had sometimes wondered then if what seemed like answers were simply coincidences that fit her desires. Now she knew it was not so. It was clear that her Heavenly Father had frequently answered those earlier prayers. And even when she had stopped praying for a time—early in her marriage to Wes, when she felt lost and unworthy—there had been loving direction pointing her gently back to the gospel she had been taught at home.

After Angela was born, she had begun praying for her daughter, still feeling unworthy to ask the Lord's help for herself. Answers had come, and she had been sure that it was because Heavenly Father loved Angela so much. But as she had begun to ask for direction for herself—timidly at first—it had become apparent that her Father also loved Kristina Kay. Sometimes she cried when she thought of specific answers to prayers: the unexpected sale of a painting just when she needed money to repair the old car her parents had given her after the wreck; the inspiration for several ten-minute gospel lessons that she could teach Angela when they were together; encouragement from the bishop, Paul, and others in preparing for the temple. In the temple she had felt her Heavenly Father's undeniable love, the burning certainty that he wanted her back.

It was easy to see now that when she had moved to Los Angeles, she had been directed to an area where her prayers for friends would be answered.

Paul was an answer to prayer in more ways than one. If it hadn't been for his strengths, she might never have come this far. And he was right about her needing to face up to Wes.

Last night, fear and doubt had made her forget what she knew about faith as a practical principle. This morning, she realized faith was all she had that could help her with Wes. She stayed on her knees for a long time, pleading to know how to deal with him. What should she do about his threat? How could she keep Angela from being a pawn in his hands?

The answers that came seemed to conflict with each other, but she had learned to trust the feeling of peace and assurance that came with them.

One answer was that she had to forgive Wes. It couldn't matter to her whether he was punished for the bad things he had done; she had to let that go. It was impossible to hold onto her anger toward him and feel her Father's love at the same time.

The other answer was that she didn't have to be Wes's victim anymore. She was a daughter of God, and he would give her strength to deal with her ex-husband. Wes's hold over her and his daughter was about to be broken.

How could that possibly be? She did not know, but the feeling in her heart was very clear: if she would move forward trusting in her Father, she would see it happen.

Kay stood and stretched her legs, and for the first time realized how hungry she was. She hadn't eaten since lunch yesterday. She walked into the kitchen and opened the refrigerator to remind herself of what she had in the house to eat; right now even a hot dog seemed appealing.

A quick bite to eat, a quick shower, and then she would turn to the most important thing she had to do today—find Paul and let him know how much she loved and needed him.

The discouragement and depression she had dumped on him

last night would be hard for anyone to carry. She smiled as she thought of a way she could lift the weight off of him. Tonight she would splurge for a couple of deli sandwiches with everything, just the way he liked them, then invite him to dinner at the beach. They could enjoy a healthy dose of wave therapy, with imaginary candle-light and a little imaginary music for dancing. She needed to feel his arms around her.

Paul parked at the curb about half a block up the street and sat looking at the house where she lived.

She had told him not to come today, but he needed to see her. If she threw him out—well, he'd have to risk that. But he couldn't stand thinking of her alone and overwhelmed, the way she had sounded on the telephone. He wanted to take away some of the hurt for her if he could.

He had spent the better part of four hours last night—before giving up on sleep and going to his office very early—thinking about Kay, and Angela. They deserved the chance to have a real mother-daughter relationship. He was determined to help Kay break free of her ex-husband—if she would. But that was a question. Just two days ago, she had let Wes take control again, and last night she had seemed ready to give up her own happiness rather than cross him.

Would she ever be strong enough to deny Wes the satisfaction of controlling her?

Would she ever, Paul wondered, have enough confidence in him to believe that they could build a future together? Or was that only *his* dream? Nothing would make him happier than knowing she wanted it too.

Last night, though, it had become clear that his feelings were not the most important consideration right now. He had to help Kay, regardless of how things might turn out between them later, because she was a daughter of God and he couldn't stand by watching while she was dominated and abused. *She* had to make the choices that would free her, of course; he could not direct her life. But he had to help her understand that she didn't need to struggle alone, even if there could never be anything more than friendship between them—that he was ready to give whatever help she would accept.

Paul had his hand on the handle of his car door, ready to open it, when he saw Kay's old sedan backing out of her driveway. She stopped in the street, turned in the opposite direction, and drove away.

What now—follow her? Wait for her here? Come back later?

While he was thinking about it, she turned the corner a block and a half away, and he realized he probably wouldn't catch her if he tried. Coming back later seemed like the best idea. Maybe he could pick up a pizza or a couple of deli sandwiches—bring dinner, and then they could talk.

He started his car and was about to pull into the street when he noticed the man who had gotten out of the gray sedan two vehicles ahead of his. The man was bald, and he wore dark slacks, a light blue shirt, and a gray jacket instead of tan chinos and a red golf shirt, but Paul was fairly sure this was the same man he had seen at the bus station the night the taxi followed them.

The man glanced up and down the street, then quickly crossed it and walked up Kay's driveway. Paul turned off his car engine as the man went out of view between Kay's house and the one next door. A minute . . . three . . . five . . . the man did not reappear.

Paul got out of his car and crossed the street, removing the small camera from the pocket of his jacket. Whatever this man was doing, he was about to get caught in the act.

Kay's driveway was empty. Paul walked to the back corner of the house and peered around it cautiously. No one. He turned toward her door. There were two deep, V-shaped impressions in the small flower bed under the window next to it. *The toes of his shoes—he stood on tiptoe to look in.*

Matching dirt from the flower bed was on the step in front of Kay's door. As he reached for the door handle, Paul noticed fresh scratches around the slot in the knob where the key would be inserted. Putting his ear to the door, he heard nothing, so he turned the knob experimentally. It was unlocked! The man inside had either gotten careless because he was overconfident, or he wasn't planning to stay very long.

Paul knew from experience that this door creaked on its hinges when it opened wide. Slowly, he opened it a crack, then stopped as he heard the man speaking.

"Sure, just like last time—but uglier. . . . Yeah, that's the number here on her phone, so you can . . . no, I'm *not* calling from *her* phone, it's my—listen, you should know by now that you're not dealing with some stupid schmuck who . . . yeah, well, I'm getting ready to take care of that part. You just make sure you have the rest of the money in my account by tomorrow morning."

There was the *beep* of a cell phone being turned off, and then—nothing.

Paul pushed the door open just enough to step through quickly with his camera ready. But the living room and kitchen were empty. Carefully he shut the door behind him.

He could see into Kay's bedroom. It had been at least partially ransacked already; clothes and papers were strewn across the bed and the floor.

On the kitchen counter to his right was a picture, torn from a magazine, of a smiling woman with a large, red X drawn across the face. Even at an angle, Paul could read the words scrawled in red across the bottom: "I told you I'd find you."

Trying to terrorize her again—but he's tried it once too often. Paul didn't even try to control the anger rising inside him; he ignored the fleeting thought that he needed to be careful. *Whatever he's doing, he's trapped in that bedroom, and I'm getting answers from him, even if I have to—*

There was a noise from the bathroom—the medicine cabinet opening.

In there? What would he want in the medicine cabinet?

Paul readied his camera before he stepped to the bathroom doorway. The man didn't see him at first because he was turned partly away, pouring capsules of Kay's pain reliever into the toilet. On the edge of the sink, there was an unopened plastic pharmacy vial of the same pain reliever—the one that she took for her migraines.

Paul aimed the camera and touched the shutter release; a flash lit up the small room. Startled, the man took a half step back as he turned to look at Paul. The two men stared into each other's eyes for three or four seconds before Paul touched the button on his camera and took another picture. It was a perfect shot of the man standing next to Kay's medicine cabinet holding the empty pain reliever bottle in his hand.

"Whoever you are, you've got a lot of explaining to do after I call the police," Paul said, trying to make it sound authoritative.

The man did not answer. He carefully put the empty bottle on the edge of the sink with his left hand. Slowly he smiled—it was not a friendly smile—and put his right hand behind his back to reach under his jacket.

Hair stood up on the back of Paul's neck. He hadn't stopped to think that the man could be carrying a weapon.

Running seemed pointless; if the man had a gun, there would be no way to get out of the apartment fast enough. Instead, Paul stepped into the bathroom, thrust his camera into the man's face, and pushed the button. The man's eyes went wide and he stumbled backward as the flash went off. Paul parried the man's pistol with his left hand and swung at the man with his right, letting his camera dangle from its strap. The man tried to dodge away, but Paul's forearm caught him across the face. The man staggered backward and clutched at a towel on the towel bar as the throw rug on the floor slipped out from under him. He managed only to pull the towel off the rack as he went down. There was a *clang* from the bathtub as the man's head hit it, then he lay crumpled in a heap on his side next to the tub.

Paul stood rubbing his arm and looking down at the man. *Wonder how bad he's* . . . Dropping to one knee, he put a finger against the man's neck below his jaw. *Strong pulse . . . and he's breathing OK.*

He stood up and aimed his camera at the man, wondering if it would work; he might have slammed it against the intruder's jaw just now. But the flash fired as he snapped one more picture. He slipped the camera into the right-hand pocket of his jacket, then leaned over and took the automatic pistol out of the man's limp fingers. Releasing the clip, he pulled it out of the pistol and dropped it into the other jacket pocket, then ejected the shell that was in the chamber and put that into his pocket too.

He laid the pistol on the edge of the sink and picked up the unopened vial of pain reliever. Holding it carefully by the base, he twisted the cap off. The capsules inside were the same color as Kay's—but on close inspection, some looked crooked, misshapen. Someone had opened them, then put them back together. *So he's tampered with these. What next—pour them into Kay's vial? Then when she comes home and finds the picture on the counter and the mess he made . . .*

It was an ugly thought—drive Kay to another migraine so she would swallow some of the medicine that had been doctored with —with what?

His hands were trembling. He wanted to put them around this man's throat, or . . . or, if the man were conscious, hit him, again and again and again until he spilled everything there was to know about the capsules, and why he was doing this, and then . . .

No! No, don't . . . can't think like that. He gripped the sink and leaned on it, letting the anger drain away. He would get the answers to his questions somehow. If this man didn't regain consciousness before the police came, then they'd get the information out of him—whoever he was.

Paul looked at the wallet protruding invitingly from the man's right hip pocket. Probably it would be a good idea to call the police right now and let *them* find out who this man was when they got here—but he had to know.

The driver's license was easy enough to locate. *Nevada. Harry Diedrich, Las Vegas. So—who's Harry Diedrich?*

Searching through the wallet, Paul found several business cards. *Harry Diedrich, Private Investigator. Well, you're a long way from home, Harry, and this doesn't look very much like an investigation. You're nailed—you won't be bothering Kay anymore.*

Putting one of the cards into his jacket with the camera, Paul closed the wallet and slipped it back into the private investigator's pocket.

The man moaned. His face was pale, and there was a small pool of red spreading on the floor beneath his head. Paul took the towel that had been clutched in Diedrich's left hand, folded it up, and put it beneath the man's head.

Diedrich opened his eyes and looked at Paul groggily. Then suddenly his eyes went wide and he struggled to get up. Paul held him down. "Easy—you're bleeding. Hold the towel against the back of your head."

Grimacing, the man laid back and complied.

"Now—what were you doing here?"

The man looked at him in silence for several seconds, obviously measuring him. "Sorry—my work is confidential," he said finally.

"Is that what you're planning to tell the police when they get here? You're way out of your area, Diedrich, and I want to know what Riddley sent you here to do."

It was a guess, but Paul could see in the other man's eyes that it was correct. Shock and fear mingled momentarily on Diedrich's face. He felt for his wallet, and when he found it in its place, his look changed to speculation—obvious wariness about how much more Paul might know.

"My business is between me and my client," he answered.

"You know the police aren't going to buy that, and neither am I. You're carrying a gun and a vial of medicine that has been tampered with, and that message out there on the counter isn't the first one you've left for Kay Reston. Now tell me why Hugh Riddley hired you!"

Diedrich closed his eyes, laid back, and seemed to relax a bit. Paul frowned. *No reason for that. He ought to be worried. Don't let him have time to think—keep the heat on.* "We're talking felonies and jail time. Tell me the truth! What's this all about?"

"All right! I'll tell you." Diedrich winced as he shifted his position slightly and moved the towel. "I was, um, supposed to scare her . . . keep her away, keep her from trying to take the kid back." He glanced at the vial sitting on the edge of the sink. "If there's something wrong with the medicine, I don't know anything about it."

"Liar! You were ready to put those new capsules in Kay's old vial, and I'm sure the police will test them to see if a little something extra has been added to the pain reliever. So far, you're up to breaking and entering, assault with a deadly weapon, and maybe—"

Diedrich shifted his body to the left suddenly, his arm moving toward Paul's ankle. Paul stepped back quickly and grabbed the pistol off the edge of the sink, wondering now if he should have called the police earlier. He was careful not to let the other man see the bottom of the pistol grip, with an empty space where the clip should be. Diedrich looked into the barrel of the gun and lay still. "Just trying to get up," he said. His eyes gave away the lie.

Paul backed out of the bathroom. "Slowly, and very carefully," he said.

When Diedrich was on his feet, Paul moved to his right, toward the kitchen. "This way."

He retreated backwards, gun in his hand, as Diedrich followed him, still holding the towel to the back of his head. Paul motioned with the pistol toward one of the dinette chairs in the kitchen. "Sit."

Slowly, Diedrich complied.

Paul picked up Kay's phone and dialed a number. When an operator answered, he said, "Lieutenant Henderson, please."

Diedrich frowned and looked away.

A clipped voice said in Paul's ear: "Henderson."

"This is Paul Webber. I've got—"

"I know—a hot story and you want me to verify it." He sighed. "What could you possibly have today? I don't know of anything going on."

"No, it's, uh—I need some help. A guy broke into my girl-friend's apartment. I have him here, and—"

"You're *holding* him? Burglary isn't my assignment, Webber, but I'll have Dispatch send a car. Where are you?"

Paul gave him Kay's address.

"I'm sure we have somebody in the area. *How* are you holding the guy? How urgent is this?"

"He had a gun. I have it, and—"

"You're holding a gun on him right now? Just a minute."

Lieutenant Henderson covered the phone, but Paul could hear part of the conversation: " . . . this address. Tell them to hurry it up . . . citizen's holding a gun on some . . ."

The lieutenant turned his attention back to Paul. "All right, we've got officers on the way. Keep your cool. Talk to me for a couple of minutes until they get there. What was the guy doing?"

"Planting some pain reliever in my girlfriend's medicine cabi-net. It's been tampered with."

"How does he know her? Do you know him?"

"He broke into her apartment a couple of times when she lived in Las Vegas." Diedrich shifted uncomfortably in his chair as Paul gazed at him. "He's a private investigator up there. He tracked her down here to—"

"Whoa! Back up. The guy who was leaving the stuff in your girl's apartment is a private investigator from Las Vegas? What does he look like?"

"About my height, bald, brown eyes, forty-fivish. His name's Harry—"

"Diedrich! The part about planting something clicked when you said he's from Vegas."

"You *know* him?"

"Oh, yeah, we've met. He's blown a couple of cases for the department. Latest was a year and a half ago. A young girl, a singer, OD'd on pills in the home of a recording industry honcho here. We thought we had the guy for supplying the drugs. Then Harry suddenly steps forward to say he was working as the man's bodyguard up in Vegas the night she died. Harry recommends that we check *her* apartment, and what do we find there but some of the same pills. So this studio exec walks, and Harry gets a *very* large check for a couple of days of bodyguard work. The Las Vegas police know him too. Seems like Harry is Mr. Fixit when somebody with money needs a dirty job done."

Paul smiled slightly in Diedrich's direction. "Yeah. That's him."

"If you've got Harry in Los Angeles with evidence of a crime, I want him. I'll be there in half an hour." The lieutenant hung up.

Paul put the phone down and grinned at Diedrich. "Sounds like the police are going to be *very* happy to see you."

"Yeah, well, that's too bad because I can't wait around." Slowly Diedrich stood. "Listen, no real harm's been done here." He took a step toward the door. "I promise I'll leave your girlfriend alone." He glanced at the picture on the counter. "No more, OK? It's all over."

"Sit down. The police are on their way, and I'm not letting you leave."

Keeping his eyes on the pistol in Paul's hand, Diedrich took another step toward the door. "This doesn't have to be a big problem. I told you, Kristina will never hear from me again." He took one more step. "That's what you want, isn't it?" He reached out tentatively for the door handle.

"Sit down!" Paul commanded.

Diedrich shook his head. "You'll have to use that gun on me, and I've learned a few things about you too, Webber. I don't think a good churchgoing guy like you would do that. Besides, your friend the lieutenant wouldn't like it."

"You've been hurting somebody I love," Paul answered. "Do you really think I'm going to let you walk out of here?"

Diedrich nodded. "Yeah. I'll take that chance." He opened the door and stepped outside.

The man was shrewd, Paul thought—a good judge of people. He had not known the gun was unloaded, but he had known the man who held it would not use it on another person.

Paul put it down on the counter and stepped outside. Diedrich was walking quickly across the street to his car, still holding the towel to the back of his head.

Paul jogged after him. "Come back here, Diedrich! Stop!" If he had to, he would hold the man down in the street until the police came.

But he was too late. Before he could cross the street, the other man got into his car and locked the doors. Paul pounded on the window with his hand. Diedrich laughed as he started his car and drove away.

Paul pulled his ballpoint pen out of his pocket and wrote Diedrich's license number on his hand. He stood in the street watching as the car pulled around the corner a block and a half away and disappeared.

Chapter 13

"I can't believe you just let him walk out of here," Henderson said. He turned to the officer who was examining the bathroom. "Bag both of those vials—the empty one too. Put a priority on finding out what's in those pills. I want as much to hold this guy on as I can get, in case we find him."

"I touched the one with the pills in it," Paul said to the officer. "You might find my prints on it too." He turned to the lieutenant. "So if I'd shot him you'd be happier? You'd be putting me in jail, and nobody would ever get anything out of Harry."

"If he was bleeding the way he did here on the floor, you could probably have tied him up with cellophane tape before he walked out," Henderson answered. "We'll need to take your fingerprints so we can match them against any we find in here."

"I gave you Diedrich's license number and a good description, and you know where to find him. He won't get away with this."

"Yeah, but everything would be a lot easier if we could pick him up before he slips back into Nevada—no worries about jurisdiction or extradition. Unfortunately, we can't cover every road out of the state."

"Well, you were the one who sent him running," Paul muttered.

Henderson looked at him quizzically.

"He knew who you were. He got very nervous when he heard me talking to *you*. He wasn't inclined to stay put just because *I* told him to."

Henderson laughed. "It's OK, Webber. You've given us enough to make *something* stick, so Harry will stay out of L.A.—at least for a while. I just wish we could put him away for a few years." He looked at the two plastic vials on the sink. "Maybe if what's in those pills—"

"What *is* this?" It was Kay's voice, from the living room. "What are you doing in my apartment?"

"We're, uh . . . we're investigating a break-in, ma'am," one of the officers in the living room answered.

Paul stepped out of the bathroom, followed by the lieutenant.

"Paul!" Kay said. "What . . ."

"You had a visitor." He nodded toward the marked-up picture that still lay on the kitchen counter.

Kay looked at the picture, sucked in a breath, and retreated from the counter as if a snake were coiled there.

Paul put his arms around her. "Don't worry, we know who he is, and he's not going to bother you anymore. The police will get him."

She leaned against his chest and let him hold her close. "Who? How do you know they will . . ."

"A private investigator from Las Vegas—Harry Diedrich. Does that name mean anything to you?"

She shook her head.

"You've never heard of him?"

"No."

"He knows all about you. And he admitted to me that he's been working for Hugh Riddley."

"Hugh?"

"I asked him what Hugh Riddley sent him here to do, and he said he was supposed to scare you—make sure you stayed out of Las Vegas and didn't try to take Angela back."

"I know Hugh doesn't like me, but I never thought he'd actually . . ."

"There's more. Diedrich was planting something in your medicine cabinet when I caught him—pills just like you take for your headaches, but they've been tampered with."

"You mean you think he put something *in* the pills, so when I . . ."

Paul nodded. "He messed things up in your bedroom, too, but I don't know whether he took anything."

Henderson turned toward them. "We'll need you to check that out, Miss Reston."

"Kay, this is Lieutenant Henderson of the Los Angeles police," Paul said.

She nodded at the lieutenant as she walked past into the bedroom. She stood looking at the clothing and papers strewn on the floor then, mechanically, began picking things up. She paused, knelt, and gathered up a dress that lay on the floor. Paul recognized it—the one she had worn to the singles dance the night he had given her the necklace. There were tears in her eyes as she held it up for him to see. "He ruined it." The dress was torn in the back from the end of the zipper almost to the hem at the bottom.

"We'll need to have you give us a list of the damage he did and anything he took," Lieutenant Henderson said softly. He turned to the woman officer in the living room. "Medina, will you take Miss Reston's statement when she's ready?"

Then he pulled a notebook out of his pocket. "Webber, I want you to tell me everything you saw Diedrich do, and everything he said."

"It's still hard to believe that Hugh could send that man to do what he did." Kay shivered.

"Cold?" Paul asked. He put his arm around her.

"No. It's just . . . thinking of him in my apartment . . . going through my things, leaving those pills. Even with everything they've already done, I didn't want to believe that they would actually . . ." She leaned her head on his shoulder and stared out at the waves. "I got caught in *half* believing—half believing that they could be dangerous and half believing that they wouldn't *really* let something bad happen to Angela's mother. Now that I know, it's still hard to accept. Is that strange?"

"No. I can understand how you feel."

Before she had spoken, they had been sitting in silence for a long time—watching the waves, thinking their own thoughts. Paul had been thinking that the pieces of this puzzle didn't fit together.

The one time he had met Hugh Riddley, the man had been arrogant and autocratic—and yet tender with his granddaughter.

Riddley was proud, hard when he wanted to be, but he was not stupid. And it seemed stupid to depend on a weasel like Diedrich, who apparently had no animosity toward Kay as a person but was capable of being vicious simply for money. Diedrich would turn on anyone if he saw a buck in it. Hugh Riddley's background and accomplishments said he was too smart to confide in a man like that. It didn't make sense—unless Riddley was slipping or getting careless.

"I was gone to look for you," Kay said.

"What?"

"When you came to my apartment today, I had gone to find you. Last night was a big mistake—everything I said to you—so I wanted to tell you how much I need you, and how much I appreciate the support you offered to give me. I'm going to need that too."

She stared out at the breakers rolling toward shore. "I'm ready to fight them. But I learned something important this morning—I can't do it Wes's way."

"What do you mean?"

"I'm not mad this time—I didn't *let* him make me mad. I've learned I can't fight him with hate. I can't hold that in my heart and expect Heavenly Father to help me." She smiled at him. "It's like you said, I have to love—love Angela, and you . . . even Wes and Hugh. Or at least I have to forgive them and let go of all the past."

She took hold of his hand. "I learned all that when I was praying this morning. And I realized just now that I don't want anything bad to happen to Wes anymore. I just want to be free. Heavenly Father let me know that if I'll trust in him and give up all my ugly feelings, it will happen. But I don't know how yet."

"I know some things we can do to help it happen."

Kay touched his face with her fingers. "Promise me you won't do whatever you do just because you want to hurt Hugh and Wes. That would be bad for both of us. One of the things I admire about you is that you're not like them."

"I'm going to do it because I love you." He leaned over and kissed her, wrapping his arms around her and holding on. "I've *got* to do it," he said when the kiss was over. "I was going to tell you today that even if you didn't love me, I couldn't just walk away and leave you at their mercy. I couldn't do that to anyone."

"Well, there's no need to worry about the love part." She pulled his face gently to hers and kissed him again.

He stood, and held out his hand to her. "Come on. The sun will be going down in a few minutes, and you must be hungry by now."

She took his hand and pulled him back down beside her. "Watch the sunset with me—and hold me. Right now I need that more than I need food."

"Sister Webber, you have visitors."

"In here, Paul."

He took Kay's hand and led her into the living room. "Mom, I have someone I want you to meet. This is Kay Reston. Kay, this is Francine Webber. Her close friends—and that's almost everybody she knows—call her Franci."

"And that's what I want you to do," Franci Webber said as she rose from her chair and extended her hand for Kay to shake. "It's a pleasure to meet you finally." She glanced at Paul. "My son hasn't told me nearly enough about you. But he's happier since he met you than he has been in a long time, and anyone who can give him that is my friend."

Kay smiled. "Your son has been a lifesaver for me. Literally."

Paul put Kay's small suitcase down on the carpet. "I have a favor to ask, Mom. Kay needs a place to stay for a few days where no one can find her—where she can be safe."

Franci raised her eyebrows. She looked at Kay. "You were serious when you said 'literally'?"

Kay nodded.

"I caught a guy in her apartment," Paul explained. "He may have been trying to poison her. I'll let Kay tell you the details if she wants. But there's no danger to either of you as long we're the only ones who know where she is."

Franci considered the request for only a moment. Then she smiled. "You can stay here as long as you need to, dear, and you don't have to tell me a thing unless you want to. Make yourself at home."

"I won't mind telling you anything you want to know. But right now I'd like to call my parents to tell them where I am. I'll pay you for the call."

"I think it's *very* important for children to keep their parents informed about what's going on in their lives," Franci said, looking at Paul. He laughed. Franci gestured toward the telephone on the end table next to the couch. "Take your time, and don't worry about the cost."

When her father answered, Kay explained briefly where she was and why she had had to leave her apartment. The conversation went on as he drew out details. "I'm fine," she reassured. "But if anyone calls or comes there asking for me, don't let them know that you know where I am."

She nodded. "Yes. And I love you too." Then she held the telephone out to Paul. "Dad would like to talk to you."

"Thanks for being there again," Bill Reston said. "Tell me about the man you found in Kay's apartment. What did he look like?"

"Your height, bald, thin, about forty-five, brown eyes."

"That's the guy who came to our house looking for her. Do you think the police will get him?"

"I hope so. We know who he is, and I believe we can make things hot enough for him and the Riddleys that they won't dare try anything else like this."

The two men said good-bye and Paul hung up.

"I should have told you to have them call my lawyer in Las Vegas and let her know I want another custody hearing," Kay said.

"I could tell her tomorrow. If you don't mind, I'd like to talk with her after I see Hugh Riddley."

"I still think I should go to Las Vegas with you."

Paul shook his head. "Not just yet. I don't want Hugh and Wes to have any idea where you are until we're *sure* we have enough on them to keep them at bay. And I hope we can turn up more to use at your hearing."

Kay thought about it for a moment. "All right, for now. But I need to face them, Paul—let them know I'm through giving in—and I want it to be soon."

"You know I'll support you on that."

Paul punched in another number on the telephone and waited while it rang. "Henderson," a voice on the other end answered.

"You're still there? This is Paul Webber. I was going to leave you a message."

"I've been arranging accommodations for our mutual acquaintance from Las Vegas."

"*Harry?* You've got Diedrich?"

"Yeah. He made it easy for us—passed out in the restroom at a service station before he could get out of town."

"How bad . . ."

"He's OK—mild concussion, and he lost enough blood to be weak. But he's feeling good enough to say he won't answer any questions without a lawyer present."

The lieutenant paused. "He's saying he doesn't know anything about the pills, and he claims *you* jumped *him.*"

"Oh, yeah. He's an upstanding citizen who just happened to be in the apartment of a woman who doesn't know him, and I pulled *his* gun on him."

"Do you think your girlfriend could come down tomorrow and identify the bloody towel we found in his car? That would be one more tangible thing to put him in her apartment. We don't have a lot of those."

"Would photos help?"

There was silence on the other end of the line for several seconds. Then: "Somehow in all the excitement today you forgot to tell me you shot pictures."

"I wasn't holding out. I wanted to be sure of what I had. How about Diedrich standing in front of the medicine cabinet holding the pills, or laying on the bathroom floor with his gun in his hand?"

"I think Harry might change his story with that kind of evidence."

"Send someone to my office in the morning to pick up an envelope with your name on it. I'm leaving early for Las Vegas. I'll call you from there."

"Webber?"

"Yeah?"

"I called in a favor and got those pills checked this afternoon. There was cyanide in them."

152

Paul closed his eyes to absorb the thought. *So it was more than just scaring her. Diedrich knew that—he must have. . . . Guess they didn't care* how *they got her out of the way.* He felt a knot growing in his stomach; heat rose in his neck and face. "If she'd taken two or three of those . . ."

"Yeah. But Harry seems pretty confident we'll never be able to pin the poison on him. You said you know who's behind this?"

"I only have Harry's word for that, and he'll probably deny it now."

"You want to tell me the name?"

"Not until I know more."

"What have I told you about trying to do the job of the police? If you have knowledge of a crime, you have to tell me."

"I will. But right now I can't tell you anything you could hang a case on—nothing I'd be willing to print on Harry's word alone. Tomorrow I'll know more. I'll call you."

"There's a story in this for you somewhere, isn't there?"

Paul was silent for a moment. When he answered, his tone was firm. "I want you to understand this—my first priority is protecting Kay. What I have to do in Las Vegas could get the people who sent Harry off her back. But, yeah, it could help me with a story—and maybe help your case." He paused. "I'm asking you to trust my judgment this time."

"Webber, if most of the reporters I know asked me that, I'd laugh. But—OK. I'll be expecting a call from you tomorrow afternoon. There are fingerprints on that pill bottle that don't belong to Harry or to you, and if you have any idea whose they are, I want to know."

"Tomorrow. You have my word."

He hung up the phone and sat staring at the opposite wall.

"Paul?"

He turned to look at Kay. Both women were watching him. "They have the man?" Kay asked.

"Harry Diedrich. Yes."

"What did you mean about protecting me? And if I'd taken those pills, what?"

Paul put his arm around her. "There was cyanide in them."

She laid her head on his shoulder. "It's hard to believe they hate me that much."

Franci Webber looked thoughtfully at Kay for several seconds, then at her son. "Are you planning to stay here tonight?"

"I was going to go back to my apartment and get an early start from there, but if . . ."

"I think it might be a good idea for you to stay here—if you don't mind the couch."

"Please," Kay murmured. "I'd feel better if you were here."

"Kay," Franci said, "I hope you don't mind sharing the guest bedroom with one of my paintings. It's set up on my easel in there—a seascape, not finished and not very good, I'm afraid. I'll move it against the wall, out of your way."

Kay sat up and brushed her hair back from her face. She smiled weakly. "It won't be a problem. I'm just grateful to you for taking me in."

Chapter 14

Paul sat in the driveway of Hugh Riddley's home staring at the front door, trying to think out exactly how he was going to handle this when he got inside.

Essentially, he was going to throw everything he had at Hugh—and it had better work because his job was probably on the line.

Early this morning, he had called Reg Morris, the wire service's Los Angeles bureau chief, to say that he was going to Las Vegas for a few days because the banking kickback story was suddenly coming together.

"Can't spare you this week," the bureau chief had answered. "I'm already one short."

"Look, Reg, as of yesterday, the story involves attempted murder," Paul had said, hoping he would be able to tie Diedrich, the Riddleys, and the banker neatly together somehow. "This story's important to me for more than one reason. If I have to, I'm taking my vacation to work on it—starting today."

There had been silence on the other end of the line for several seconds. Then Reg had said: "This had better be good, Webber—*very* good." And he had hung up.

Paul got out of his car, walked slowly up to Hugh Riddley's front door, and rang the bell. It seemed like a long time, but it was probably only half a minute or so before Max opened the door. "Please tell your boss I need to see him," Paul said.

Max simply nodded and closed the door.

A couple of minutes later, the door opened again. Max stepped outside, shutting it behind him. "He says he don't want to talk to you, Mr. Webber."

"Put it to him this way, Max: the Los Angeles police want to know what I know about him, and the Las Vegas police would be very interested in it too."

Max frowned. He shut the door and went away again. But he was back in less than a minute this time.

He ushered Paul into the office, where Hugh Riddley sat behind his large walnut desk. Riddley did not look up. Paul did not wait for an invitation to sit down; he took the chair across the desk. Max stood by the door.

Slowly, Riddley raised his head and looked Paul in the eyes. "I don't take kindly to threats, Webber. What do you want?"

Paul tried to do what Kay had told him—he tried not to hate this man. But he wasn't going to let him off easily—he couldn't if he was going to help Kay. "No threat, Riddley. I just want to know why you tried to have your ex-daughter-in-law killed."

Hugh didn't flinch. A red flush began to spread up his neck and across his jaw. "That's a lie. Get out!"

Paul opened the envelope he held in his hand, took out a picture of Diedrich holding the bottle of medicine, and slid it across the desk. "This man says it's true. He says you hired him to put those poisoned pills in Kay's medicine cabinet. Then the little love note you had him leave would stress her out, she'd get a headache and take a couple of those, and she'd be dead. Is that the way it was supposed to work?"

Hugh's eyes opened wide when he saw the picture. He sat staring at it.

"What I'd like to know," Paul went on, "is why you want so badly to get rid of her. What do you have to gain?"

Hugh looked up at him, again slowly. "I *don't* want . . . I hired this man to keep an eye on her—and you. I wanted to find out what kind of relationship you have. I still have my doubts about whether Kristina's a fit mother for my granddaughter."

Paul held his anger at the other man's insinuation. "If you believe anything your hired detective told you about Kay or me, you're making a mistake."

"My only instructions to him were to *watch* and report back. That bottle of pills doesn't mean anything to me. Why should I believe *you?*"

Paul slid a picture of the unconscious Diedrich, pistol in hand, across the desk. Again, Hugh's eyes widened in surprise. "Harry Diedrich would have killed me too if he could have gotten away with it," Paul said. "He told me he was working for you, and I heard him talking on the phone to you from her apartment about money. *You* hired him, so who else—"

"I haven't talked to him about money since—"

"Who else could have known what he was—"

"Wes knew," Max said quietly.

Both men turned to look at him in surprise.

"Wes knew," he repeated. "Boss, you asked me to find you a good detective. I wrote the name down on a piece of paper and left it on your desk. Wes saw me coming out of here that day. And Diedrich wasn't the name I wrote on the paper."

Hugh sank back in his chair and stared down at the desktop. Paul said nothing, watching him. Finally Hugh reached down and opened a drawer in the desk, took out a piece of Riddley Construction letterhead, and held it up so Max could see the name and telephone number printed neatly on it. "This wasn't the name you left me?"

Max shook his head. "No, sir, Boss. I *wrote* it—with a pencil. I'd never touch your computer."

Hugh laid the paper on the desk and stared at it.

Paul spoke to Max. "You think Wes typed that?"

Max looked at Hugh as though waiting for his permission to speak, but Hugh said nothing. Finally, Max nodded. "Couldn'ta been anybody else."

Hugh cleared his throat. "I phoned this guy. When he showed up, I told him I wanted Kristina watched. That was all. He gave me one report." Hugh looked up at Paul. "He said she met a man— he described you—at a bus station in Los Angeles. He said the man took her home—and stayed there."

"That's a lie," Paul responded. "He made it up because he didn't want to tell you I lost him when he followed us in a cab. I didn't know who he was at the time. I took Kay home and sat down the street in my car for nearly an hour to see if he'd find the place somehow. He never did—at least not that time."

Hugh's fingers toyed idly with the paper on his desk. It was a long time before he spoke again. "You have a son . . . try to raise him the right way . . ." His voice sank almost to a whisper. "By yourself, after your wife's gone . . ."

It was impossible now to hate the man slumped in the chair behind the desk. Paul felt sorry for him. Were there tears in the corners of Hugh Riddley's eyes? *Hmm—probably not. He wouldn't let himself cry—not in front of me.*

Hugh looked up at him. "I don't like you very much, Webber. I don't trust you. What do you want from me?"

Paul thought for a moment about what Hugh had said. "This may be hard for you to understand because of the way your son . . . because of your experiences, but people don't always want something from you." He leaned forward, resting his arms on the desk. "I know Kay doesn't want anything from you, and I don't want anything either—except to see her free."

Hugh sat looking at him without saying anything. Paul wondered what was going on in the man's mind; his eyes gave away nothing. *If he ever had to negotiate with the unions, I'll bet he was good at it.*

Finally, the other man nodded. "Maybe I've been wrong about her. I don't know now if I can believe anything Wes ever told me." He sighed. "I'm not going to let him harm the mother of his daughter. I'll call the police myself." He leaned forward and reached for the phone.

Paul put his hand on top of Hugh's to keep him from lifting the receiver. "No. Don't do that yet—please. She's safe for now, and I need some time."

Hugh looked at him in surprise. "Time for what?"

Paul took his hand away. "He told Kay that if she ever got him in trouble because of what he's done in the business, he'd see that she went to jail with him. I'm asking you for time to find what I need to clear her so he can't do that."

Hugh took his hand off the telephone and leaned back in his chair.

"I'm not out to get your son," Paul continued. "I'm just trying to protect Kay—and your granddaughter. If Wes managed somehow to get Kay sent to jail, then what would happen to Angela?"

"She'd have me!" Hugh answered. "Me and Max. We don't do such a bad job, do we, Max? We know how to take good care of her. We can give her everything she needs."

Max cleared his throat and opened his mouth, but then said nothing.

Hugh turned to look at him. "Well, what is there we can't do? We've been taking care of her for almost two years now. I've gotten her fed and bathed and dressed just like she was *my* little girl. You know how I play with her. You take her to the park and play with her. You take her to preschool. What could a father do that we aren't doing?"

Max shifted uncomfortably under Hugh's gaze. It was obvious that he was trying to pick his words carefully. "You and me, we're gettin' older, Boss. You've got that bad heart." Hugh glanced at Paul and frowned at Max, but the chauffeur went on anyway. "And me, I don't walk so good anymore. Don't know if I'll be able to keep doin' that when I'm old. Don't know how long either one of us'll be around. And there's other things. What about when she starts gettin' interested in boys? What about when a little girl starts turnin' into a grown-up woman? What are two old guys gonna do for her then?" Max shook his head. "She's gonna need a mother." He paused. "And Kristina's a good one."

Hugh bowed his head and looked down at the intertwined fingers of his hands resting on the desk in front of him. He looked at them so long that Paul wondered if he was going to answer. Then he seemed to come to some kind of decision.

He looked up at Paul. "My son usually leaves his daughter with us until Friday night—when he wants to use her to look good with one of his girlfriends, I think—or Saturday morning. When he comes for her next time, I'm not letting him take her, and I'm going to tell him why. I guess that gives you until Friday night."

Three days. "OK—Friday night."

Paul stood and walked toward the door of the office, then stopped and turned around. "Riddley?"

Hugh didn't answer. He was looking down at the desk, and this time the tears were plainly visible in his eyes. "Thanks," Paul said softly, then turned again and walked outside.

He was about to slide into the driver's seat of his car when Max opened the front door of the house, stepped outside, and shut the door behind him.

"Follow the money," Max said.

"What?"

"Since he was a kid, Wes never cared about anything as much as he cared about money—bein' richer than his old man. This has gotta be about money."

He opened the door again and disappeared inside.

What money? Paul thought as he drove out of the driveway. *Kay doesn't have any money, so what does Wes gain financially by seeing her dead? And where am I going to find out about that?*

There was someone who might be able to give him answers.

But first, he had promised to call Lieutenant Henderson in Los Angeles. He reached for his cellular phone.

The lieutenant's first words were: "Glad to hear from you, Webber. I need the name of Diedrich's client in Las Vegas. He's still stonewalling, and I need leverage to pry more out of him. I want to be sure some clever lawyer can't get him off without hard jail time."

"I was wrong about that name," Paul said.

Henderson groaned.

"But I've got something better. Try this on Diedrich—tell him that *Wes* Riddley is about to get nailed by the police in Las Vegas and ask him if he thinks his good friend Wes will take the fall all by himself. Ask him if he believes Wes is going to say, 'Sure, I was the one who poisoned the pills. Harry didn't know a thing about it.' "

"You think that will loosen his tongue?"

"I think it's worth a shot," Paul said. "Harry may want to get his version of the story on record before Wes has a chance to talk. Wes is the one who put him up to this, and I think I'll be able to tie them together."

"Well, Harry's the one *I* have in hand, so he's the one I have to wring out."

"If you need extra leverage with him, try dropping the name of Mitchell Harrison along with Wes's. Harrison is a lawyer up here. He and Wes are running a kickback scheme. I don't know yet if Harry is tied into it, but if he reacts to Harrison's name, you can play him."

"You mean let him sweat about whether the other two will turn on the one who blew it by getting caught?"

"Yeah. I'll call you tomorrow to see if any of this lights Harry's fire."

"You're on. Can you give me anything else?"

"Not right now. And Henderson?"

"Yeah?"

"Wes Riddley and Mitchell Harrison don't know yet that they're in trouble. Can you leave them alone for a few days—at least until Saturday?"

There was a short pause. "Sure, no problem. I have plenty to do until then."

After Paul said good-bye to Henderson, he dialed Scott Pike's number at the television station.

"News desk, Pike."

"I've got a hot tip for you."

Scott laughed. "You need a bed tonight?"

"Yeah, but that's not it. The story on the greedy banker from California and the larceny twins from Las Vegas is a go. Right now."

"*Hmm. Bad!* Bad timing. This is an ugly week."

"Sorry. There's no other way. Remember I told you somebody was leaving threatening notes for Kay in her apartment in Las Vegas before she moved?"

"Yeah. He showed up again?"

"The Los Angeles police have him. I found him in Kay's apartment yesterday planting poisoned migraine medicine."

Scott whistled.

"He told me he was working for Hugh Riddley, so I came up here today and confronted Hugh. It turns out that Wes is our boy instead, and Hugh's ready to call the police himself. He's given us until Friday afternoon to get everything we need on Wes."

"OK, all right, I'll, uh . . . I don't know . . . I'll work something out. I can't talk now, but I'll see you at my place about seven-thirty."

The tiny, stuccoed office building had obviously once been a private home. It was located next to a small strip mall on a busy street in an older section of Las Vegas. The shiny brass plaque on the front door read: "Cynthia Ramirez, Attorney at Law."

Paul opened the door and stepped inside.

It was not what most people might expect in a lawyer's office. There were bare venetian blinds over the windows. The furniture was old, and so was the receptionist's desk.

The woman behind it was not. She looked like she might have been out of high school a year or two. Her dress was short and she wore four earrings in the pierced ear that Paul could see. Her red hair looked like it might have been blow-dried by the wind on the way to work in her car. She was chewing gum vigorously, but she stopped as she turned to smile brightly at him. "Hi, can I help you?"

"I'd like to talk to Cynthia Ramirez."

"I'm sorry, but she's not taking any more appointments today." The girl was still smiling, but the words were firm.

Paul tried to make his own smile as engaging as possible. "I don't need an appointment. I just wanted to talk to her for a couple of minutes. It won't take long."

"I'm sorry, but she left instructions not to be disturbed." Again, it was firm. She still seemed friendly, but there was something steely about this girl—this *woman*. Maybe she was more experienced with life than she looked. If the two little children in the picture on the desk were hers, she was older than she seemed or she had been very young when she had them.

Webber, either you're not as charming as you think, or you're not using the right approach. "I'm not trying to be pushy, but this is very important," he said pleadingly. "Please tell her I'm a friend of one of her clients, Kay Reston. I think that might make a difference."

The woman looked dubious, but she picked up the receiver of her telephone and punched in two numbers. "There's a man here who'd like to see you about . . . I know, I told him that, but he said it's about somebody named Kay Reston, and maybe you'd . . . well, OK, I'll tell him."

She had barely hung up the phone when the door to the inner office opened.

Framed in the doorway, Cynthia Ramirez seemed small. She was short and petite, and she wore a conservative gray skirt and white blouse ensemble that looked like there must be a dark blazer somewhere to go with it.

She looked him over curiously. "We've never met, have we?"

"No. Kay told me where to find you."

"Come in."

She shut the office door behind him. Her dark blue blazer was hanging on the back of the door.

Cynthia Ramirez's office was plain, the furniture nice but not expensive. Her desk was neat and well organized. Her framed law school diploma hung on the wall, along with a photo of two older people who had to be her parents and pictures of others who looked like family.

"You called her *Kay* Reston," Cynthia said as she sat down in her chair. "Where do you know her from?"

"Los Angeles." Paul sat in one of the two straight-backed office chairs.

Cynthia waited as though she expected more. Paul got directly to the point. "I'm trying to help her out of a tough spot, and I need some information about her divorce settlement with Wes Riddley."

Cynthia's expression changed; it was as though a barrier had gone up between them. "Any information about that is between me and my client. I can't share it."

Paul realized he had been *too* direct; maybe that was because he could almost hear the clock ticking toward Friday. "I'm sorry, I shouldn't have just jumped into that. She said I could ask you—"

"If Kristina sent someone to me who was trying to help her, I think she'd let me know, Mr. . . . ?"

"Webber. Paul Webber. There hasn't been time. I only found out an hour ago—"

"Just what is your relationship with Kristina, Mr. Webber?"

"We're friends—*close* friends."

"Really? I think I'd like Kristina's word for that before this conversation goes any further."

"Listen, I can explain—"

Cynthia shook her head. "I'd like to talk to *her* first." She picked up the handset of her phone and pushed two buttons. The phone in the outer office rang. "Stephanie, will you get Kristina Reston on the line for me, please?" Cynthia hung up and sat staring at Paul. He stared back.

Her telephone rang and she picked it up. "No answer? All right, we'll try again later—maybe in the morning." She hung up once more.

" 'Close friends,' Mr. Webber? What does that mean? You walk in here and start asking for personal information, and you could be anybody—a guy she doesn't know, maybe somebody else sent by Wes Riddley. Is Webber really your name?"

" 'Somebody *else*'? It sounds like you've met Harry Diedrich."

"Who?"

"The private detective who's Wes's evil alter ego. A little shorter than I am, about forty-five, bald, brown eyes, mean."

"I can't say I've heard the name."

It was evasive. She had recognized the description; he had seen it in her eyes. "Look," he said, "I want to break the hold Wes has on her, and Kay told me you could help."

Cynthia said nothing.

Paul sighed, and stood. "You won't find Kay at her number right now. Harry got caught trying to plant some poisoned migraine medicine in her apartment yesterday, so she's staying someplace safer."

Cynthia looked stunned. "How do you know—"

"I can tell you where to call her if you decide you want to help. I'll check with you tomorrow. But right now there's a lot to do and not a lot of time." He walked out of her office.

He was unlocking his car when Cynthia stepped out of the office building and walked toward him. "They, uh . . . they really tried to kill her?"

"Yes."

"And you *know* what hold Wes has on her?"

"Yes."

"She tied my hands. She never would let me go after him."

"There's no choice now. I promised I'd help her fight him. She needs all the help she can get."

"That man *was* here, a couple of months ago—the detective. He claimed he was from the state, investigating their business, and he wanted to know where to find Kristina. But he left when I started to call the state offices to check up on him. Then today, when you started asking questions . . ."

"Sorry. I'm a reporter. I'm used to asking questions, not answering them."

"So there's a story in this for you?"

"Yes. Kay is on the edge of it. But protecting her from Wes is more important to me than any story."

She stood looking at him for several seconds, studying his face. "You really care for her. I mean, this is more than just friendship, isn't it?"

"Does being in love fall in that category?"

For the first time, Cynthia smiled. "It does for me." The smile faded. "But if you knew how many women I've helped who lived with men that said they loved them, and then beat them, or used them . . ."

"Women like Kay?"

She nodded.

"And Stephanie?"

Cynthia raised an eyebrow.

"Sorry. Reporter's instinct," Paul said.

"All the women I help have my promise that their situations are strictly confidential."

"You've made a believer out of Kay. She trusts you as much as anybody she knows."

"She's not just a client. We're friends—we lived in the same apartment my last two years in college." Cynthia frowned. "That's why it hurts so much to know she's one of my failures. I hated leaving her tied to so many of Wes Riddley's strings."

"I think we can break those if we work together. But you need to put your mind at ease before you answer any questions from me. Can we use the phone in your office to call Kay?"

Kay's first words when Paul's mother put her on the line were: "I'm bored, Daddy. Can I go down to the beach and play?"

"Will you be a good girl and wear your wig and sunglasses?"

"You really think I need to? Here?"

"I'm just trying to make sure the guys on the beach don't get a good look at you. I don't want any competition while I'm away."

165

Kay laughed.

"I have someone here who needs to talk to you." Paul handed the telephone to Cynthia.

"Kristina?" Cynthia smiled when she heard her friend's voice. "Are you all right? Is it true they tried to poison you?"

Cynthia's side of the conversation was cryptic. "The same man who left you those notes?" Her eyes widened as she gazed at Paul. "Really? He didn't tell me that part. . . . So it's OK to tell him anything I know?" Slowly Cynthia smiled again. "Oh. How long has this been going on? And why didn't you share any of it with me?" She listened, then laughed again. "OK." She handed the telephone back to Paul.

"My ears were burning," he said to Kay.

"I was telling her what a wonderful man you are—and I told her to remember who saw you first. So, did you talk to Hugh today?"

"Yes. He's not our man. Wes is the one who's been pulling the strings. He tricked his father into hiring Diedrich."

Kay sighed. "Why doesn't that surprise me? Well, I'm glad to know about Hugh, at least. Let me know if you learn anything else." She paused. "I miss you."

"Don't go watching the sunset on the beach with anyone but me. I'll call you again tomorrow—or maybe tonight." He said good-bye and handed the phone back to Cynthia.

"You skipped over the part about how you handled the detective," she said as she hung it up.

He rubbed the bruised spot on his forearm. "Simple self-preservation."

Cynthia took a file folder out of a drawer, laid it on the desk, and folded her hands on top of it. "Before we go any further, I have to know—what is it that Wes has been holding over her?"

"Prison—and maybe losing her daughter. She found out that he was overbilling customers and charging for service they didn't get, but he doctored the books to make it look like she approved it. Wes promised her that if he got in trouble and went to jail, he'd take her with him."

Cynthia frowned. "It's hard to predict what a jury will believe sometimes, but I doubt he could pull that off."

"She wasn't willing to risk it, so Wes had her right where he wanted her. I'm not sure yet why he was willing to take a chance on pushing her to the breaking point—or why he thought he needed to kill her."

"Because he's rotten scum?"

Paul smiled. "Try not to hold anything back—on a scale of one to ten, tell me honestly where you'd rate your lack of trust in Wes."

"Around twelve."

"Yeah—me, too. But 'rotten scum' would just go on toying with her the way he always has. There's got to be some payoff in this for him if she's gone."

Cynthia opened the file folder on her desk. "Well, he wouldn't have to share the profits from the business with her. But he's never put up a fight about that. In fact, I'm surprised at how cooperative he's been in providing information."

"Even about expanding into California?"

Cynthia's brow furrowed. "California?"

Slowly Paul smiled again. "That's what I needed to know. I think we've got him."

"What do you mean?"

"Motive for murder. Last year Wes won a contract to sell copying machines and supplies to CommerceBank of California. I'll bet he hasn't offered to share *those* profits, has he?"

"No—and there was nothing about it in his year-end report. Does Kristina know?"

"I haven't told her—I'm still putting it all together—and I'm sure Wes hasn't told her. It involves bribing a banker, and he knows Kay wouldn't go along with that. So he might be worried that if she finds out, she could use it against him—or maybe that she'd demand half of the profits."

Cynthia looked dubious. "But *killing* her. Even for Wes that's . . . I mean, how much could half of the profits be?"

"The problem is that Wes is in no position to share. He's trying to pay off the loan to his father so he can hold onto full control of the business. He has to be worried about what Hugh would do if he found out about the kickback scheme. And it looks like Wes is already splitting the profits from California with somebody else—a lawyer named Mitchell Harrison. They're—"

"*Mitch Harrison?* The attorney that attorneys love to hate! He makes us all look bad. I should have known! He represented Wes in the divorce."

Cynthia swiveled her chair to the side and gazed out the window. "Expanding the business . . . Wes can't do something like that without Kristina's permission—not legally. It's in the agreement they made when they were divorced." She turned to look at Paul again. "So if there's a contract with the bank, and if Kristina didn't sign it . . ."

Paul looked at his watch: 4:35. The bank offices should still be open. "Can I use your phone again?"

Anna Leeds answered as usual: "CommerceBank of California. This is the office of the administrative vice-president."

"This is Paul Webber. Sorry to have to call you there again, but I need some information. Can you answer yes or no questions?"

Her voice level dropped. "Yes."

"When the bank accepted that bid from the company here in Las Vegas, was there a contract?"

"Yes."

"It has Weston Riddley's signature on it?"

"Yes. And his partner's."

"*Both* signed? Are you saying Kristina Riddley's signature is on it?" Cynthia, listening, raised her eyebrows.

"Yes. The legal department insisted," Anna answered. Paul nodded at Cynthia. She made a note on her legal pad.

"The woman's signature has to be a forgery," Paul said into the telephone. "Can you fax a copy of the contract to me at her lawyer's office?"

Anna hesitated. "I don't know."

"Because it's confidential?"

"Yes."

"OK, I want you to do what you feel is right, and I'll respect your decision. But if we can show that her signature is forged, I think it could help get the bank out of a bad deal." Paul looked questioningly at Cynthia. She nodded. "And I know it would help protect Kay—Kristina—from being charged with something she didn't do."

Anna's voice was almost a whisper. "This is the woman you told me about?"

"Yes. Her lawyer will be making a formal request for a copy of the contract." Again, Cynthia nodded. "But we need to see it right away."

There was silence on the other end of the line for several seconds. Then: "Can you give me a number?"

"The fax number here is . . ." Cynthia wrote the number hurriedly on her pad and turned it toward him. Paul repeated it into the phone.

"It will be about thirty minutes," Anna said, "after the office closes."

The next words were muffled. Paul could tell she was covering the phone. "My boyfriend. He wants me to meet him after work."

A woman laughed. Paul could hear her words faintly: "I wish *my* husband would think of things like that."

Anna spoke into the phone again: "I'll be there as quickly as I can. Bye," she said sweetly. Then she hung up.

Cynthia made more notes on her paper. "I think I won't ask for that contract officially until we're ready to confront Wes. That way there won't be any chance for somebody to warn him." She looked up at Paul. "There's a lot more I need to know about this, isn't there?"

"Yes—and a lot more you can tell us."

"*Us?*"

"I'm working with a friend on this. Scott Pike. He's a—"

"TV reporter. I thought you journalists never shared stories."

"Not ordinarily. Not with lawyers, either. But if this will help get Kay free of Wes . . ."

"You really *are* in love, aren't you?"

169

Chapter 15

"There," Franci Webber said, "you'll look just like another one of us middle-aged girls on the beach trying to keep from going to flab." She laughed.

Kay looked in the mirror, adjusted the floppy brimmed hat Franci had loaned her, and put on her sunglasses. Franci was right. The sweatsuit, also borrowed, was shapeless, and the hat and sunglasses would keep anyone from recognizing her.

Maybe there was no need for the disguise. It wasn't likely Wes had sent anyone after her besides Harry Diedrich, and if he had, how would someone find her here?

Still . . .

"Let's go enjoy what's left of the sunshine," Franci said. "We've been cooped up too long today."

They strolled along the asphalted path that ran above high-tide level on the beach. Bicyclists, joggers, and even other walkers passed them, but Kay matched Franci's leisurely pace. She judged that Paul's mother was in her mid-fifties and not especially athletic. Franci seemed to enjoy the walking just for being out of doors, and today because she had company.

Kay drank in the beauty of everything she could see and feel—the warm afternoon sunlight on the waves, the cool ocean breeze on her skin, the splashes of color in bathing and jogging suits that stood out against the beige sand and monochromatic buildings on the horizon.

Franci talked and Kay listened. Franci talked about her daughter, Lisa, and Lisa's family; about Paul, and what kind of boy he was growing up; about Robert, her husband, and how happy they had been in their nineteen years of marriage.

"Franci, did you ever think about getting married again?"

"For a long time I thought I couldn't, and then . . . well, sometimes I get lonely now—but I've never found another man who makes me feel happy the way Bob did."

"I'm sure it was wonderful to live with a man like that," Kay said. They walked a little farther before she added: "I thought I had one like that once—but I was wrong."

"I, ah, hope you don't mind my asking this, but was your husband abusive to you?"

"Not at first. Before we were married, he made me feel like he wanted me for me—for what I was. It turned out later that he only wanted to *own* me, like a possession he could use when it was convenient for him and then ignore. He had to feel like he could control me. He couldn't live with me any other way."

"I'm sorry—sorry you had to go through that."

"How much has Paul told you about me?"

"That you're a wonderful person. That he loves you. I haven't asked him to share anything that might be deeply personal to you. I thought it was your right to share those things if *you* wanted to. Knowing that Paul thinks you're wonderful is good enough for me."

"Thank you for being so kind. But I want you to know the truth about my past. My parents taught me the gospel just the way you did Paul, but when I went away to college, I let other things get in the way of what I'd learned at home. I was pregnant when I got married. I quit going to church because it just reminded me of all the things I'd done wrong. Then, after my daughter was born, I realized I couldn't live without the gospel anymore." She sighed. "I also found out that my husband couldn't handle the idea of marriage as a long-term commitment if I insisted on things like fidelity and trust in the relationship."

Kay glanced at Paul's mother. Franci looked straight ahead as they walked. It was impossible to tell what she was thinking. "I'm deeply ashamed of what I did," Kay said. "But I can't go back and change that part of my life. Now I'm trying to find my way to the kind of happiness my parents have because of the way they've lived. I used to think I'd lost that chance forever, but your son has helped me see that I can still do it."

Franci stopped walking. Kay stopped beside her to see what was wrong. Tears were running down the other woman's cheeks.

Kay stood in awkward silence, wondering what she had said that brought this on. A small knot began to grow in her stomach. If Paul's mother felt deeply disappointed at learning the truth about her . . .

Franci moved a step closer, then slowly reached out her arms and pulled Kay into a hug. Kay put her arms around Franci, tentatively at first, then hugged her too.

"It must have been so *hard* for you!" Franci said. "I hope your parents are proud of you. I know they're a long ways away, so if you ever need someone to talk to . . . another woman . . ."

"Thanks. Thank you for . . ." Kay blinked away the tears in her own eyes. "Thank you."

They turned and started back toward Franci's condominium, walking in silence until Franci looked toward the beach and saw a woman and child wading in the edge of the surf. "Tell me about your little girl," she said to Kay.

"Angela?" Kay smiled. "She's four and a half, very smart, beautiful—everything a mother could want. And she loves Paul because she can tell that he really cares about her. I couldn't be luckier with her."

"I'd like to meet her sometime. I have some books and toys at home I think she'd like, and I know some games—"

Kay laughed. "Being a grandmother is habit-forming, isn't it?"

Paul's mother turned red. "I'm sorry. I wasn't trying to, uh . . ."

"Franci, I'd love to have my daughter meet you. She needs all the good role models I can find for her, and she'll like you."

When they came to Franci's street, Kay said, "I think I'll sit out on the beach for a few minutes and watch the sun go down. It's one of my favorite things to do."

Franci smiled. "Paul did tell me that part. Mind if I watch with you?"

They sat on the sand without speaking for a time, until Franci sighed and said, "I wish I could capture that light in my painting."

"You're actually doing pretty well," Kay responded.

"You peeked!"

Kay smiled. "I couldn't resist. It's a good beginning. There are a few little pointers I could give you if you wanted."

"Thanks. I'd appreciate that."

They fell into silence again, until Kay said: "I should be there."

"Where?"

"Las Vegas. It's *my* problem, but Paul and Cynthia, my lawyer, are doing all the . . . well, I'm not sure exactly what they're doing. I want to know what's going on. And I have to face Wes sooner or later—I want to get it over with. I should be there right now."

"Then why don't you go?"

Kay turned to look at Franci. "It's not that I don't appreciate what you're doing for me."

"I understand. What I'm telling you is, if you feel you need to go get involved, do it. Don't let Paul put you off with his investigative reporter mumbo jumbo. Sometimes he lives and breathes that stuff."

Franci smiled at her. "My son needs someone to help him get his priorities right in life. I'm hoping you're the one."

"Mmm—the only enchiladas I've ever tasted that are better than these are my mother's," Cynthia said. "Where did somebody named Scott Pike learn to cook Mexican food like this?" She put the last bite in her mouth and chewed slowly, savoring it.

"In Albuquerque, from the mother of a girl I dated just after I got out of high school. Her mother said, 'Connie, pay attention to what I'm doing. If you're ever going to get married, you need to know how to cook.' I paid attention too."

Cynthia smiled. "But now Connie's cooking enchiladas for somebody else?"

Scott nodded. "I was in Ecuador being a missionary for our church when she met a guy who'd just come back from Mexico. I think they have two little kids now."

Cynthia looked at him quizzically. "You two are Mormons, aren't you—just like Kristina?"

Scott nodded again.

Cynthia looked at Paul, then back at Scott and smiled. "You were one of those guys who goes around in white shirts and ties knocking on people's doors and . . . and what? Preaching?"

Scott smiled too. "Teaching. Yeah—me."

Her smile faded. "Well, it's not that I thought *you* couldn't, uh . . . I mean, it's just that I used to wonder why young guys would . . . and I never talked about religion very much with Kristina."

Paul chuckled. "You thought those guys in white shirts and ties never did anything but preach and pray and study scripture books, and maybe they laughed out loud once a week or so, if nobody else was around. Is that it?"

"Well, sort of. And, uh . . ."

"The only Mormon you knew wasn't like that?"

"No, she wasn't. I mean, Kristina was a good person—we all looked up to her, and we knew she cared about every one of us in the apartment. But she was fun, too. She could have more fun at a party than anybody else I knew—*without* drinking. Everybody loved being around her because of what she was."

Cynthia frowned. "Except Wes. He wanted to make her change—make her like him. That's how I knew he was wrong for her. But he was good at making her feel like he needed her, and I think she believed she could help him. She was a lot happier before she met him. Sometimes I wished I could be happy that way."

"That's what those guys in the white shirts and ties are all about—teaching people that God wants us to be happy, and how," Paul said.

Cynthia looked at Scott again. "But you didn't . . . you were never mad at God because he let Connie find somebody else while you were out doing what you thought he wanted?"

"I hurt for a while. But she and I never promised anything to each other, and she had every right to choose what would bring her the greatest happiness. That's what I wanted for her."

"Umm. I don't know if I could, ah . . . if I could be that charitable."

"Sure you could—you're that kind of person," Scott said. "Think about it. You could be making a lot more money if you didn't spend so much time helping all those women who come to you, but you do it anyway. Why?"

Cynthia thought for a few seconds, then shrugged. "Because I feel like I can make a difference for them. Most of them don't have anything—no job, no education, sometimes no family around. If it were my sister or my mother, I'd hope there'd be *somebody* who'd help them."

"We're *all* family—we were family before we were born—and we're supposed to make a difference in each other's lives while we're here."

"*Before* we were born?"

"Yes."

Cynthia looked at Scott curiously. "I'd like to hear more about that sometime." Slowly she smiled. "Over enchiladas—the ones my mother taught me how to make. I'll cook when—"

Paul laughed. "The gourmet meets his match!"

Scott winked at Cynthia. "Jealousy—just because I can cook when I want to. This is a guy who single-handedly supports a burger outlet, a fried chicken franchise, and two frozen pizza companies." He looked at Paul. "Be nice and we might invite you to dinner."

"Boys! Please," Cynthia said. "I was offering to cook dinner for four to celebrate—*after* we get Kristina free from Wes Riddley. This is a chance to do what I couldn't do for her the first time, and I'm going to make the most of it. Paul, you said Mitch Harrison arranged payoffs to go into an account in the name of a banker's wife from California. Can you tie Mitch or Wes directly to the money?"

"Mitch maybe, through the account number I saw him give to the banker. But he may not be the one handling the money. We'd probably have to look at bank records to know for sure."

"That could take a subpoena. So, who's the lucky winner, Mitch Harrison or Wes Riddley? I can't think of any legal reason Kay could give for looking at Mitch's account. But if we pick Wes and we're wrong, that will tip our hand and Mitch will have time to try to cover his trail."

Paul thought it over. The day he had seen Mitchell Harrison having lunch with James Delaroi in the restaurant, the lawyer had taken pains to crumple up the keno card with the account number written on it and dispose of it—or so he thought. "Harrison's probably too careful to leave a paper trail. My pick would be Wes."

Scott nodded.

Cynthia's brow furrowed. "Me too. But I wish we knew whether—"

"Don't we have the law on our side with him?" Paul asked. "Kay's still a partner in the business. She should be able to look at the company's account."

"Yes—according to the agreement when they were divorced," Cynthia answered. "But I wouldn't put it past Wes to use his personal account, which is against the agreement. Or I wouldn't be surprised to learn he has an account we don't know about."

She sat gazing past the two men, into the night outside Scott's living room window. "I wonder if they've got any more of these kickback deals going? I can see Mitch Harrison making a persuasive case. 'Let's help each other out here. Give us a chance to make the best bid and your company still gets a good price, but you and I walk away with a little profit. Everybody wins, nobody gets hurt.' "

Picking up the contract that had been faxed from the bank in California, she turned to the last page. "This top signature is definitely Wes's. The one below it is definitely not Kristina's. I don't have anything with Mitchell Harrison's handwriting on it to compare, so—"

The ringing of the telephone interrupted her. Scott reached for the cordless unit on the wall. "Hello?"

He smiled. "Sure, he's here. It's dinnertime—where else would he be?" He listened, then laughed. "You remember when Paul took us out to dinner three weeks ago and I said I'd cook next time? Well, you missed out on my enchiladas. But Cynthia promises to cook up a batch for us later."

He tossed the phone to Paul. "Kay wanted to know if I cooked or if you ordered in."

"Hi. We were just talking about you," Paul said into the phone.

"My wit, my charm, or my great talent?" she asked, and laughed.

Paul smiled. It was good to hear her say positive things about herself, even jokingly. "All of the above. But Cynthia was just saying you must not have been yourself the day you signed the contract with the bank in California. We have a copy of it here, and the signature doesn't look at all like yours."

"California?"

"That's what I thought. You never saw this contract, or anything else involving a bank in California, did you?"

There was silence on the other end of the line for several seconds. "Wes forged my name?"

"Did he ever say anything to you about moving into California to do business?"

"No. He said something once about picking up bigger clients—corporations, hospital systems, institutions like that—but I told him I wouldn't have any part of it if he was going to cheat them the way he cheated smaller customers. He never brought it up again."

"Remember the banker in the pictures I took in the restaurant here? He's getting money from Wes and Mitch Harrison somehow because he set Business Line Office Machines up for this contract."

"Paul, I'm coming up there. I want to know what's going on. You'll probably tell me you're taking care of everything and I should stay out of sight, but I can't just—"

"What time do you want me to meet the bus?"

"What?"

"You're right. You need to be in on this, and we need your help. What time to do want me to meet the bus tomorrow?"

"Meet me at the airport. My flight gets in at nine-forty-five."

"Well, I'm not sure it's quite that urgent. The bus would be fine, and probably a lot cheaper."

"Doug's paying. He insisted. He found out from Mom and Dad what happened. He said to tell Cynthia they're all in this to help me pay the cost of whatever she needs to do."

Paul looked at Cynthia across the table. "I don't think she's worried right now about what it will cost."

Cynthia shook her head vigorously and held out her hand for the telephone. Paul gave it to her.

"All I want is a chance to go at this without restraints. Will you give it to me?" she said to Kay.

She was silent for a moment. "All right, we can talk about the money tomorrow if it really worries you. But I want to take this on without one hand tied behind my back this time. Do we have a deal?"

Cynthia listened again, then smiled. "I'm going to hold you to that."

Chapter 16

The woman behind the desk turned to examine the man who had opened the door. Her gaze lingered momentarily on the words above the pocket of his khaki uniform shirt: Kwik Runner Messenger Service. "May I help you?" she asked.

He handed her a large manila envelope that had been taped shut. "Confidential documents for Mitchell Harrison." He held out a clipboard with a printed form on it. "I need to have him sign for them personally. Just ask him to write, 'Received from Kwik Runner Messenger Service,' then the date and time and his signature."

The woman smiled a slight, official smile. "I'm sorry, but Mister Harrison isn't available right now. I can sign for him."

"The sender of those documents wants to be certain that they've been delivered to Mister Harrison personally. I was told to get his signature."

"I'm sorry, that won't be possible." The woman folded her hands carefully on top of the envelope lying in front of her. She sat primly behind the desk in her navy blue dress, her honey blonde hair pulled back and tied neatly with a white ribbon. She was in her late thirties or early forties, and posed behind the desk that way, she almost looked the image of a teacher or librarian—or perhaps the perfect executive secretary—from a generation earlier.

"I'm not authorized to deliver those documents to anyone but Mister Harrison," the messenger said, and reached for the envelope.

The woman rolled her chair back from her desk and pulled the envelope out of his reach.

"Look, the sender said he needed a reply from Mister Harrison immediately." The messenger pointed to the Kwik Runner name on his shirt. "And I have other deliveries to make. Are you going to see if your boss will sign for those?"

The woman kept her eyes on the messenger as she picked up the telephone and pushed the intercom button. "There's a messenger here with some documents. He says they're important and have to be delivered to you personally." She listened for a moment, then smiled her official smile again. "Yes, that's what I told him." She hung up and reached for the clipboard the messenger had laid on the edge of the desk, then removed a gold Cross pen from its holder in front of her. "Mister Harrison says my signature is acknowledgement enough that he received the documents," she said as she wrote on the form. She held the clipboard out with the form toward the messenger.

"Well, it may not be good enough for our customer," he said. "I have my instructions."

The woman glared at him and continued to hold the clipboard at arm's length.

"You understand that we can't be responsible if—" The messenger stopped speaking as he stared down at the form. Slowly he reached out and took the clipboard from her hand. The way he looked at her made her feel somehow that he was sorry for her. "All right," he said softly, "I suppose the responsibility is yours." He turned and walked out the door.

He had been gone for less than a minute when Mitchell Harrison stepped out of the inner office. "What's so important that I need to leave my morning coffee getting cold?"

The woman behind the desk smiled at him as she handed him the manila envelope, but he didn't notice.

He turned the envelope over in his hands, examining the tape that sealed it. "How did they expect me to open this?"

Quickly the woman searched out a letter opener in her desk drawer and handed it to him. He slit the flap of the envelope, pulled out the papers inside, and stood looking at them. Then he frowned as he positioned the documents so she could see them. "What do you think this is supposed to mean?"

"What is it?"

"An article from a legal journal. It's about disciplinary actions against attorneys."

"Mitch! Do you think someone—"

"Where's the messenger who brought these?"

"He left about a minute ago."

"What did he look like? Anybody you've seen before?"

"No, nobody I . . . he had on a uniform—a shirt that said Kwik Runner Messenger Service—and jeans."

"Look the company up in the phone book," the lawyer said as he stepped into the hallway. He stood peering out a window at the street, two stories below.

Half a minute later, he was back. "Thin guy, brown hair, glasses?"

She nodded.

"Alone?"

"Yes."

Harrison frowned again. "He got into a car driven by someone else."

The woman closed her telephone directory and stood looking at him quizzically. "There's no messenger service by that name in Las Vegas."

His lips compressed into a thin line and he looked away.

She understood that she had let him down. "I'm sorry," she said contritely.

"Well? Did you get it?" Cynthia asked as she maneuvered her car out into the traffic.

"Yeah." Paul held out the clipboard for her to see.

She smiled broadly. "The K and the R match, don't they? Mitch Harrison won't be able to walk away from *this*."

Paul shook his head. "It's not his writing."

Cynthia glanced at him in surprise, then looked down at the clipboard again. "Who, then?"

"His secretary."

"Roberta! Roberta Kramer."

"That was the name on the desk." Paul sighed. "This is one of the things I hate about my job."

She looked at him questioningly.

"Seeing how people like Mitch and Wes suck other people in and ruin them," he said.

Cynthia frowned. "Do you think they might have told her it was just for convenience—that Kristina said it was OK to sign her name so they could send the contract off right away?"

"Maybe. You're the lawyer—would that do her any good if she's charged with forgery?"

"Technically, no—but if Wes or Mitch would tell the truth and stand up for her in court . . ."

"Put their necks on the line for somebody else?" Paul shook his head again. "And she'll have to testify against them if she wants to save her own skin."

Cynthia's lips compressed into a thin line. "I wonder if Mitch has some kind of hold on her."

"True love, maybe? The feel of status and power? I don't know, but from the way she acted, my guess is she'd do just about anything for him."

Cynthia muttered something that Paul didn't understand.

"What?"

"*Sinvergüenza*—somebody shameless. He doesn't care how much he hurts other people so long as he gets what he wants." She paused. "If it wouldn't be a conflict of interest, I'd volunteer to defend her in court."

Paul was waiting near the door when Kay came up the ramp into the airport lounge. She put her carry-on bag down on the floor, took his face in her hands, and kissed him tenderly. "I've missed you," she said.

"Pretend you haven't seen me in a *really* long time and do that again."

He held onto her as she kissed him this time—until they heard giggling. They looked down to see a little girl of about six watching them. Both of them smiled at her. Paul picked up Kay's bag and put his other arm around her waist as they walked up the concourse.

"I like your outfit," he said, looking at the black dress slacks and satiny white blouse she wore. "Get tired of the green dress?"

Kay sighed. "I used to like that shade of green. But I dropped the dress off at a thrift store yesterday." She smiled. "Your mother and I went shopping. I hadn't bought anything new for myself in a long time, and she convinced me I needed it."

Paul laughed. "She would—and she's right. But you weren't exactly keeping a low profile while I was away, were you?"

Kay patted the wig on top of her head and pulled down her sunglasses so he could see her brown contact lenses. "Nobody could have recognized me." She stopped him to gaze at their reflection in a shop window. "This is the *last* time I come to Las Vegas in disguise, like I have to hide from somebody."

She turned and started walking up the concourse with him again. "By the way, I love your shirt too. That's a very fashionable shade of khaki, and the name patch on the front is just the right color accent. Moonlighting?"

"*My* disguise—a little playacting for Mitchell Harrison's benefit. I didn't have time to change."

"Just how deeply is Mitch Harrison involved in what's going on?"

"Up to his *habeas corpus,* I'm sure, but we haven't got much that's concrete to prove it, except for the picture I took and an account number. We haven't got a lot on Wes either, as far as the business is concerned. That's why we need to know *everything* you know."

Kay inspected the signature below Wes's on the contract. "I wonder who they got to sign my name?"

"Roberta, Mitch Harrison's secretary," Cynthia answered, putting the contract into the folder on her desk.

"This should *prove* that I'm not involved in any kind of fraud with Wes," Kay said hopefully.

Cynthia looked at Paul, then Scott. "Probably."

"*Probably?*" Kay responded. "But that signature's a forgery. How could they think—"

"Wes's attorney would hammer on the fact that you knew, or should have known, about his cheating some of the other customers. Why didn't you come forward about that?"

"There was Angela. Wes said he'd see that I lost her if—"

"But maybe there was the money, too. If they can show that you got some of the profits from the company while Wes was cheating people, then his attorney could suggest that you're just trying to get back at Wes because you found out that he was cheating *you* too, on the California deals."

Kay gazed out the window of Cynthia's office. "I never wanted any of his dirty money."

"*We* know that. But could we make a jury buy it? Wes's lawyer or a prosecutor might say you hung onto part of the company because you didn't want to be left out of the profits. I have to tell you the truth, Kristina—it's hard to predict what a jury will believe."

"Prosecutor? There's no way they'd ever prosecute Kay," Paul said, reaching out to take her hand. "Not if she's testifying against Wes."

"No, probably not. But I don't know how strong a case they'll be able to make against Wes here. And if all they've got against him in California is the detective's word, I don't know how strong a case they'll be able to make there either. He probably won't serve the jail time he really deserves."

Cynthia paused. "A custody fight could be tricky, too."

Kay looked at her again. "But *why?* We can prove that Wes is a forger, and he tried to have me killed."

"*If* we can prove he was involved in that last part, I'd feel a lot better about our case," Cynthia said. "If not . . . well, those things he told the doctor after Angela got hurt when she was a baby could come back to haunt you."

"But that was a lie!"

"I know. But the doctor can't testify to that. All he could say is what Wes told him. You and Wes are the only two people who *know* the truth—and you moved away, leaving your little girl in her father's custody, so you must not have thought he was so bad." Cynthia paused. "If we can't prove that Wes was some kind of threat to you . . ."

Tears began to roll down Kay's cheeks. "But they would see . . . wouldn't they? I mean, they'd see what kind of man he is."

"I hope so—I think so. I'm just playing devil's advocate so you'll understand we don't have a sure thing," Cynthia said. She opened the bottom drawer of her desk and handed Kay a box of tissues. "I wish we had more evidence. I wish we had *proof* that Wes cheated those clients without your knowing about it, or that he's connected to the detective, or—"

" 'Follow the money,' " Paul muttered.

"What?"

"Hugh Riddley's chauffeur told me to follow the money if I wanted to get at the truth about Wes. So if we could find some evidence that Wes paid Harry Diedrich, or that he bought the poison . . ."

Cynthia nodded.

Kay wiped at her eyes with a tissue. "About the overbilling—I know of two companies that quit Wes and signed service contracts with someone else. Maybe somebody at those two places would tell us why."

Paul looked at Scott. "We've got the rest of today and tomorrow. We can each focus on part of the problem. You take—"

"Kristina and I will take the bank," Cynthia said. "She's got the best chance of getting information about Wes's business, and if they don't want to give it, I know the legal buttons to push."

Paul looked at her speculatively for several seconds. "OK, counselor, you're on." He turned to Scott. "I want to get the latest from Los Angeles on Harry Diedrich this afternoon, and I'll take one of those companies Kay was talking about if you'll take the other."

"Sure." Scott glanced at Kay. "But if you *really* want to wrap Wes up, why don't we let *him* tell us about the California contract? Let him explain forging Kay's name."

The other three looked at him strangely. "And how do you think you could get him to do that?" Cynthia asked.

"I couldn't." He looked at Kay and smiled.

Paul gazed at him blankly for a moment, then slowly he smiled and looked at Kay too.

"What?" she asked.

"You're an actress," Scott said. "How good are you? Good enough to get Mister Ego to open up?"

Kay's brow furrowed. "You're thinking of some kind of hidden microphone?"

Scott nodded.

"With Wes? Well, I . . . I don't know. He likes to keep me guessing—he won't usually admit to anything. But maybe if I played it right . . ."

"If he thought he could brag to you and get away with it, he might be glad to wallow in his own cleverness," Cynthia said.

Kay thought for a moment, then shook her head slightly. "I don't know. With him, I can't . . . I just don't know."

Paul took her hand between his. "Kay, you can handle him, whatever happens. You've always been able to handle him. You just have to believe."

"I'm sorry I've kept you waiting," the bank manager said, gesturing toward the two chairs in front of his desk. "I understand you want to see your husband's business account, Mrs. . . . ?"

"Kristina Kay Reston—but it used to be Riddley," Kay said as she and Cynthia sat down.

The man tapped a few keys on the keyboard of his computer. "Yes—a joint account with Weston Riddley." He looked up from the computer monitor. "What would you like to know?"

"Actually, your assistant has already shown us the record of that account," Cynthia said, sliding one of her business cards across the desk. "We need to see the record of his other account."

The banker studied her card, then frowned slightly as he turned to the computer and tapped at the keys again. "I, ah, can't show you that record, since Mrs. Riddley isn't . . ." He looked at Kay. "You aren't listed on it, so I can only confirm for you that he has another account with this bank."

"Opened within the past year?" Cynthia asked.

The banker glanced at the computer monitor. "A little more than eight months ago."

"That account may be hiding assets that should be shared with my client," Cynthia responded. "I believe she has a right to see it."

"You may believe that—and you might be correct under the

law," the man said evenly. "But you'll have to go through legal due process to look at this record."

Cynthia hesitated, then leaned forward, hands folded in front of her on his desk. "We don't have very much time to get the information. It would be better for the bank if you cooperated with my client."

Kay glanced at her in surprise. It sounded like a threat, or a bluff—something that Cynthia simply hoped would work.

It didn't.

"Better for you and your client, but not for the bank," the man said. His tone was no longer congenial. "I presume you know the laws I'm bound by?"

Cynthia flushed. "And I presume you know I can get a subpoena?"

"Maybe you can. If you do, I'll cooperate—as far as the law requires."

Cynthia stood. "Come on, Kristina. Let's see if we can get a subpoena this afternoon before—"

Kay reached out and took hold of Cynthia's arm to keep her from walking away. She glanced at the nameplate on the banker's desk and spoke to him. "We're not trying to make things difficult for you, Mr. Brackman. It's just that I'm in a very risky position—and I don't mean financially. This isn't about money at all."

Cynthia sat down again. The banker leaned back in his swivel chair, listening. Kay reached for the small, framed family portrait sitting on his desk and turned it toward her. It showed the banker and a woman, both apparently in their mid-thirties, with two girls and a little boy.

"You and your wife have a lovely family," Kay said, studying the portrait. She put the picture down and pointed to the youngest child. "My ex-husband and I have a little girl about the same age as your son. Wes made me give up custody by threatening to blame me for some of the illegal things he's done in the business. Then when he knew he couldn't make me go along that way anymore, he tried to have me killed—just a couple of days ago."

Kay stared into the eyes of the banker as she spoke. "When he finds out I'm still alive, if we can't prove he was behind it, he might try again. That's why we need to see your record—to help us prove he paid somebody to do it."

The banker glanced at Cynthia then looked back at Kay. "Your lawyer knows I can't . . . I mean, even if what you say is true, I—"

"It's true, Mr. Brackman," Kay said softly. "And I have until tomorrow to find the proof."

"But under the law . . ."

"Please. Please help me. I don't want you to do anything that could get you in trouble, but if we could just find out whether Wes made a large cash withdrawal recently . . ."

"I'm sorry. I . . ." Brackman frowned, and sat gazing at the picture of his family. Finally, he turned toward his computer and typed a string of numbers. "Without a subpoena, I can't legally let you see this record. I can't even tell you what's in it." He scanned the screen, stopped, and raised his eyebrows. Then he followed the lines down the screen with this eyes, stopped again, and whistled softly. He turned to Kay and spoke very deliberately. "I can't tell you anything about the cash withdrawals your ex-husband has made recently."

Kay smiled at him. "Thank you."

"*Withdrawals?*" Cynthia asked. "More than one?"

The banker smiled slightly but said nothing.

Cynthia turned to Kay. "A man like Harry Diedrich wouldn't do anything without cash up front."

Kay thought for a moment. "And Paul said Harry called Wes from my apartment to talk about money. Wes probably wouldn't give him all of it until he had some assurance . . ."

"At least *two* payments, then," Cynthia said. "One sometime before last Monday, and one after."

The two women turned to look at the banker. "Probably enough together to pay for a nice vacation in Brazil," Cynthia added, "but not enough at one time that a banker would have to report the transaction."

Brackman still did not reply, but again he smiled slightly. Then he leaned forward, arms on his desk, and spoke to Cynthia. "In my company, when a bank officer suspects illegal activity tied to an account, he's obligated to report it immediately to Security."

"What happens then? If the owner of the account tries to use it, he might find out that there's a problem?"

"Not necessarily—at least not right away. We'll monitor the

account, but I'm sure there'll be no other action within the next twenty-four hours."

Cynthia nodded. "When I come back tomorrow with the subpoena, I may be able to share information about some regular cash withdrawals over the past five or six months that could be part of a kickback scheme."

The banker turned to the computer monitor again and scrolled the cursor down the screen, then picked up a pencil and began to make marks on the note pad next to his phone. When the first row had three marks in it, he frowned and started another row, then soon another. When he finished, the first row had eight marks, the next had five, and the last had three.

Kay sucked in her breath and looked at Cynthia. "He's got more than one of these deals going! It looks like one started *before* the banker's wife in California."

"I wonder how much income he's hiding?" Brackman asked no one in particular.

He reached out to put the family photo back in its place, gazed at it for a moment, then shook his head as he looked at Kay. "Your ex-husband sounds like the kind of person I see too often in my business—somebody who doesn't know the difference between being rich and being really well-off in life."

"Paul! We've been waiting for you," Cynthia said as he slid into the booth next to Kay. "What did you find out?"

Paul grinned. "I'm starved. Kay looks hungry. Aren't you hungry? I think we should order first."

Cynthia wadded up a paper napkin and threw it at him. She turned to Scott, sitting next to her. "You said you'd talk when he got here. What did you learn?"

He looked at her soberly. "In my extensive investigations, I've learned that the steak here is great done medium-well. Enjoy. Paul's buying."

"Cute!"

Kay took hold of Paul's hand. "I think I know how to persuade this one to talk." She smiled at him. "Do you remember the time when you were thirteen and your friend Tom had a goldfish, and you—"

He put his hand over her mouth. "My mother told you *that?*"

Kay laughed and pushed his hand away. "And I could tell everyone else unless you—"

"All right!" He put his arm behind his back as if someone were holding it there. "I'll talk!" He straightened up and put his arm around Kay. "But it isn't pretty. The police in Los Angeles have traced the last call made on Harry Diedrich's cell phone. It was to Wes's number at the office here. Harry's sticking by his story that Wes gave him the bottle of pills, and there are fingerprints from three different people on the bottle—Harry, me, and one as yet to be identified."

Kay shuddered. "Cynthia and I stopped at the pharmacy here where I used to buy my migraine medicine. My prescription was refilled three weeks ago—the Sunday you took Angela and me to church, then drove me back to Los Angeles. Whoever signed for it wrote 'K. Riddley.' The handwriting looks like somebody was try-ing to copy mine."

Scott took two pieces of paper out of his pocket, unfolded them, and slid them across the table to her. "Did the writing look like this?"

The papers were copies of invoices from Business Line Office Machines billing an auto dealership for copier service and supplies. Kay studied the initials at the bottom. "*K.R.* That's Wes's hand-writing. It looks like he tried to disguise it, but if you compare this with his *W.R.*, you'll see the R's are alike."

"The dealership dropped its contract with him as soon as they caught onto the overbilling," Scott said.

Kay held one of the invoices out to Paul, her thumb under the date. "That's only fourteen months ago. But I quit doing any work in the Business Line office before the divorce—more than eighteen months ago—and I never handled any of the invoices."

"Is there anyone who could back you up on that?"

"Yes—Jan, the secretary he let go. She used to make up all the bills, but Wes reviewed them personally, and sometimes he made adjustments before she mailed them out. Then, about the time Wes and I got divorced, he decided he didn't need her anymore. I won-der if she found out too much?"

"Do you think she'd talk to you about it?"

"Probably. We got along well."

"Well, we're two for two so far on the companies that dropped Business Line," Paul said. "The office manager at the real estate company was glad to tell me why they canceled their contract; they got bills for repairs when Wes's technician hadn't done anything but service the machines."

He looked at Cynthia. "And the bank?"

She smiled coyly. "Oh, I think we've got enough on Wes already." She reached for a menu. "Let's eat. Isn't anybody else hungry?"

Paul directed a stage whisper at Kay's ear. "What do we have on this woman that she wouldn't want to come out? If I checked in the UNLV yearbook at the library . . ."

Kay wrinkled her nose. "Well, she wasn't too fond of a couple of the pictures. But we could do better than that. I could tell you about the time she was locked out of our apartment in her bathrobe at four in the morning and the police came by, or—"

"Tell the man about the bank!" Cynthia said, rolling her eyes. "Tell him everything he wants to know."

Kay laughed. "The banker couldn't give us specifics, but Wes does have an account for the business in his name only." Her smile faded. "He's made two large cash withdrawals recently—one before Harry Diedrich tried to plant the poison in my apartment and one after."

"Eight months ago," Cynthia said, "he started making regular, smaller cash withdrawals, then another series five months ago, and—"

"That's about when the deposits in Mrs. Delaroi's account would have started," Paul interrupted.

"And three months ago, he started another series of cash withdrawals." Slowly Cynthia smiled.

Scott looked at Paul. "*Three* kickback deals—and one of them started *before* they hooked Delaroi."

Paul held out his hand with three fingers showing. "Delaroi golfs every Wednesday afternoon with two other guys. One of them is vice president of a chain of small hospitals, and the other manages a string of travel agencies owned by one of those used-to-be Hollywood stars."

Scott raised his eyebrows in surprise. "You never told me about . . ." A smile played around the corners of his mouth. "Remember when you asked me to check out whether Mitchell Harrison was tied to any *local* businesses? I couldn't find anything. But there was an interesting lawsuit a year or so ago, just after you moved to L.A., involving a travel agency owned by an ex-actor. The plaintiffs sued for fraud because they were promised that some of their old favorite movie stars would be on their tour with them, but it didn't happen. As part of the settlement, the agency had to close its offices in Nevada. Care to guess who the defendant's attorney was?"

"Mitchell Harrison! And I'll bet if we check we'll find out his client in the case is acquainted with a California banker named James K. Delaroi!"

Scott held out his hand across the table, palm up, and Paul slapped it.

Cynthia looked at Kay. "Is this the part where we smile like we didn't have anything to do with this and say, 'Great job, guys'?"

Kay laughed. "Oh, I don't think their egos need any more stroking." She put out her hand and slapped Scott's palm, then Paul's. "How about on-air credits and bylines for the two of us?"

Kay pushed open the door and the two women stepped outside while Paul and Scott waited in line at the cashier discussing the story each was going to write.

"What is it that's different about you, Kristina?" Cynthia asked as they walked across the parking lot. "I haven't seen you so happy since . . . well, you're like the Kristina I met in our second year of college."

"Happier," Kay answered. "I'm happier now."

"How is that, with the divorce, and dealing with Wes? How can you be so happy?"

"Because I'm doing things I should have been doing all along, and my life is beginning to straighten out. I'm not worried about Wes anymore."

Cynthia stopped next to Paul's car. She folded her arms across her chest and stood staring down at the ground. "Look, we've got

Wes where we want him—I think. But you need to understand that things still could be tough."

"I *do* understand. Wes won't give up without a fight. But I'm not *afraid* of him anymore—and I don't hate him, either. Whatever he thinks he can do to me, I'll handle it."

Cynthia frowned. "How can you be so . . ."

"So sure? Cynthia, when I was nineteen and I first met you, I'd never done anything seriously wrong, but I didn't realize how much I was drifting. That was before I let Wes make me . . . before I started doing things with Wes that I knew I shouldn't do. Those things brought me hurt and pain. But I've learned God can help me put them behind me. I'm not drifting anymore."

"This has a lot to do with your church, doesn't it?"

"Yes. I never talked to you about it very much back then because I wasn't really living the way I'd been taught, and I knew it. If I'd just . . ." Kay shook her head. "But I'm still learning, and I'm glad my Heavenly Father understands. If I handle life his way, everything will work out."

"You talk like we're *really* his children, not . . . not just accidents, or . . . well, I always thought of him as our Father only because he created us. How could we really be children of someone—something—that we can't . . . but you talk like he's actually watching over us while we grow up."

"I think it's a lot like that," Kay answered. "He knows what we can do, and he's giving us the chance to find out."

Cynthia was silent for several seconds. "And this doing what God wants you to do—is that what makes a couple of guys like Paul and Scott? They're, uh . . . they're like what you are now—happy, or at least not afraid of . . . well, there's something about them—I don't know what it . . . peace?"

"Yes."

"I haven't seen many men like that. My father—but I thought he was rare, one of a kind. This caring about other people the way those two do"—she nodded toward the restaurant—"being willing to put themselves on the line to help somebody out just because the person needs it—I don't see much of that in my work."

"Well, to start with, there's you."

"I mean *men*. I don't see many men like that."

Cynthia was silent again for several seconds. Then: "If what you believe does this, some of the women I work with need to know it. I need to know it." She paused and looked at Kay. "But please don't send a couple of those young guys in white shirts and ties to see me. I'd like to hear about it from somebody who *knows* what it really does—what it feels like inside. Somebody like you."

Kay smiled. "Any time. And I know Paul would be glad to tell you about it, too. Or Scott." She thought for a moment. "But Paul will be going back to California, and you know I can't be sure where I'll be or what my life will be like for a while. If I'm not around, I know Scott would be glad to help."

Cynthia nodded. "OK. Don't prime him for it. Just let me ask him my questions when I'm ready, after this is all over." She watched the two men as they came out of the restaurant. "Maybe over dinner sometime." She smiled. "Just the two of us."

Kay laughed. "I think Scott would like that." She put her arm around Cynthia's shoulders and hugged her. "I'm going to check to be sure it happens. I want you to have the chance to feel like this."

Scott was talking earnestly to Paul as they crossed the parking lot. He looked at Kay and gestured, and Paul nodded in agreement. Kay and Cynthia heard Scott's last few words as the two men came to the car: ". . . but it wouldn't be hard to do technically, if she's willing to give it a shot."

Kay looked at them questioningly.

"Talking about meeting with Wes," Paul answered. "Have you given any more thought to that?"

Kay took a deep breath and nodded. "Can I use your phone?"

Paul unlocked the car, pulled his cellular phone out from under the driver's seat, and handed it to her.

Kay punched in a number and waited. "Hello, Wes. We need to meet tomorrow."

She put her hand over her mouth and stifled a laugh. "You're surprised to hear from me? Yes, I'm in town, and no, I won't tell you where I am. I'm *not* at Marcy's, and I don't even know yet where I'll be staying tonight."

She rolled her eyes and shook her head. "No, I *don't* need you to book me a room somewhere. . . . Yes, I know that, but . . . but you . . . listen to me, Wes! You're busy every day, but this meeting can't wait."

Her tone when she continued was not angry or demanding, but it was firm. "We have to talk about the business—tomorrow, you and me, no Mitch Harrison. Believe me, you can't afford *not* to talk to me—you'll be better off if you do."

Kay glanced over her shoulder, in the direction of the Strip. "The hotel where you had me stay last fall when you bought me that green dress. . . . Yes, in the restaurant."

She looked at Scott, pointed to her wristwatch, and raised her eyebrows questioningly. Scott held up all ten fingers, then ten fingers three times in rapid succession. "Ten o'clock," Kay said into the phone, and silently mouthed to Scott: "He'll be late."

She listened again, nodded, and said, "Tomorrow."

Turning off the phone, she took another deep breath, then smiled. "Two things Wes won't be able to resist—a challenge from me, and a hint of something in it for him."

Chapter 17

The smoked mirror on the wall of the restaurant gave Paul a full view of everything behind him. Kay was sitting alone in a booth across the room. Paul had put his back to her so that Wes would not be able to glance this way and see his face.

But Wes was not here—at least not yet. Paul frowned and looked at his watch.

Scott, sitting opposite him, laughed suddenly as he looked in Kay's direction. "She says to tell you not to get nervous. Wes is late on purpose, just to show her that she can't tell him what to do."

"You're getting the sound from her OK?" Paul asked.

Scott adjusted the earphones in his ears. They were connected to what looked like a slightly-larger-than-usual tape player in a belt pack on his waist. "Yeah, the sound's fine. I wouldn't plan on using it in a high-class production—too much room noise. But it'll be OK as long as she doesn't cover up that sunburst pin she's wearing."

"You think the picture will be all right?"

"Hey, I checked all this out with Kay at the studio an hour ago, OK?" Scott straightened the cap he wore; the lens opening for the tiny video camera inside it was a small dark spot in the Las Vegas design on the front of the hat. "All I have to do is look at her and she's covered."

Paul took another bite of cold pancake. The breakfast crowd was mostly gone, and it was too early for lunch. There was a handful of other people in the restaurant—late risers, or early gamblers taking a break from the casino.

Kay had told Wes ten o'clock. It was almost ten-thirty.

If he's not going to show, I hope Cynthia can at least get something good from the bank, Paul thought. She had planned to be at Wes's bank with a subpoena when it opened.

Scott glanced across the restaurant, then fixed his gaze on something and slowly turned his head to follow it. "Heads up," he said as he pushed the record button on the tape machine at his waist. "Looks like our man is here."

Kay managed not to shrink back in her seat instinctively as Wes slid into the booth across the table from her. No time now to think about the tightness in her stomach. *You're on—and this had better be the best acting you've ever done. . . . Try to* look *confident, at least—but don't play out what you know too fast. Give him time to talk.*

Wes smirked at her. "Still wearing the same old wig, Kristina? You really ought to try a new style. Or stop being afraid of your shadow and let everyone see the gorgeous hair underneath that thing." He laughed—taunting her.

It didn't have the effect he intended.

I don't have to hit back. I don't have to let him make me mad, or make me feel inferior. He can't make *me hate him.* The hate was dead, Kay realized, and she did not need to resurrect it to resist him. She felt her apprehension about this meeting drain away.

"I haven't been running from shadows, Wes. It's all been real, and you know it." Reaching up to lift the wig off of her head, she dropped it in a heap on the seat beside her, then shook her head and ran her fingers through her own hair to straighten it. "That's over. From now on, I refuse to live in fear. I won't let you have a hold on me anymore."

Wes was obviously surprised. He sat back against the seat cushion studying her curiously for several seconds. Then the mask came down over his face—the look he usually wore, eyes cold and blank, when he was about to let her *feel* the power he had over her. "You know what I can do to you, Kristina—what I *will* do."

It was more crude and harsh than usual. He was trying to take control of the situation quickly.

"I know what you *thought* you could do, Wes. I know you put my name on some of those invoices when you overcharged customers. But it won't stand up in court." She paused. "And I know you had my name forged on the contract with the bank in California, without bothering to tell me you were expanding the business out of state. Did you think I'd never be able to find out?"

This time he looked shocked.

Good—he's off balance. Wonder if I can keep him that way? "Was it only the money? Did you forge my name just because you didn't want to share the profits with me?"

"No, uh . . . it was . . . how did you . . ."

He had dropped his guard momentarily because he was surprised. But Kay knew him well enough to know his mind was racing, trying to recover.

"I would have told you," Wes continued. "I'll give you your share . . . if you'll . . ."

Slowly Kay shook her head. "I don't want the money, Wes—not the way you got it."

He reached out to try to touch her hand, resting on the table, but she drew it back.

"Kristina, you're smart," he said. "I have to give you that. You're smarter than I am in some ways. But you never would listen when I tried to tell you what we could do with the business together." He paused. "We belong together." He leaned forward and smiled the charming smile she remembered from the first day she met him. "You belong to me."

"No! No one can ever really *belong* to someone the way you want. I know I can't." She tried not to make the next words harsh, but she was no longer afraid to say them to his face. "You have to understand that it could never work for us again. What *you* want I can't give, and there's nothing you have to offer that *I* want anymore."

His smile went away, and expression faded from his eyes as he retreated behind the mask again. "If *we* can't be together, Kristina—well, I really can't see you with anyone else."

"Is that why you sent that man to kill me?"

She could see that Wes's disbelief had reached yet another level. He was stunned. *Good. Have to keep this going—can't let him think.* "You couldn't contact Harry Diedrich last night after I called, could you?" His eyes told her she had guessed correctly. "You thought maybe he was off spending the money you paid him? He's in jail, in Los Angeles. Now, is there anybody else I have to watch out for—maybe some of those mysterious people you've hinted about before?"

For just a moment more, Wes looked uncertain, confused. Then he managed to recover. She saw the mask drop into place again. "I don't know what you're talking about," he said.

He's trying to buy time. "Harry Diedrich was in my apartment to plant poison. He says he was working for you."

Wes managed to keep his composure. Kay could see he was determined not to let her outmaneuver him.

"This . . . Harry Diedrich knows my name? Just because *he* says something—whoever he is—doesn't make it true. And as for other people out there . . ." Wes shrugged. "Well, I really couldn't say."

"You don't know—or you won't tell me?"

Wes leaned back in the cushioned booth and smiled enigmatically at her.

"Speak to me, Wes. You're in no position to play games right now."

His smile faded. "Was that all you had to say to me, Kristina? Because I don't think it was worth the trouble." He moved as though to slide out of the booth, but Kay could tell it was a feint. He wanted—needed—to know how much more she knew.

Scott pressed an earphone against his ear and frowned.

"What are they saying?" Paul asked.

"Not much now." Scott stared across the restaurant. "She's good. She got him to admit that he forged her name. But he's stonewalling now. He claims he doesn't know the detective. She's up against a pro at lying."

Paul frowned. "Hmm. I wonder how he'd handle a pro at asking questions?"

Scott smiled and clenched his fist. "Yes!"

"What?"

"She just smashed an ace across the net at him. He made like he was going to leave and she told him to sit still, she wasn't through yet and he'd regret it if he didn't hear her out. He's staying. She's playing him just right, but I don't know if she has anything else to throw at him."

Paul stood. "I have the tiebreaker right here." He patted his shirt pocket. "Something I haven't had time to tell you about yet. I want to see how he handles this when we throw it across the net at him."

Scott glanced at Wes, sitting on the edge of the seat in the booth. "What if he decides to bail out when he sees you? You could blow this."

"Maybe. But I think his ego's too big to let him run from me. Just keep the tape rolling."

"Wes, I'm asking for the truth. I'd never want anything like that to happen to the father of my daughter. Did you really want it to happen to her mother?"

"I'd never touch you, Kristina."

"But you sent somebody so you wouldn't be connected—"

Kay looked at Paul in surprise as he slid into the booth beside her. This wasn't part of the plan.

The smile Wes gave Paul was evil. "I *knew* you were behind this."

A wiser man might have read a warning in Paul's expression or the look in his eyes, Kay thought. But Wes was too caught up in trying to manipulate the situation—too cocky.

Paul turned to her. "What did he say when you told him about Harry Diedrich?"

"That he doesn't know him."

Paul looked at Wes. Wes smirked.

"Did you tell him *everything?*" Paul asked, looking into Wes's eyes as he spoke. "Did you tell him what a good friend Harry was? How Harry said he got the pills from Wes? How Wes had told him it was just LSD in the medicine to give his ex-wife a bad trip and scare her? How Harry wants to cut a deal with the police in L.A.— dump everything on good old Wes, who'll be left holding the bag for conspiracy to commit murder?"

Wes Riddley's face was white. He couldn't hold the mask

anymore; he stared back at Paul in obvious fury—*helpless* fury. The helplessness must be a strange feeling for him, Kay thought. Still, he had admitted nothing.

Maybe if she turned up the heat?

"The police in Los Angeles found fingerprints from three different people on the bottle of poisoned pills—Harry's, Paul's, and one other person's." She leaned forward, closer to Wes, resting her arms on the table. "Do you think they might be planning to find out if the fingerprints of Weston Riddley match those last ones?"

"Harry's lying!" Wes exploded. "He knew *exactly* what was in those pills. He asked me—" Wes stopped himself suddenly. There was panic in his eyes now. "I mean, whatever was in those pills, he knew. . . . He asked me if . . . if I wanted him to get something to take care of you. I thought he meant to scare you, like he did before. All those phone calls were his idea."

Wes moved closer so he could look across the table into her eyes. "Kristina, I never would have let him . . . if I'd *known* what he—"

"*You're* lying," Paul interrupted. He took a folded piece of paper out of his pocket and flipped it across the table at the other man. "Kay doesn't even know about this yet. I got lucky this morning, just before I came here." Wes stared down at the paper. "Open it!" Paul commanded.

Wes reached out slowly and unfolded it. His eyes gave away his surprise when he read the name at the top of the photocopy: ChemShop.

"There are four or five places in town where somebody could buy cyanide," Paul said. "The clerk at the next-to-last one remembered you when I showed her your picture. You were such a handsome devil, and so well dressed—not like the miners who come in to buy cyanide for processing ore. You had some kind of requisition on school district letterhead—that was a nice touch—and you talked about chemistry classes."

"She made a mistake. I've never—"

"Been there? Won't fly." Paul put his finger down on the "paid in cash" notation on the receipt. "She remembered that you tried to sweet-talk her into letting you order less than five hundred grams, as if you really couldn't afford it—then you pulled a fifty out of the wad of bills in your wallet."

Kay let out a long breath. "Oh, Wes!" Intellectually she had been prepared for this, but still it hurt to know for sure.

He refused to look at her.

"My lawyer can handle all this," he said, folding his arms across his chest. It was a retreat, Kay recognized—an admission that he was not in control. His enigmatic mask was gone. She wondered what he was feeling—what he was telling himself inside.

"Do you really believe you can count on Mitchell Harrison?" she asked. "Paul says some people from the state attorney general's office will probably be talking to him about your kickback arrangement with the banker from California and his golfing buddies. You know Mitch pretty well. Do you think he's going to be the good guy and tell them the whole thing was his idea?"

"It *was!* He came to me and said—"

"*Maybe* he did," Paul interrupted. "But I have a witness who saw *you* make the first contact with Delaroi."

Wes looked at him wide-eyed. "There's no . . . you can't prove . . ."

"Are you willing to take a chance on that? And remember, you have to worry about what Delaroi is going to say when he's trying to save his own skin. I'm sure the state of California will also be looking into your deals with him and his friends."

Kay watched Wes's expression as he thought about what Paul had said. It was the first time she had ever seen Wes look scared.

Then hate came back into his face and she knew he was not going to go down easily. "I can get another lawyer," he said defiantly. "My father—"

"Your father was ready to turn you over to the police four days ago, but I asked him for time to break down your case against Kay," Paul answered.

Wes's look showed that he didn't want to believe. "No. He would never—"

"Wouldn't he?" Kay asked. "You've heard your father talk about integrity and how important that is in life."

Wes sagged back in his seat.

"You owe it to me to clear my name," Kay pressed. "Why did you lie to the doctor when Angela was a baby—when you told him that I hurt her?" She watched as Wes turned the answer over in his mind. *He's trying to find something here that can be used to his advantage.*

He leaned forward and looked into her eyes. "Kristina, *you* can tell them I didn't know what Mitch Harrison was doing. I'll leave you out of all the business stuff, and I'll say I made a mistake when I talked to the doctor, if you'll—"

"No deals, Wes." She shook her head. "I won't help you hide from what you've done, and I'll fight you for Angela if I have to."

Paul turned to her. "He doesn't have anything left to fight with. His credibility's gone and he stands to be prosecuted in two states for crimes including trying to kill the mother of his child." Slowly he turned to look at Wes again. "Just so he wouldn't have to share his profits."

Wes glared at him and said nothing.

"Sometime soon," Paul continued, "you're going to be hoping a court or a jury will see some trace of decency in you. I'd say your chances are slim. But it would be a start if you'd give up using your little girl against her mother." He paused to let Wes think about it. "There's no doubt Kay could win custody in court now. Her lawyer would lay out what we know . . . maybe bring in a couple of your old girlfriends and ask them if you ever hit them . . . or if you're a good example for a four-year-old girl. But if you gave her up on your own before—"

Wes leaned back suddenly and waved his hand as though to dismiss them. "All right! Take her."

Kay spoke slowly and distinctly. "You're giving me sole, uncontested custody of our daughter, Angela?"

Wes glared at her. "Yes."

"You admit that you lied to the doctor when you made him think that Kay hurt her own daughter?" Paul asked.

Wes hesitated. His hatred for Paul was unconcealable. But: "Maybe I was wrong about what I said."

"Maybe?"

"I didn't tell him what to think! I told him I thought things were tough for Kristina with the baby. He came to his own conclusions."

"But you didn't bother to correct him." Paul looked steadily into Wes's eyes. "And you admit that you tried to poison your ex-wife, with the help of a detective named Harry Diedrich?"

Wes's laugh was short and ugly. "You're enjoying this a lot, aren't you, Webber?"

"Not especially. Tell me the truth."

"I'm not telling you anything else until I see a lawyer."

Paul looked at Scott, across the restaurant. Scott tapped the tape machine with his finger and made the OK sign.

Wes had followed Paul's gaze and had seen Scott's gesture. He looked at Paul speculatively, then at Kay. Suddenly he leaned across the table, took hold of the silver sunburst Kay wore, and turned over her lapel to expose the small wire running away from the back of the pin. Just as suddenly, he let go of the lapel, drew back his hand, and slapped Kay across the face.

Paul was halfway across the table when Kay grabbed his arm to pull him back. "*No!* Don't be like him! Please, Paul."

Slowly, Paul put his hands down flat on the table and leaned forward, his face close to Wes's.

Keeping his eyes on Paul's, Wes settled back into the corner of the booth, pressing against the cushion, as far away as he could get. Paul eased down into his place next to Kay.

She rubbed her cheek and spoke softly to Wes. "Do you think hitting me is going to accomplish anything? Did it ever?"

Wes looked away.

"You've never answered my question," Kay said. "You used to hint that there were people out there who'd try to get rid of me if I don't do what you say. Are there?"

Wes's smile was cruel. "I don't have anything more to say to you." He slid across the booth as though to leave.

"Don't be in too much of a hurry," Paul said. "I don't think you're going to be leaving alone."

Wes sat on the edge of the cushioned seat looking at him quizzically.

"I told a friend in the police department what we were going to be doing here today," Paul continued. He nodded toward two men at a table in the center of the restaurant. "Do you think those two guys are just gamblers? Think the one with the earphone in his ear is just listening to his ball game?"

The man with his back to them quickly turned his head so the earphone was out of sight—but not before Wes had seen it. Wes watched the two men for several seconds. Then, slowly, he turned around and settled back in his seat, folding his arms across his chest and staring down at the table.

"Please answer my question," Kay said. "It won't hurt you to do that."

There was no response.

"Maybe mob types?" Paul asked.

Wes smiled slightly, then suppressed it. He continued looking down at the table without answering.

Paul sighed. "Let me give you a quick lesson in journalism. There will be follow-up stories on this. Other TV stations and newspapers will pick it up—maybe even the tabloids. If you leave this hanging, and they keep digging, they'll ask questions that will get back to some of these people you've been hinting about. Maybe the police will be asking questions too. Pretty soon some of the mob people will start asking themselves, 'Who is this Wes Riddley? What's he after? Maybe we need to shut him—' "

"No!" Wes spat.

"What?"

"No—there aren't any more people out there like . . ." Wes glanced in Scott's direction as he realized what he had been about to admit. "I mean—"

"I know what you meant." Paul stared at him for several seconds. "I wish I could believe you."

"Believe it! You made your point."

Paul sat staring at him until Wes could no longer meet his gaze; he looked away. Finally Paul said: "I don't know how long they'll be able to put you away, but if I thought you'd be meddling in Kay's life again when you got out, I'd be at every parole hearing, every review—"

"You keep your hotshot journalist nose out!" Wes pointed his finger at Paul's face, then quickly withdrew it and sat back against the cushion again. "Leave me alone, and I'll leave you alone." He turned his gaze very deliberately on Kay. "You don't have anything I want anymore."

Paul nodded. "I hope you can be a man of your word—for once in your life." He took Kay by the hand. "Let's go."

They slipped out of the booth and walked toward the front of the restaurant. Kay looked back. The two men Paul had pointed out were moving toward the booth where Wes sat.

Scott followed Kay and Paul out of the restaurant. Cynthia met them just outside the entrance. "Well?" she asked.

"Everything we wanted," Paul said, smiling. "You see any of it?"

"The last few minutes. I was behind one of the machines out here," she said, gesturing toward the casino. "I saw him slap her. Scott, did you get that on tape?"

"Yeah, it should show up well."

Cynthia turned to Paul. "How come you were sitting in the booth too? That wasn't the plan."

"We improvised. Kay was standing up to him well, but I had the final nail for the coffin. I found proof this morning that Wes bought the poison."

"You did?" Cynthia laughed. "I'll bet *that* left Wes speechless. Wish I could have heard it all."

"Come back to the studio with me," Scott said. "We can watch the tape together."

"How did things go at the bank?" Paul asked.

Cynthia smiled as she held up a sheaf of papers. "Two large cash withdrawals from Wes's account, the week before and the day after Harry Diedrich visited Kristina's apartment. And cash withdrawals in the middle of the week before each one of those dates when you followed the banker and his wife to Las Vegas. When the police check the accounts for Harry Diedrich and Mrs. Delaroi, I'll bet they find matching deposits."

She turned to Kay. "If the videotape is everything Paul says it is, I'll have Stephanie call Hugh Riddley this afternoon to let him know that you'll be picking up Angela—to keep her."

Paul intertwined his fingers with Kay's. "Fine. While you two go watch the instant replay in the studio, I'll take the real, live witness along to help me finish my story."

"*Finish* your story?" Kay asked.

"Yeah. I wrote part of it last night, some of the things that wouldn't change—the kickback payments, Wes's part in that scheme, and Mitch Harrison's. With what we've learned today, I can write the lead, add some details, and call Delaroi and Mitch Harrison to ask if they have anything to say."

"What do you think they'll tell you?"

Paul laughed. " 'It's nothing but lies. I'll see you in court with a libel suit.' "

Scott grinned. "Paul has the story all to himself until tomorrow morning. That's our agreement. By the time I call, after they've had time to think about it overnight, they'll be saying, 'I can't comment, you'll have to speak to my attorney.' "

"And tomorrow," Paul continued, "after they've actually read the story or seen Scott's version on the six o'clock news, they'll know there's not anything they *can* say. Everybody else will be picking it up. Delaroi's golfing buddies will be running for cover—but they'll be too late."

Cynthia took Scott's arm. "Come on. I've got to see that tape." They walked quickly out through the casino and toward the exit from the hotel.

Kay held onto Paul's arm as they strolled along behind. "I'm glad I had you on my side. I don't know whether I'd ever have been able to stand up to Wes without someone like you to believe in me."

"Of course you would have. You had it in you all along. But I'm glad I could help the process."

His brow furrowed. "We did what we had to do to get you free of him. But I wish we'd had more time to develop the story—find the links to those other people he's paying. And I wish I had an undeniable link between him and Delaroi. The woman at the bank only saw Wes once, and she can't identify him for sure. I wish I had something like the keno ticket that Mitch Harrison wrote that account number on—something tangible."

Kay stopped walking and looked at him strangely. "But you have—haven't you? I mean my painting—the one I gave to Angela. Hugh said Wes used it in a deal with an important client. When I found out the banker in California is an art collector . . . well, I just assumed . . ."

Slowly Paul smiled. "Sharp. I missed that. Next thing I know, you'll be taking a shot at my job." He thought for a moment. "I wonder if . . . come on, I need to make a phone call."

When Anna Leeds answered her telephone at the bank, he said, "This is Paul Webber, and I have more questions. If I can find a tangible link between your boss and the two men here in Las Vegas, your testimony might never be needed. Can you talk?"

"Yes."

"Have you ever seen your boss with a painting of a desert scene, looking out over a valley with ranges of mountains in the background?"

"Yes."

"Do you know if he still has it?"

"On the wall in his office. He's very proud of it."

"In his *office*? Where anyone who comes in can see it?" Paul grinned at Kay. "He must be awfully confident that his tracks are covered."

Kay whispered: "My initials—KR—would be in the bottom right hand corner, and the year."

Paul spoke into the phone. "Have you ever noticed the painter's initials in the lower right corner, and a year?"

"I think there's something there. I'll check later."

"Thank you. And one more favor, if you can do it without calling attention to yourself. Do you think you could shoot some pictures of the painting after everyone else is gone today? From across the office, and then just the painting on the wall. In case he panics and moves it, the pictures will prove it was there."

"Are you close to, uh . . . finishing your project?"

"You might want to check your paper tomorrow morning."

"Well, I'd like to help with what you ask, but I'm not exactly prepared for that today."

"If you could buy one of those disposable cameras at the shop down the street on your lunch hour, I'll pay you back. Just send the camera to my office when you're through."

"I'll see what I can do." Anna paused. "How are things working out for your friend?"

"Just fine. And thanks for asking."

"Thanks for protecting me," she said softly. Paul heard a door open in the background, and Anna's tone changed abruptly. "Yes, sir, I'll watch for that information. Thank you for calling." She hung up.

Paul turned his phone off and stood looking at Kay speculatively for a moment. Then he smiled.

"What?" she said.

"I was just wondering whether you could get your painting back from Delaroi if you let it be known that you wouldn't sue on Angela's behalf provided—"

"No!" She shook her head. "I'd like to have it back, but no. I'd never sue. I'm tired of fighting. No more."

"I didn't say you *should* sue. Maybe there's not even a case. Just let it be known that you *wouldn't* if he'd cooperate, and see what happens."

She smiled. "I'll worry about the painting later. Angela first."

"Want to take my car and go get her while I'm working?"

"No. I need to give Cynthia time for that call to Hugh." She took Paul's arm. "And when I go, I want you with me."

Chapter 18

Max was stonefaced. "Come in," he said finally, leaving the door open as he turned his back and walked away.

Paul glanced at Kay questioningly. She shrugged, and stepped inside. He followed.

"Wait here," Max said over his shoulder. "I've almost got Angela's bag ready." His words seemed curt, and he didn't look at them. "She don't know you're comin' to get her."

Kay frowned. "Is Hugh here?"

"Yeah." Max glanced at the office door, which was closed.

"I need to talk to him," Kay said.

"He don't want to talk to you."

"Max, I don't think it's wrong to want my daughter back," Kay said softly. "Do you?"

"No—I guess not." Max nodded toward the office. "But *he* don't think much of the way you're doin' it. And I guess I don't either."

Kay looked puzzled. "What do you mean?"

"What that woman said—'Just have her ready when Kristina gets there, you're in no position to argue.' "

Kay frowned. "Cynthia would never—" Her eyebrows went up. "Oh—Stephanie." She put out a hand to touch Max on the arm. "I'm sorry it was handled that way. The woman who called had to fight to keep her own children when she was divorced, and she thinks all men . . . well, she just doesn't know *you*."

Kay turned to look at Paul. "I can't leave it this way with Hugh."

She knocked on the door of the office. There was no answer for

209

several seconds. Then they heard footsteps inside, and the door opened.

"Are they gone? I—" When Hugh Riddley saw who it was, he stood glowering at Kay. It looked like there might have been tears in his eyes just now, but she couldn't be sure.

"I told Max I didn't want to talk to you," Hugh said. He started to shut the door.

Kay put out her hand to stop it. "Please? I'm sorry Cynthia's secretary talked to you the way she did. It wasn't right." Gently she pushed the door open a bit farther. "She probably doesn't understand how much you love your granddaughter."

Hugh's expression softened.

"May we come in?"

Hugh left the door open as he walked back to his desk and sat down behind it. Kay motioned for Paul to follow as she stepped through the door. She sat in one of the leather chairs facing Hugh across the desk; Paul took the other.

Hugh pointed his finger at her face. "I could fight you. I'll—"

"You'll lose," Paul interrupted. "If you think—"

"Paul! Don't, please." Kay put her hand on his arm. She looked at Hugh. "I don't want a fight. I don't think you do either. My daughter loves all three of her grandparents, and I don't want anything to change that. I want her to grow up being close to *all* of them."

Hugh looked at her as though he could not believe what he was hearing.

"I need her with me," Kay continued, "and a little girl needs her mother. I hope you can understand that, because there's nothing you can do that would ever make me give her up again." She paused. "But I'd never tell a grandfather who really loves her that he can't be part of her life."

Hugh's expression softened again, and there was something in his eyes that Kay had never seen before—respect. He blinked several times to clear his vision but sat perfectly still without saying anything.

Paul leaned forward in his chair. "I owe you an apology for the way I reacted just now. And I'll tell you before you see tomorrow's newspaper that I'm sorry about what we had to do to Wes. It would have been a story only about the business if he hadn't . . . if he'd just been willing to leave Kay alone."

Hugh Riddley looked at him and nodded.

Kay reached out to take hold of Paul's hand, then turned to Hugh. "Tomorrow morning I'm taking my daughter out to my parents' place for a couple of days, but I don't know what's going to happen in my life beyond the weekend. I won't be taking Angela out of state—at least until there's a custody hearing—and the business is probably a mess that I can't walk away from, so for now I'm going to have to find a place to live in Las Vegas. Can I leave Angela here during the days next week while I look for someplace I can afford?"

"Yeah. Sure, you . . ." Hugh blinked again. "Anytime."

Kay smiled at him. "Thank you. I know she's in good hands with you and Max, and she loves the swing set and the pool, so—"

"Mommy!"

Kay and Paul stood, and Angela ran to her mother with her arms outstretched. Kay picked her up and held her close. "Hi, baby! Umm, I've missed you."

"Me too!"

"Would you like to go visit Grandma and Grandpa on the ranch and ride the horsey?"

"Yes! Yes! Yes!" Angela looked over her mother's shoulder at Paul. "Is Paul coming?"

Paul reached out and touched her hand. "I wouldn't miss it."

"Can Grandpa come too?" Angela asked. "And Max?"

Kay looked at her in surprise. "Well, uh . . . yes, if they want to."

Hugh Riddley smiled at his granddaughter. "Not this time, Princess. Maybe another time."

He looked at Kay. "Maybe on Monday afternoon your mother can come swim in the pool with you here . . . and stay for dinner?"

Kay smiled at him. "I'd enjoy that."

She walked out of the room leading her little girl by the hand. Paul followed, accepting Angela's bag as Max handed it to him. He was opening the front door when Hugh stepped out of the office behind them. "Kristina?"

They turned to face him. "Yes?" she answered.

"I forced you into the business with Wes. I owe it to you to help you get out—if that's what you want."

"Thank you, Hugh. I'd appreciate that."

Bill Reston undid the cinch beneath the mare's belly, then heaved the saddle off of her and positioned it carefully on the top rail of the small corral. Paul leaned on the rail watching him work with the horse.

"Seems like my wife and I are getting deeper in debt to you all the time for the things you've done for our daughter," Bill said.

Paul shook his head. "No. I could enjoy spending a lifetime doing things for your daughter."

Kay's father smiled slightly. "So—what now?"

"You mean, 'Young man, exactly what are your intentions?' " Paul intoned. Both men laughed. But Bill stood waiting for an answer.

Paul glanced over his shoulder toward the house, where Kay had gone with Angela after their ride. "I've never wanted anything more than I want to ask your daughter to marry me."

Bill nodded.

"But if she's got to be up here and I'm in Los Angeles . . ."

Bill gazed off toward the west, in the direction of Las Vegas. "There's no way you could . . ."

"Maybe. I hear there might be an opening at the *Review-Journal*." Paul paused. "But if I stay with the wire service in L.A., I could have a shot at moving to bureau chief somewhere in a few years."

"That's a pretty big thing in your line of work?"

"Yeah, it is. If you want to go up in the organization, it's, ah, . . ."

He didn't like the way the words were coming out. He had always told himself that when the right time came, he wouldn't have any trouble determining what was most important to him in life. But now there was the orderly plan he had laid out for his career, or there was Kay—and Angela. His choice ought to be simple. Why was he talking in terms of alternatives?

Kay's father slipped the bridle off of the mare. "For me, it was horses. I wanted to raise them—champions, breeding stock. But after my wife and I got married, I never was able to scrape together enough money to buy brood mares and a good stallion. I finally figured out that life was happening anyway while I was waiting for my herd to come in, and if I wasn't careful, I was going to miss some of the best parts." He turned his head slowly, surveying the rangeland beyond the house and barn. "Raising cows hasn't worked out so bad."

He looked at Paul. "Something will work out for the two of you—if you pray for it and work hard at it." He lifted the saddle to his shoulder and walked toward the barn. Paul watched him go.

"Hungry, cowboy?"

He hadn't heard Kay walk up behind him. She was eating a cookie and holding one out to him. "Grandma Reston's special recipe." She laughed. "Angela's helping her put them away in the cookie jar—one by one."

Paul took the cookie, then intertwined the fingers of his other hand with hers. "Let's go for a walk."

He led her across the patch of lawn behind the house to a small rise where the sagebrush began. In the distance, craggy, barren mountains faded away into lighter shades of blue above the desert floor.

"Is this where you painted your picture for Angela?" he asked.

"No—there." Kay pointed to a rocky knoll a hundred yards farther to the southwest. "Come on, I'll show you." She threaded her way through the sage ahead of him, and as they came to the base of the knoll, she tightened her grip on his hand. "Don't do one of those track star things and run ahead this time. Stay with me."

They sat on the rocks at the top of the knoll and looked out over the valley that stretched away in front of them. Neither of them said anything for a time, until Paul turned to her. "There's something important we need to talk about now."

"What?" she said innocently.

Paul laughed. "I saw you looking over at the temple when we were driving out of Las Vegas this morning. You looked for a long time. And your Dad asked me a few minutes ago what's next for the two of us."

Kay groaned. "Mom brought it up while I was in the kitchen with her. I'm sorry, Paul. I didn't want there to be any pressure."

He smiled. "As if you and I weren't thinking about it already." The smile faded quickly. "There are things we need to settle."

"I know. And we can now. I'm *free*. For the first time in five years, I can do what I really want with my future."

"That's the question: what do you *really* want? When you were looking at the temple this morning, I wondered . . ." He stared out at the desert.

Kay turned to look at him. "What?"

"I was wondering—*worrying*—about what you really feel inside. Maybe a lot of it's gratitude? I mean, you've been chained to Wes for a long time, and I'm glad I could be the one to help you break free, but if you're not sure—"

"Paul, if there's anything the past couple of years have taught me, it's how to know my own mind. Yes, I'm grateful to you—but that's only a small part of what I feel. I've found somebody worth giving my life to—every part of me, for now and for always. I *need* to be with you."

He kissed her lightly on the cheek. "I need that too. I just had to be sure it's what *you* really want."

She put her arm through his and leaned her head on his shoulder.

He looked out over the valley again. "That leads to the next thing—Las Vegas and Los Angeles. I don't want to wait to get married *someday,* when we can work out how to live in the same city. I want to start spending my life with you *now*." He turned to look at her. "Scott heard that the *Review-Journal's* political reporter is retiring, and the managing editor told me when I left a year ago that if I ever wanted to come back and he had an opening, I could have a shot at it. The job probably wouldn't mean a step up in salary, but the hours could be a lot better for family life."

Kay's brow furrowed. "But you wanted to move up to bureau chief for the wire service, maybe overseas somewhere—and if you leave . . . well, I don't want you to wake up someday and regret letting go of the dream. Maybe you ought to think this over."

"I don't need to. I made the decision a long time ago, really." Paul leaned over and kissed her. "A wise man I know just reminded me why it was so important. He helped me see that I could raise cows instead of horses and still be happy."

Kay smiled. "How hard did he twist your arm?"

Paul put his arm behind his back and winced in mock pain. "All right, Bill, I'll marry your talented, beautiful daughter. How many cows for the dowry?"

She laughed. "A dozen, at least." She took his hand between hers. "Maybe if I tell the court I'm getting *married* and I *need* to take my daughter and move to California—"

"We can try that." He put his arm around her and pulled her closer. "And maybe I'll find out the paper already has somebody lined up for that job. But we'll make something work for us. The important thing isn't *where;* for me it's *when*—now, together."

"If you leave the wire service now, you won't be able to follow your story."

"No problem. I'm off of it anyway, as of today. It's somebody else's."

"Why?" Kay looked puzzled. *"You* dug it out."

"The bureau chief asked me yesterday if I'm too close to it. That's the right question for him to ask. If I go on writing about Wes while I'm getting ready to marry the former Mrs. Riddley, or when I may have to testify against him in court . . . well, you see the problem."

"Mmm. Yes." She frowned. "When I testify, Wes's lawyer will try to make me look like a liar, won't he? And he'll probably bring up you and me."

"I wouldn't be surprised at anything. It could get ugly."

"Will you be there? Close?"

"I promise. As close as I can—if we have to testify."

"If? Why wouldn't we? I mean, if we don't, then—"

"What happens to Wes and Harry?"

"Yes."

"Harry's trying to cut a deal with the prosecutor in Los Angeles. He'll give up Wes and give the police information about some other cases they'd like to solve if they'll give him immunity in those cases and a lesser charge in this one instead of conspiracy to murder. The police will probably go for it provided they get what they want—Harry spends time in jail and stays out of California ever after."

"And Wes?"

"They can probably try him for both bribery and conspiracy. The prosecution would likely go for whatever will put him away the longest, but they might offer some kind of plea bargain to avoid the expense of two trials. A smart lawyer would probably advise Wes to take it, because the stakes are pretty high for him."

Kay frowned thoughtfully. "That's frightening. They try to poison me, and then they may get off with . . . but . . . I . . . well, I don't know what I want most. I hate the thought of having to testify—dragging through all the ugliness again in court. But I want Wes out of our lives for a long, long time."

Paul nodded. "When I found out for sure that Wes bought the poison, I wanted to work him over before he ever got to court. I admire the way you can forget your anger with him—and with Hugh. You're showing me some things I need to do better."

"It's simple for me. If I let go of the anger I can still feel what I felt in the temple. Now that I've found that, I'm trying to hold onto it."

"Well, it's still too early to know which way things may go with Wes in the courts." Paul put his arm around her. "When we find out, we'll deal—"

"Mommy!"

Angela made her way toward them through the sagebrush, with her grandmother watching from the backyard. Paul and Kay stood and walked down the slope to meet her.

"Mommy, Grandma says it's time for you and Paul to wash up if you want lunch."

Paul lifted Angela up to sit on his shoulders and held onto her hands. "Do you think your mommy will always be Grandma's little girl?"

"Grandma says so."

Kay smiled. "I used to want to come home and be Grandma's little girl again." She put an arm around Paul's waist. "Not anymore. I get to be the mommy now."

"Is Paul going to be my daddy?" Angela asked.

Kay looked at Paul.

He squeezed Angela's hands. "Maybe I can. What do you want a daddy to do, Sweetheart?"

"Love me—and play with me."

"I can do that."

"Go places with me and Mommy. Mommy says you could take us to the beach!"

He smiled at Kay. "I can do that. I know a place where they make waves you'll really like. What else?"

"Be nice to Mommy, and love her."

"If that's what you want, I can do that too." He put one arm around Kay's shoulders and pulled her close. "For now and for always."